COUNTY LINE

Amanda Cadwell

ISBN: 0692049223
ISBN 13: 9780692049228

To my Greg; may I forever be your Dharma.

1

HARLEY

Yellow road markers act as little counters to let me know the path has already come and gone. I frequently drive this road, and often wonder why I still live out in the middle of nowhere in a town called Middleton.

The road curves around the mountainside. I increase my speed after the switchbacks and glance down at the dashboard to check my speed. His picture rest next to the gauges and he is smiling back at me. My fingers instinctively stroke his face and my heart aches for the laugh that was caught behind those crinkled grey eyes. The thought of my father always chases away any doubts I have ever had about my life choices. He built a life for us in a desolate town and made the town what it is today. It was from him that I learned how to support a community, to strive for a better way of living, and to see the ugly for what it could be.

My lead foot cuts loose on the edge of the county line. Rarely do the cops patrol this area so I tear through this last set of switchbacks. The road winds around Mt. Kale one more time and I feel the pull against my seat belt as my speed increases. I don't have many thrills in my life, so I take them as I get them.

The road swings back to the right where the river cuts its path through the land. When the road stretches out to the valley between the mountains, I notice a shiny black Chevelle sitting on the shoulder with smoke leaching out from under its hood.

Pulling my truck up beside the car, I spot a trim figure standing in front of the hood with his hands resting on his head. I lean over the passenger seat to crank the old window down. A pungent motor-oil smell drifts into the cab. I glance under the stranded car and see something dripping into a black puddle on the ground.

Taking in the driver, I realize he is taller than I expected and considerably under-clothed for the winter weather that is almost upon us in late October. He is wearing a thin, long-sleeved t-shirt, washed-out jeans with holes in the knees, and flip flops. The only things he has on that can be considered winter wear are the knit hat on his head and the full beard.

"Need a ride?" My mouth speaks before my brain registers how unkempt and ragged the stranger looks. The small prick in the pit of my stomach brings to my attention that I am alone on the road and stopped for a stranger.

He briefly glances away from his hands to me. He seems annoyed by my sudden appearance. "No, I've got my phone," he replies coolly.

He holds his phone up like everyone does when they are searching for service. I'm amused because that trick never works, but we all try it. I examine the car, his phone, and his appearance one last time before I let my mouth speak again. Weighing my options out, I calculate the unlikely chances that a serial killer would purposefully break down out here unless this is where he dumps his bodies. Then happening to break down here could be a more likely possibility. But then again, his car is facing the direction I am heading - which is away from civilization. *Apparently the "flight" part of my brain decided to take a hiatus today.*

"You won't get reception out here due to the valley, but I can give you a lift into town." He doesn't acknowledge my comment so I ask the question again.

"I heard you the first time." His voice snaps like a whip at me as he studies his car.

I do not appreciate his brashness after risking my well-being for him. My snippy attitude quickly seeps into my voice. "Listen, I can give you a ride or you can wait for the next car to drive by and try your luck."

Glaring eyes aim to shoot daggers at me, but change as they study exactly who their target is. His lips quirk to the side. Looking at the scenery and deserted road he asks, "How do you know I am not a murderer?"

Figuring this is a game to him, I start to get cocky. "How do you know I'm not psychotic and fixed on torture?" I retort. His Adam's apple bobs. I couldn't help but find pleasure in that reaction, which confirms the danger might be a little less than previously thought.

"Are you in or out?" I ask again with a kinder smile.

The truck door squeaks open. He looks around the rough interior of the truck and gives a low whistle. The floorboards are dirty, trash is littered here and there, and the seats are tattered and faded. "Sorry it's not a limo for your pompous derriere," I state defensively.

He smirks at me and climbs in. I put the truck into drive and head towards town. He has a slight funk like he hasn't showered in a few days. I appreciate the cracked windows.

"Didn't your daddy ever teach you not to pick up strange men on the side of the road?" This makes me laugh- if he only knew how unsure I am at this moment.

"My daddy taught me how to protect myself and never to go anywhere without Sig." I pat the door where I keep my handgun. He nods in respect and we fall silent.

The fields in the valley look empty and barren in the autumn. Most harvests have been cut, bundled, and shipped to the nearest co-ops.

"Where is 'town' exactly?" he asks, making finger quotes. "Just so I know where you might kill me and dump my body."

"We're about fifteen miles out." It feels like those measly miles are ticking by more and more slowly. The music plays through the speakers, and I drum my fingers to the beat, lost in my thoughts. I am repeating my to-do list over and over to distract me from the awkwardness that surrounds us.

"Does my captive have a name?" I ask. Again, he acts as if I haven't spoken a word. "How long have you had the car?" I'm hoping this line of questioning will help speed up the diagnostic tests that will need to be run on his car.

"A few months."

"Where did you get it?"

"In Georgia."

"Where did you buy it?" I feel like we are playing 20 Questions and hardly getting anywhere. Luckily, we only have a few more miles to go thanks to my lead foot.

"Saw it on the internet and bought it off a guy." Each answer is clipped and cool. I glance over at him and catch his jaw clench. "I just had the oil changed."

"When did you start noticing there was something wrong with it?"

"After I left the city and had been on the road a bit, I heard something knocking but I thought I could make it back to California and have it worked on there." The poor guy just ruined his car based on what I saw leaking under it. I try to fight back my grin, but he catches it and glares. I can't help but grin wider.

"I am sorry," I choke out. "It's just... my friend... it sounds like they destroyed your engine." His glare grows darker. "Do you remember where you took it? We can try to see if we can hold them liable for the damages."

He gives me a nod but his eyes stay on the road. "The shop you are taking me to, what do you know about it?" His tone is even icier than before.

I cough to help recover my composure and quietly add, "It's a small-town shop that has been in business for years. They are known for their engine repair. From what I see and can gather from you, it sounds like they will be your best bet."

"Small-town huh...just my luck. Charge an arm and a leg?"

"I will make sure they take you for a ride. Saddle up." He rolls his eyes at my mockery.

"Yeah, I'm sure." His sarcasm matches mine and drips from every word. "What, do you have the shop-owner's balls in your hand?"

"You could say it's something like that," I quip.

Middleton comes into view. The only thing that keeps it alive is the cheap lodging for the ski resorts on both sides of the town. Middleton is about a twenty-mile drive to either resort. There are a few bed-and-breakfast establishments and a hotel that looks like it came straight from a horror movie, with stained carpets, flickering lights, and blackened bathroom fixtures. No one wants to stay there except maybe the few college kids who are looking for the cheapest trip possible. My father started helping the Michaelsons renovate the hotel gem a few years ago, and they are still trying to revamp it. With such little cash coming in, they are only making ends meet.

"We're here," I announce, throwing the truck into park. I realize it might have been an abrupt stop when I see my passenger thrown against his seat belt. I sheepishly look over at him and climb out.

2

REED

We finally arrive at the shop. My driver slams on the brakes, hops out like a country girl, and saunters into the office before I get her name. A few minutes later, a tan, dark-haired guy who looks like he is familiar with the police department comes out. He climbs into the nearby tow truck and takes off.

I glance at my wrist to calculate how much time I can spare here in this desolate town. It's a bad habit I have developed over the years, but I view my time as an equation for money. I have already spent too much time away and the pressure to get back is building not only by my standards but by obligations as well.

I slowly get out of the truck and survey the area around the shop. The cabin-styled houses across the street look kept up, but settled. A few cars are parked in driveways and on the streets, but overall there is no activity in the quiet town. As the sun sets behind me, I imagine most local families are home and eating dinner. I turn to face the shop, taking in the open bay doors showcasing the clean and organized work spaces - the complete opposite of the interior of her truck. The siding on the building could use some touchup and minor repairs. It's a rather dull and uninteresting place.

Walking inside the shop, the bell above the door jingles, taking me back to a time that is only displayed in movies. "Can you give me the number of the shop you used?" Her tone is clipped and straight to business. I'm slightly confused as to why she is sitting behind the counter, but I scroll through my phone, pull up the auto shop's name, and I pass it over. She scans the screen then looks at me. Her eyes are full of pity. My irritation spikes. It's a look I know too well and despise.

"Well, the person you took it to is a shady mechanic. I know the shop and they screw up a lot of cars. Evidently, you are their latest victim." She reclines back on the stool and crosses her arms. "Since we don't have proof they didn't attach the oil pan bolt correctly, I don't think your repair will be covered under their warranty."

"And you would know about the other shop because…" I prompt trying to understand her knowledge in the business.

"I've dealt with them before."

"How do you know that's the problem when you haven't looked at my car?" I ask doubtfully. *She is really puffing herself up for just being a receptionist.*

"Experience," she states matter-of-factly. Arrogance oozes from her relaxed posture. Arrogance typically turns me off, but I want to toy with this arrogance. I want to ruffle her feathers, so I let my brain calculate her, waiting for any moment I can attempt to chip away at her haughty demeanor.

"How much is this going to cost me?" I ask.

"We'll know more when George gets back and I can really look at it." She shifts in her seat as her fingers drum on the counter.

The way she avoids a real answer feels like she knows it is going to be bad but wants the facts first before moving forward. I stand in awkward silence and look around the shop. It looks out of place for the town. There are old car parts mounted on the wall giving it a vintage, rustic feel, but it has an artistic new-age look that grabs my attention. The style is very contradicting but it seems to flow nicely as I walk around to take it all in. But it just doesn't fit in the rural atmosphere. "Did you design the shop?" I ask, still calculating.

"No, George did." Her eyes are on me.

"How long have you guys been together?" I mosey down the dirty shelves storing mechanical parts. It's obvious that she manages the store side because it matches her disorganized truck. The shelves are full with boxes of parts, but nothing matches inside the boxes. My hands twitch to organize them.

"We aren't. I hired him on a few months ago to help me out."

I replace a greasy part back in the box, not realizing my OCD kicked in. Wiping my hand on my jeans, I catch a whiff of myself. I realize I've gone a few days without a shower. When I look at her, she is still sitting there watching me move along the shelves.

"You hired him on?" I must have heard wrong or else she misspoke. She shifts in her seat and rolls her shoulders back in a show of pride and prissiness.

"Yeah, the name on the building is *Harley's Auto*." She points to the sign on the wall behind her. "Harley Anderson," she introduces herself.

"I guess that would be why you hold the owner's balls," I mumble. I see a smile creep across her lips and amusement dances in green eyes that are almost too small for her face. Looking at her more closely, I realize her eyes look tired, almost like she hasn't slept in a few days. Her cheeks look sallow. She is a little ratty and homely. She could be cute, but it's as if she hasn't quite figured out how to embrace her beauty.

"Who is the mechanic that will be working on my car?" She rolls her eyes to the ceiling then settles them on me with a pointed look. I shake my head with a chuckle at her response and start walking up and down the aisles again.

She had told me the shop had been open for years and they were known for their engine repair, but anyone can say that, especially the owner. "How long has this place been open?" For the experience she boasted about, she isn't old enough to have that type of reputation.

"My dad started the company when I was little." She fidgets in her seat and moves to start straightening the shelves. I eye her closely.

"Are you trying to call bullshit on my reputation?" she accuses. I shrug my shoulders nonchalantly, just to toy with her.

"You never told me your name." She changes the subject.

"My name is Reed."

"Nice to meet you." She sticks out her hand and it feels small in my hand. She keeps eye contact and her grip is firm. She knows how to conduct business. I give her props for that.

It feels like the hour is dragging on but we finally hear the tow truck honk in the garage. Harley goes into the shop to help George unhook my car. As George climbs out of the cab, I see the tattoos wrapping around his biceps and neck. His features are cold and he reminds me of my body guard. I know he is not a man to be messed with. The way he sizes me up makes me realize that Harley has no clue how George feels for her. If George wants her, he can have her. We make the manly eye contact and non-verbal agreement that it is his territory and that I am merely a passerby. I nod and avert my eyes to the car.

"Thanks George, you can call it a day. Tell Kate I said hi." He nods to Harley's words but his eyes never leave me. She catches the silent exchange between us and shoves his arm, laughing, "just go." She shakes her head as she wheels a tool cart towards the car. George's car revs up and peels out of the parking lot. She sighs in irritation and starts digging through the mess of tools on the cart, looking for what she needs.

"How can I help?" I ask.

"Can you pop the hood?" Her eyebrows cock up, making me smile. I climb into the driver's seat and I can feel Harley's smirk bleeding through the windshield as I hunt for the lever. I catch a glimpse of her out of the corner of my eye, right when she reaches under the hood and pops it herself.

I roll my eyes while climbing back out of the car. She laughs robustly. "Who is Kate?" I blurted, trying to recover my fumble and not wanting to give her arrogance any edge.

"George's wife. Why?" Again, no reaction from her – her eyes are focused on the engine. She pulls a stick out and I assume she is looking for a reading on the oil level. She then wipes the end, re-inserts the stick, and checks it one more time. She looks smug with the results.

"Are you sure nothing is going on? Guys only stare each other down like that when they are having a pissing war," I ventured.

"George is protective. He's had a troubled past and protects anyone he cares about." I suddenly have a unique connection to George.

"How did you guys meet?" I ask while she continues checking the fluid levels.

"We grew up together." Her simple statement has a gentle tone of more meaning than I think she intended. I sense I am not welcome to push this matter any further. "Will you push that top button? You'll have to press and hold it." She points to a box on the nearby support column.

The car starts to elevate. When it's high enough for her to walk under, which isn't very high, she starts poking around under there. With her focus on the task, we settle back into awkward silence. "What kind of work do you do?" she asks. I look at her from the corner of my eye. My jaw clenches because I don't know how to answer this question.

"What?" Harley asks, confused by my hesitation. "Nothing…." I mumble, "I…I just work on… You really don't know?" I stumble while my brain tries to think of a good answer. I typically would lie, but for some reason I don't want to lie to her.

"Am I supposed to know who you are?" She looks at me with disgust, likely thinking my ego is rather large. The longer she looks, the more switches click on. I can tell when she figures it out. "You're Will Montgomery, the movie star," she states.

3

HARLEY

While still under the car, I finish my mental checklist and struggle to collect my racing thoughts. I try hard to remember our conversation from the last hour and hope I didn't say anything stupid. Knowing my smart-ass mouth, I am sure I said something embarrassing.

I stare up at the car's under-carriage and rest there for a minute, allowing embarrassment to bleed through my body. When I feel more settled, I holler to Reed, "It appears the last mechanic didn't install the drain plug for the oil pan correctly and your car leaked all the oil."

I want to celebrate my *I told you so* moment, but I'm still off kilter from the discovery that William, Reed, whoever he is, is standing in my garage. "You need a whole new engine block. This one is seized up," I report as I step out from underneath the car deciding to error on the more professional side.

"How long will that take?" Annoyance is heavy in his voice.

"Couple weeks," I say while lowering the lift.

"Is this just a ploy to keep me here? If I sign something will you hurry it along?"

I drop my tools on the cart as anger surges through my body. His constant misogynistic comments are getting under my skin. The last one wasn't that bad, but now that I know who he is, I am ticked off that he thinks I would string him along to get extra money or an autograph.

"You can sign the tow-charge paperwork," I spit out.

"Harley, I am kidding," he states, sensing my mood change. My cheeks are warm but he proceeds with his remarks. "I don't think I was that bad," he utters under his breath.

"You aren't, I…just…" I stumble for words and feel embarrassed at my reaction.

"Can I ask why it's going to take a couple of weeks? Do you know how to fix my car, because it's okay if you don't." And just like that I hate him all over again.

"Reed, listen, I know how to fix your damn car better than anyone around here. I deal with pompous pricks like you all day long that want to act as if I don't know how machines work." My voice stays calm and cool but straight to the point. "It's going to take a couple weeks because that's how long it takes! Now if you want to take it somewhere else, I will gladly tow your car into the city tomorrow and drop you off onto someone else."

I slam the hood and turn to face him once more. "Your call, but the shop is closed for tonight. There is a hotel a mile north you can stay at. We will open at eight in the morning. You can let me know what you decide then. But until then, have a great evening." I turn and stride to my office.

Reed sighs heavily. "Wonderful," he mumbles more to himself but loud enough that I hear him. "What do I do now?" He asks tightly, "Do you have a rental car?"

"You have legs, don't you?" I retort with my back to him. I shut my office door, thankful the blinds to the shop are closed. I rest against the door and let my frustration simmer.

Opening my computer to search for the nearest mechanic shop in the city, I begin looking for the worst one possible. As I take out my frustration on the keyboard, I hear a knock on my door.

"Hey Yamaha, you know you have a customer out there, right?" I look up at my best friend, Milo, as he comes into the room. His strawberry-blonde hair pokes awkwardly out from underneath his baseball hat.

Milo's dad and my dad had been best friends since childhood and the relationships go back through the generations from our grandfathers to our great-grandfathers. It would have made more sense for him and my brother to have been friends since they were the same age, but Ben was never big on the small-town stuff. Ben's distaste and inflated ego caused Milo and me to team up. Since then, Milo has been a better brother to me than Ben.

"You know I hate that nick-name," I growl at him.

"Ah, one of those customers," he states. There is a twinkle in his eye as he watches me fume, which makes me fume even more.

"What's that supposed to mean?"

"The ones that put you in a bad mood. Like how Mrs. Tilly puts you in a bad mood. You know you guys really gotta let the Riley thing go," Milo razzes me.

"Milo, my irritation with them has nothing to do with her daughter."

Riley Tilly was my grade-school bully. One day when Milo and I were walking home, he started teaching me how to fight. A couple days later, Riley was pushing and calling me names. Milo wasn't there to protect me so I clenched my fist and gave her a good follow-through to the nose. My dad had to pretend to be mad at me for fighting, but was ultimately proud of his little girl for breaking Riley's nose. Ever since then, there has been a little animosity between the Tillys and myself.

"Lee," Milo says, calling me by nickname, "Mrs. Tilly puts everyone in a bad mood and you know it. But yes, he pissed me off. Did you even see who it is?"

"Nah, it's dark out there."

I glance up to see that the sun had pretty much gone to bed and was casting a twilight glow into the garage. I stand up to turn the lights on in the shop. My smile broadens as Mr. Montgomery squints at the sudden bright lights. At that moment, I hear Milo whisper, "No way, is that a '71 Chevelle SS?"

"Yep, and that would be William Montgomery... the stuck-up actor." I go back to my computer and resume my search.

"Holy freak show!" Milo murmurs. "You and Nikki dragged me to every one of his movies. I had to suffer through listening to you two go on and on about him."

"Yeah, I know." Embarrassment warms my cheeks as I recall how Milo's wife, Nikki, and I would get wound up to go see William Montgomery on the big screen. Milo always seemed to be a good sport about it.

"I thought this would be your best day ever!"

"They always say when you meet celebrities they tend to disappoint you. Plus, it's always aggravating when someone makes generalizations about your ability to do a task based on what you carry in your pants." My mouth tastes disgusting after those words left my mouth. It felt like I just ate dirt.

I am doubted all the time because I am a girl. I had to work hard to prove myself in this industry and have shown that I am capable of filling my father's shoes. Milo knows how hard I work and nods with a gentle understanding.

"In that case, you can't get rid of him yet." His eyes sparkle. "You know how much money we can pump out of him, right?" Milo teases.

"That's just wrong, Mi!" With this playfully chide, I punch him in the arm. "To me he's not worth dealing with."

"Yet you deal with your fam..."

"Don't," I cut him off with a steely look. Milo raises his hands in surrender, palms up, and backs away towards the door. "Will you get him set up at the motel?" Milo agrees and offers to bring me dinner later. I decline since I need to go to my second job. With a final nod, Milo leaves me to watch the introduction between him and Mr. Hollywood. Milo coos over the classic muscle car for a few minutes and then they both leave.

Alone at last, I find the mechanic's shop I was looking for online and print off the directions. I close the shop and leave for my next job.

Cheapshots is the local bar/eatery/local hang-out. It's a large building with a good-size bar top and a pool hall. My father was always working on this town trying to help with remodels. I proudly took this trait from him. Because of his influence, I saw the opportunity to revamp the bar to its current rustic-pub ambiance.

Ryan Dexter, the previous owner of Cheapshots, and my brother Ben shared the same mindset. They had no desire to hang around this town. Ryan moved to the city and took a desk job for a big business. When his dad passed, leaving Ryan the bar, he quickly learned he didn't know how to keep it up and running. Ryan wanted the business to operate in a hands-off kind of way. Neither of our fathers intended their businesses to be ran in this way. The bar became filthy, over-smoked, and nose-dived into the red.

Thanks to my dad's grooming, I offered to buy Ryan out. A few negotiations later, leveraging money from the auto shop, I became the owner of a bar. I cleaned up the place aesthetically by embellishing the high ceilings with exposed beams and copper pipes. Next, the hardwood floors were refinished. I added some mountain essence by sprinkling in head mounts, antlers, and a large bear. The bar felt like it belonged in the ski resort town my father hoped Middleton would one day be. Next, I worked on the staff and had to make the hard decisions of to let people go. In a small town, that didn't leave my likability in high standing. By the end of it all, people had moved on from licking their wounds and the bar became the new hit of the town.

Walking from the auto shop to the bar, I look around this town and see my dad everywhere. We bonded as he trained my eye for opportunities like the bar. Ben was more interested in *serving* his time and getting out. He never took interest in my dad's vision. I remember times when my dad would try to include Ben on his hotel project with the Michaelsons or in the auto shop, but Ben would make snide remarks about us needing to be *realistic*. He would tell my dad and I that we lived in a fantasy world and that the town was dying. My dad always acted as if his son's aloof attitude didn't bother him, but I could see the truth in his eyes. He was a third-generation Middleton citizen. His father and grandfather farmed this land, helped settle it, and were a part of its history. All his friends who stuck around the town took up their family farms and supportive shops. He wanted to pass his shop along to his son, too. Seeing the hole that was left, I tried to fill it.

Reaching the corner where the bar sits, I glance up at the neon sign. We had all agreed it was time for a new name. Milo, Nikki, and I wanted to stake our claim on this town and mark it for the new era. The three of us were going to achieve what my dad had set out to do. Milo suggested we call it Cheapshots in honor of the nickname (Cheapshot Anderson) Riley Tilly tagged me with after our tussle. I gave him a sarcastic laugh, but after all, the name fit.

Most weekends, Cheapshots serves as a meeting hall for the mini-reunions of those who have come back to visit. Groups of kids from the nearby colleges congregate in Middleton as a get-away because the lodging is cheap and they are now "legal" to drink. It's my least favorite time during the week because the twenty-one-year-olds don't know how to handle their alcohol.

Tonight, it's mid-week, so Fred is the last one out the door at two o'clock in the morning. He grunts his way out and stumbles into Kayden's car. Kayden is my trusty bartender. I made the mistake of offering to take Fred home one night. When we got to his house, he had passed out in the car and I couldn't move him. We also learned that night that we needed to do a better job of watching his alcohol intake and now keep track of what he orders.

Every town has one or two odd characters. Middleton is no different. Kayden waves to me on his way out and I wave back. I lock the door as he and Fred leave the parking lot.

The room is empty. A soft melody of music plays in the background. I stroll over to the jukebox and press "Closing Time" by Green Day. It always makes me smile because it's the perfect closing song for a bar. I select a few other favorites then move on with my duties.

I enjoy the quietness of the empty room. No one's here to distract me and there are enough tasks to keep my mind from wandering too far into the darkness. I stay away from thinking about the "what-if's," the "could-have-been's," and anything in between. All I think about is cleaning the counters, counting the money, logging the books, and taking inventory. I'm taking notice of the here and now.

With the music and lights off and the deadbolt in place, I sigh with satisfaction. My mental checklist is complete. I start my walk back towards my father's house, Bromley. The cold seeps through my sweater. While most people shudder and wrap themselves tighter, I welcome the biting cold as the wind rustles the fallen leaves. I glance up and see the remaining leaves hanging onto the almost-bare branches. The moon is high and bright, illuminating everything around me. Another gust of wind comes through, forcing one leaf to succumb to the pull and take flight.

I find myself pitying the leaf. All spring and summer, the leaf gave everything to the tree. It took the sun's rays and turned them into plant food to feed the tree. But the tree couldn't protect the leaf from bugs and animals that could strip it from the branch, or kids who were collecting leaves out of boredom or for some school project. Yet it held onto the tree as long as possible. When autumn came, the sap from the tree receded. The fragile leaf was cut off and abandoned and can't hold up to winter. It will be replaced next spring with a new life. At that moment, I understand why the leaf gave up. Why hold on to something that never gives back?

The wind sweeps by again, cold and empty, and matches my insides. I want to let go and take flight like the leaf - let the wind carry me where it may. I want it to show me how freeing it can be. The thought scares me.

I huff a sigh, knowing if Milo or Nikki ever knew I had those thoughts, they would think something was seriously wrong with me. Milo has been my rock. He stood by me while my family turned their backs on me, and supported me after a bad relationship. Milo has been there for me. Though our relationship has been a little rocky for a while now, he's part of the only real family I have. But his watchful eye exhausts me, and I have moments of wanting to be wild and free from it all. I want to throw caution to the wind and experience things I missed out on because I was forced to grow up too fast.

I want to make mistakes and not feel the weight of responsibility. I want to be able to pass the blame to immaturity. Another sigh comes over me as I chalk this up to being *it is what it is*. There is a reason why I am in this place. I don't know the exact reason yet, but the answer is out there.

Rounding the last corner, I see the door of Bromley, or as normal people would call it... home. It didn't feel like home, hence, my nickname for it. This place is my constant reminder that I am here and my dad is gone. It's a reminder that this is my life, which I didn't actually choose but feel stuck with.

The lights are on inside the house and I see movement in the window. Nikki's laughter rings out in its distinct, infectious way. Nikki and Milo met in college at one of the fall parties Milo and I attended. Nikki knew that Milo and I were a package deal from the very beginning. She didn't like me at first, but who could blame her? Milo and I spoke with our own code without ever speaking or uttering a word, forcing her to feel left out and insecure. She stuck around though and fell in sync with us. Now, the three of us have our own code. She has become one of my best friends – and a part of my new family.

Nikki and Milo were married right after they finished college. After the diplomas were delivered, they moved back to live in Middleton. Milo works at the family lumberyard in preparation for taking over when his dad decides to retire.

I push all my thoughts and emotions down to my toes and force my body to take a step forward. By the time I step past the threshold, I have myself back together.

"I couldn't stand to see him staying at that horrible hotel," Nikki said before I could even process what she was talking about. My eyes find Reed sitting on the couch with his feet propped up on my coffee table, looking very relaxed and comfortable.

"What do you suggest then?" I ask, already knowing where this is headed.

"The Bromley." Nikki wags her eyebrows at me like she is doing me a favor. "Trust me, he isn't as cranky now that he is warm and has been fed. He has also been lectured on his car issue." Nikki continues to try and convince me to let Reed stay at my house.

"I have made arrangements to take your car into the city tomorrow morning," I say to Reed.

"So you can't fix it?" His eyebrow arches up a bit and the "I knew it" attitude seeps in his deep voice.

"Yeah, it's out of my league." I take my shoes off and walk over to the couch.

Milo and Nikki just gape at me. "I have never messed with a muscle car like that. I can drive you into town tomorrow morning. Towing will be free." I grab the remote that is sitting on the coffee table and begin flipping through the channels. I try to go for a casual attitude, but it isn't smooth and I feel awkward.

"Thanks." He eyes me as if trying to see the punchline to a joke.

"At least I know how to pop a hood," I murmur.

"I just got the car yesterday," he shot back. His face split into a grin.

"News flash, old cars don't have release levers inside the car."

"Well, now I know." Sarcasm drips from his voice. The smirks that play on our lips turn into grins. *Is this what they call flirting?* I wonder to myself and start questioning my flirting ability.

"Anyway, we leave tomorrow at six a.m. That work for you?" My voice rings out smooth, not reflecting the nervous energy that is building up inside of me right now.

"Yeah, I'll be ready."

Milo stands up, stretching, complaining about having to open the store tomorrow. He takes Nikki's hand and they head to the door. We bid each other goodnight and Milo and Nikki exchange pleasantries with Reed. The standard "Nice to meet you! Don't be a stranger," ends with handshakes. They say goodbye once more and go on their way.

I shut the door behind them, blocking out the chilly wind. "We leave at six?" Reed asks. I am startled by how close he sounds - which causes me to flush. I try to convince myself that it's just the warmth from the house and not his voice that reverberates in my bones.

"Yep." I sound a little off. I turn in his direction and almost bump into him. We stand in awkward silence a little longer, looking everywhere but at each other. "You can take the room on the far right." My voice is soft and shy, a response that is abnormal for me. "Towels are under the sink; feel free to use whatever you need."

I look up to see him nodding; looking at him, I realize exactly who is standing before me. This is the American heartthrob. The guy whose posters are plastered on pretty much every teenage girl's bedroom wall. "In fact, use whatever you can. I know I can make a ton of money selling the bath mats you step on."

Amused, Reed grins, "I will do my best."

Another head nod from one another and he heads towards the back room. I shut off the lights in the living room once he has the bedroom lights on. I retreat to my room, which is upstairs. Inhaling deeply for the first time in several minutes, I am thankful for the space between us.

4

HARLEY

I don't sleep well at night to begin with. Having a stranger at Bromley didn't help. I slept for a few hours and then gave up the fight after another hour of tossing and turning. I tried reading a book I had started months ago but end up reading the same paragraph multiple times before realizing that it isn't capturing my attention like I need it to. I snap the book shut, glance over at the clock, and calculate that I only have two more hours before I have to be up anyway.

With a huff, I move to my computer and search for the car parts that will need to be ordered to get William's car repaired. Even though I will be taking him to town to a different mechanic, I still want the opportunity to show him that I can fix his car. Plus, I am bored.

Sitting at my desk, clicking on parts and adding them to the on-line cart, I envision the simple machines being taken apart and put back together. I could prove that I was like one of those army guys who can assemble their gun blindfolded. That, like them, I could re-assemble his car with my eyes closed. But in the end, it didn't matter. It would just be another car on the list. Another car in and out of my shop. Another customer in and out of my life.

After some debating with myself, I decide I need to take William's car to a better mechanic than I originally chose earlier this evening. Today, I was so frustrated with him that I let my reaction dictate my action. From a business standpoint, my dad taught me better. I make a mental note to call the other shop in a few hours to set up arrangements.

I glance at my bedroom door, which stood open to the dark hallway. I wonder what it would be like to be William Montgomery. I wonder what he saw when he looked at Bromley. Did he see the same shabby house in the country I saw, or did he think it was "nice" considering the surroundings?

It's not that I care what he thinks about me or my father's house. I just want to see it through someone else's eyes and from someone else's point of view. I look around my room and see the green paint that had been up there since high school, and my awards still hanging on the walls. I see the pictures of my father, my brother Ben, and our cars. I let my mind wander…

> *I tape the last box up. Looking around my room, I make sure I have everything I need. I glance at the pictures on the wall, taking in the picture where my family was still together. All four of us kids have our arms slung over each other's shoulder and big goofy grins on our faces. I always thought we were a happy family. The sad part about pictures is that they always show the good times. But when I really looked at the picture in my hands, I catch the distant stare of my mother's eyes.*
>
> *She had a smile across her tanned face but it never reached her eyes. I stretch my finger out and cover her nose and mouth, revealing her cheerless expression in a very happy-filled snapshot. I realize then that she had mentally left long before she had physically left.*
>
> *My dad steps in the doorway and pulls me from my thoughts. I pick up the box and turn towards him with a beam on my face, shoving the sadness aside. He gives me a tight smile and reaches for the box. With it propped under one arm, he wraps the other around me as we walk out of my room and*

down the stairs. "Lee, please don't be a stranger. I won't touch your room. It will be just the way you left it."

"Dad…" I whine, "I will come see you. I am not abandoning you, I am simply growing up."

"I know, but that is what I don't like. I miss my five-year-old little girl who carried that ratty doll around, who wanted me to have tea parties with her and the little girl who would sit on my back and put ribbons in my hair so she could play beauty shop."

We reach the bottom of the stairs and I look up at him to see the shine in his eyes. I throw my hands around his neck and kiss him on the cheek.

"I promise I will be home in two weeks. I will need you to do my laundry,"

He smiles at me and ruffles my hair. "I knew there was a reason I didn't teach you everything about being independent. Now go so you can get there before dark."

Staring at the picture of my dad on my desk and looking around my room makes me feel like I haven't gone anywhere. There is nothing to show for the experiences I have lived through. I went to college and then dad got sick during my fall semester of sophomore year. Ben was finishing his senior year at college, and I knew neither my sisters nor my mother would come back to take care of him. Someone had to step up to the plate, so I did. I wouldn't have changed anything about how it happened. I got to spend the rest of my dad's days with him.

People say I will always cherish those memories, which I do to an extent, but no one talks about how difficult it is to take care of an ailing family member. Sure, I remember the smiles, funny mishaps, and awkward times. But no one mentions the constant clean up or the sleepless nights making sure they don't need help. Or making sure they didn't pass away in their sleep. No one mentions those depressing thoughts or moments.

I hear some movement in the kitchen, startling me. I laugh to myself and think *how could I forget someone is staying with me?*

I can't be in my room any longer so I make my way downstairs too. The kitchen light is dim and the open refrigerator door is open casting a bright, yellow light on a very square jaw and very bare, tight abdomen. He scans the empty shelves and I see him grab my much-favored tube of raw cookie dough. "I don't think so."

His head pops up at the sound of my voice and he drops the cookie dough on the ground. A curse word follows. I bite back a giggle and snatch the sacred snack off the floor. I go to the counter to cut it open, retrieve two spoons, and make my way towards the table.

"Grab some drinks while you are standing there with the door open." He sat a drink down in front of me and starts to walk away. "You can have some if you want. I was only teasing."

"It's okay. I don't really need to eat your food seeing you don't have very much."

"I don't mind." I offered him the second spoon, ignoring his jab. "Just in case you are a germaphobe."

Amused, he sits and takes the spoon, "Do you even know where my mouth has been?"

"Gross." I dig out some cookie dough from the tube, remove the glob with my fingers, and pop it into my mouth. "A simple fix to the cross-contamination issue because you never know where my mouth has been either."

His eyes widen, but he smirks at me and takes the tube and does the same thing. "So, what's your story?"

"I grew up here in Middleton. Went to college. My father died a year ago after I moved back to take care of him and the business. What's your story?"

"Grew up in a small town in Georgia and moved to L.A. when I was nineteen. Two years after that, I hit it big. I was so good looking that it only took me a year to nail a job, while it takes most people several years." He leans back in his chair smugly, but sarcasm dripped playfully from his mouth.

"Ooh, maybe I should leave. There isn't enough room here for you, your ego, and me," I raise an eyebrow at him and take back the tube. "Your accent doesn't sound southern."

It was kind of nice how he didn't offer his sympathy for my deceased father. Most people pat my hand and try to explain the loss or make it ok that he is gone. The words mean more to them than they do to me, so I just say, "Thank you," and move on. I assume he doesn't say anything for the mere fact he doesn't really care.

"I moved around a lot as a kid so the original accent I learned stuck the most." He snatches the cookie dough back. I grin and twirl the spoon in my hands.

Reed sits there looking around the kitchen and asks, "Where's your mom?"

"She left when I was in middle-school. She and my sister now live in the city." My answer is void of any emotion.

"How many of you in your family?" he continues.

"One of me," I tease in reply. He gives me a "whatever" roll of the eye but laughs softly. "I have a brother, Ben, and two sisters, Shelby and Elan, all older."

When my parents divorced, they allowed us to choose who we would live with. Looking at my parents across the table from me, one on each side, my thirteen-year-old mind couldn't have known how weighted that decision would end up being. There was no way I could have known then that my mother would write me off all because I chose my dad over her.

My mother was the art to my dad's life. He grew up farming my great-grandfather's land. He went to the big city for a loan to buy the auto shop and that's where he met my mom. They married shortly after they met and he moved her from the big city.

All four of us kids couldn't be more alike yet so different from each other. Elan, the oldest, took after my mom in every form. Her independence and need to be in control is why she walked away from the family; my mom already had that role covered. Ben is a mix between my parents, more like my mom, but tends to have a few traits of my dad. He has the mentality to make sure all the ducks are where they are supposed to be, but he will back down to someone more demanding like my mom. Shelby is a mix as well, however she's a dangerous mix. She has my dad's pleasing heart and will blindly follow anyone who shows her love. Her submissiveness has allowed my mom to control her actions, but my mom isn't the only one controlling Shelby. The twisted side to Shelby is that she has the ability to manipulate those who aren't controlling her. She's learned how to take no responsibility for her own actions and make her problems everyone else's fault. Then there's me. I am like my dad. I always hoped for a family that could be together, however, like him I want to keep the peace.

"What about you, have any siblings?" I ask.

"I have a younger brother. Why isn't your brother taking over the business?"

"Do you really have a problem with me being a mechanic?" I ask, trying not to be too hasty as I take the cookie dough. I refuse to let him think that comment bothers me.

"No, it's just interesting," he affirms. I raise my eyebrow at him. He knew he needed to continue, "I am used to girls who won't pick anything up off the ground because that in itself would ruin their manicure, let alone get under a car."

I nod. "Guess that would make me a little manly in your world."

He bobs his head. "I think it shows you are open to almost anything. I guess I think your brother is more of a pansy for letting you take charge of something that should be his."

"Trust me, my dad wanted him to. He wanted something else for me, but life played out differently." We sat in silence for a little while, lost in our own thoughts as we pass the cookie dough back and forth.

My dad always thought I would be an architect. That's what I originally set out to do. He and I had plans to revamp this town and build it into a quaint mountain-valley getaway.

"Why did you tell me your name was Reed?"

"Because it is. I changed it to William Montgomery when I moved to Hollywood."

I stare at him blankly, thinking he might go on. He stares back at me, feeling me out and possibly trying to see if he wants to go further. He decides not to. I can't blame him. I don't really want to go into the nitty-gritty of my life story with someone I met a few hours ago.

"Do you prefer to be called one over the other?"

He sits there for a moment before responding. "If you don't mind, can you call me Reed? I would like to stay low key if at all possible."

It might be close to impossible to keep it low key in a small town, but I respect him for the wish.

"Reed it is then."

"You have the capability to fix my car, don't you?" He states this more as a fact than a question.

I just nod.

"How long would it take?"

"It will take about a week for the parts to get here. But once they are here, it would only be another week, maybe even less. So two weeks tops."

"Is it going to cost an arm and a leg?"

I chuckle, as we have already discussed this. "No, I am not one of those mechanics." I pull a piece of paper out of my robe pocket. I am not really sure why I hesitate a moment, but looking at him it feels like this could be more than working on his car.

I slide the paper across the table. He picks it up while I take another bite of cookie dough. I wait and watch him scan the handwritten quote. His jaw clenches and smooths out.

"Ok, then I can wait it out. I kind of like being in the middle of nowhere."

"You say that now."

Reed smirks but his eyes are focused on me. "Yeah, I say that now."

5

HARLEY

Thursday night finally arrives. It's my first night off in a long time. Since Milo, Nikki, and I all worked earlier today, Reed had been cooped up in the house by himself all day. The image of him like a puppy that needs to be let out and socialized amuses me.

I walk into the house to find my kitchen spotless, except for the one open chip bag on the table. Movie scripts are spread all around it. Immediately, I feel my world closing in on me. I know I am messy - but it's my mess.

Reed is sitting on the couch watching one of his movies, completely zoned out. My temper is building to the point that I want to reach out and slap him across the back of his head. I haven't lived with anyone but my dad. Since losing him, I have developed my own routine. It is very clear to me that Reed is definitely not in my routine.

"It's Thursday, I'm meeting Nikki and Milo at the bar for dinner," I holler down to Reed as I make my way upstairs to change.

"Am I invited or is it just you three?" he asks. I'm at the top of the stairs where he can't see me gritting my teeth. Reed has been here for four days now and I feel suffocated with his ever-present existence in my house.

"Yes, you're invited, but we have to hurry," I reply, trying to hide my true disdain.

Today's workload was light so I focused on logistics of the businesses - running numbers, ordering supplies, and checking the financials a couple more times. Getting ready will be quick and easy since I don't have to scrub motor oil off my skin. I hurry to my room and put on my jeans and a clean button-up shirt with cowboy boots. Combing my hair with my fingers, I look in the mirror and decide that's as good as it will get. When I hurry downstairs, I realize that Reed isn't ready. I check my watch, and calculate the time we are supposed to be there. Milo and Nikki are likely already there.

"C'mon Reed, I swear you take longer to get ready than my two sisters combined," I holler while I fidget with my shirt. "It's not like the media will find you all the way out…" I stop mid-sentence as he is standing before me in nothing but jeans. His toned abs, tanned and smooth like marble, look like they had walked right out of my TV and into my living room.

"Speaking of media, how can you guarantee that they won't be out here?" he asks, crossing his muscled arms over his chest. "Does small-town America not have Facebook access?"

"I can't guarantee anything but we need to go, so get a shirt," I say, shooing him away. I'm a little disappointed I can't touch his abs or stare at them. I may not like that he is in my space, but any girl would be able to put the irritation aside for the glimpse of this sight.

He shrugs and leaves me to fawn over his backside, which is just as appealing. Embarrassed by my reaction, I stare up at the ceiling and try to compose myself before he comes back. Finally, he reappears in a tight screen tee, his loose-fitting jeans, and his flip flops. Tugging his baseball cap on, he nods at me.

"Don't you want more than that to wear?" I ask, staring down at his feet.

He glances down, wiggles his toes, then looks back at me. "This is all I packed. I never thought I would get stuck in this cold climate." I reach for a lightweight jacket Milo continues to leave at my house. Reed takes it and we are finally out the door.

Reed walks up to my jeep and I shake my head. "Nope, we aren't taking Marcy; it's not that far, we can walk."

Even with his hat low over his eyes, I can still see them rolling in irritation. It's only a five-minute walk across town. He will be fine.

Along the way, Mrs. Avery waves to us from her window. She is dressed in her ever-present, ratty bath robe and is clearly melting in her house shoes while she eyes our town's newest guest. A few houses later, Mr. Jacobs is out sweeping leaves off his sidewalk. He stops briefly to gawk as we walk past him. It's apparent that our town does not get visitors often.

I can feel winter creeping around the corner. I pull my jacket on and look over at Reed to see that his hands are shoved deep in his pockets.

"If we would have taken the car, would it have been so bad?" he chides. "I mean, we are in a farming community, are you all really that concerned with the environment?"

"Yeah, but I would hate for you to lose that beautiful figure since we don't have any state-of-the-art gyms like you are accustomed to," I retort.

I swallow my pride and fight the urge to debate his other environmental concerns. I have seen the documentaries covering pesticides, farms, and everything that bashes the way our community tries to survive. It may not always be ethical according to an outsider's opinion, but until they live and breathe the choices that have to be made, their opinions don't amount to much.

We keep a steady pace while he shivers in efforts to stay warm. His flip flops scuff against the pavement as a reminder that they are not covering his feet. I force the guilt down for not taking the car.

"I've been looking at engines this week and I was thinking - since we have to replace it, we could do a whole overhaul with a bigger and better engine block. It will cost a little more, but we can make it a car buff's dream Chevelle."

"I take it that will be a longer repair?" His question is full of irritation.

"It will, but not by much."

He nods. "All I ask is that you take good care of it." His voice reveals some sentiment he has for the car. "Why does everyone keep looking at us? I know it's not normal to see me in real life but I would think after a couple days of seeing me, I would be old news." His eyes make contact with another gawker.

"You said you grew up in a small town. Did you forget your life becomes theirs too?"

Small towns are full of nosey people. They enjoy creating as many rumors and speculations as the media and paparazzi do. It doesn't matter if the visitor is a celebrity or not, the townies just like to meddle. The only difference is that the rumors they generate stay here instead of going worldwide.

"I was born in a small town but I grew up in a suburb, so I don't remember too much about the small-town life." Reed glances over at me, "question for you…" he asks with a cocky attitude "… who is Lance?"

My stomach plummets to the core of the earth. My step falters a little and I try to recover quickly, hoping he hadn't noticed. Given his arrogant smirk, I know the truth. "How do you know about him?" Internally, I criticize my shaky voice.

"Your phone kept ringing today and I noticed it was the same number. He also kept leaving messages begging you to call him back. My favorite was the one with a girl in the background, causing an immediate hang-up. What's the story on that?"

I don't respond. A triumphant grin spreads across his face. Luckily, we reach the bar. I pull the door open and wave for Reed to go in. Following behind him, I notice the room went silent. The cliché' "a pin dropping could have been heard" rings true. Everyone stares at us. I nudge Reed forward to the table where our small party is waiting for us. I scoot into the booth first as Reed takes the outside seat. I give a few stargazers a pointed look as one by one they go back to their own business.

"We have a camping trip planned for tomorrow if you would like to come," Nikki pipes up after we had ordered our food.

Reed looks at her skeptically. "You mean camping as in vinyl tent in the woods with bears, in the dead of winter? I don't think so." He shakes his head at us like we are crazy.

"It's not the dead of winter. Winter is just waking up," Milo comments.

"It's so much fun!" Nikki pushes. "You will be surprised. And there aren't bears around this neck of the woods." I look at Nikki, whose smile gives away her lie. I choke back a laugh and Reed continues shaking his head at her lame attempt at deception.

Our food arrives and everyone falls silent as we eat. Reed is the first left-handed person I have ever sat by. I quickly learn the inconvenience of this anomaly. We try our best not to bump one another, but it is inevitable. At some point in the middle of dinner, it turned into a game for us and we purposely knocked elbows.

In the short time we have known each other, an easy verbal banter has developed between us. But for the first time, our banter has become physical. I catch Nikki's gooey gaze. Our flirting was being observed. I clear my throat and adjust to be a little more out of his way.

Once the dishes are cleared, we move to the bar, order a pitcher of beer, and take over one of the open pool tables. After a couple of drinks and games of pool, we all start to loosen up. Reed starts to let his guard down, making jokes, attempting trick shots, and sharing some of the trade secrets to his movies. He talks about the funniest moments but never reveals who was the accused fool.

The more the drinks flow, the more new rules we begin to come up with for each game. Eventually, we settle into a game we called *Truth*. This is a game Nikki, Milo, and I played when we were young. Now that we are older, we have added alcohol.

I raise my glass and finish off my drink. Milo pours refills behind me. Continuing on with the rules, Nikki explains, "Whoever makes a shot gets to ask anyone in the game a question. They can either answer the question or drink. Whoever misses a shot has to drink."

"Let's play 'Truth' then, shall we?" Reed asks, leaning close to my ear. My stomach quakes from his reverberating tone. His closeness makes my toes tingle, but when I turn, I see my body has deceived me as he is not standing as close as I thought. "I have a feeling I am about to get close and personal with all of you," Reed's lips quirk up devilishly. He chuckles while he lines up his shot. The cue ball breaks the triangle but nothing makes it into the pockets. "I take a drink now, right?" We nod and he drinks.

I am next, banking Ball 15 into the corner pocket. I look at my friends. Poor Reed is the newest; of course I want to know about him, but decide to give him a break. "Milo, when was the last time you went skinny dipping?"

"You already know this," Milo said mildly.

"I know, but I thought I would give Newby a break before we unleash on him." I encourage Milo to start.

Nodding, Milo proceeds to answer, "The last time I went skinny dipping was last week on our camping trip. See, my lovely wife and Lee here decided to take my clothes, leaving only a child-size pair of Superman underwear for me to walk through the campground back to our campsite. I almost got arrested by John over there," Milo said, tipping his glass in the direction of the bar where Officer John Meeks is sitting. Officer Meeks nods over at us, clearly intrigued with our game.

"Lucky for him, I covered his…" Nikki gooses Milo in the rear. He yelps, which made Nikki giggle.

"And you want me to go camping?" Reed asks, amused.

"Just make sure you know where to hide your clothes," I tease.

I line up for my next shot, miss, and take my drink. The next couple shots end with questions for Reed about what movies are coming up next, who was the best kisser out of the kissing scenes from the last five movies, and what it was like to be in Italy.

Reed asks us questions about what it is like to grow up in a small town, how we met, why we stayed here. We share playful jabs, poke fun at one another, and work up to a nice, relaxed intoxicated level. On the last game, Reed starts asking more personal questions, mainly aimed at me.

"Harley…" He pauses, waiting for the ball to fall in the pocket. "Who is Lance?" he asks, causing my buzz to dissipate into thin air. Milo and Nikki glance over at me but I keep my composure.

"My ex-fiancé."

Reed pauses for a second, shocked that I actually answered the question. He recovers quickly. Then just as fast, he sinks another shot followed with his next question, "What happened?"

"We decided we weren't meant for each other." My answer is bland and to the point.

Another ball falls in. Reed fires off his next question, "Why is he still calling then?"

Milo's eyes harden at me, Nikki's mouth pops open, and it feels like the whole bar stops to listen to the answer. Milo didn't know about Lance's calls so I decide it is best to take a drink instead of answering. Finishing off the pitcher, I thrust it at Milo. "Go get a refill," I order quietly - not looking at him.

Once Milo and Nikki are out of earshot, I lean in close to Reed. "I don't know what game you are playing right now, but leave the topic alone." My voice is ice cold. Everyone seems to act like they aren't watching the exchange between us, but I know better.

"I thought this was a way to get to know each other," Reed scoffs, acting as if he was asking innocent questions.

"You know plenty now." His glassy eyes sober up as he realizes he crossed a line.

Milo returns with a full pitcher and keeps his glare on me. Reed intentionally misses the next shot. With the eight ball left, I call the pocket and end the game. The rest of the evening is spent in awkward tension.

Thankfully, Kayden asks me to close the bar, giving me an out of the game. Walking away from the group, I continue to avoid Milo's steady glare, at the same time trying to look anywhere but at Reed. "I think we will call it a night," Milo interjects.

I finally make myself meet his glare. It gives me the feeling that we aren't finished with the conversation but he will leave it alone for tonight.

"Milo, will you take Reed back to Bromley?" I ask. Despite his heavy stare, I don't shy away from him. I just get pissy. He nods and they leave.

With the bar cleared out and Kayden gone, the empty space gives me a little bit of relief. I need the uninterrupted space to process the events that just unfolded.

I gather my hair up in a messy bun and begin picking up empty beer bottles to take them back to the kitchen recycle bin. In the kitchen, I rest my palms on the cool metal countertop and take slow breaths.

I have tried to get Lance to stop calling me. I know what Milo is going to say, but he just doesn't get it. I am thankful for Milo's desire to protect me, but what am I supposed to do? I hate his solution and he hates my reasons, which only leaves us gridlocked in the same argument. I wish he would let it go and let me deal with my life the way I want. I see a shadow move in my peripheral vision. I jump and knock cups over on the counter.

"I thought I would hang around and wait for you, if you don't mind." Reed looks apologetically at me. I wasn't sure if it was for scaring me or if it was for bringing up Lance. Either way, I don't care. I just want him to leave.

"Why? Haven't you heard enough?" I snap. I know he only asked who Lance was to pester me, but that was the second time tonight. I feel like I already made myself clear that this subject was off limits. Apparently, pointed looks don't register with him though. Right now, I need a break from his prying, especially after Milo's heated glare.

His jaw clenches, "I thought you could use some help." I fight the smile caused by the twitch of his strong jaw line. It makes him that much hotter. His expression reveals I didn't hide my grin very well. "What?" His voice holds a ghost of a laugh as he looks me in the eye inquisitively.

I shake my head as I push past him and try to hide my heated cheeks. There is no way I am going to tell him what I was really thinking. I won't let him have the upper hand on me like that. I head towards the bar to begin cleaning. "Well, if you are going to hang around, you might as well make yourself useful. Could you clear off those tables?"

Turning on the water and checking its temperature, I focus my pressing anger towards the sink in front of me. My fury isn't spurred by Reed or that he exposed a secret to Milo, it was the fact that Lance is still a part of my life. He is a constant reminder of what happened between us and how his slimy hooks still have a firm grip on me.

I let all the frustration about him boil inside. When my hands plunge into the hot soapy water, all I feel is the sting prickling my palms. I try to drive Lance as far from my mind as I can by focusing on the water's heat. Reed returns with his arms full of bottles and glasses, and a confused look on his face.

"Never seen anyone actually wash dishes before?" I snort. "Have you ever washed dishes?"

"You have a dishwasher back there, is it broke?" he points over his shoulder, "and yes I have washed dishes before," he mocks back.

"The washer is not broke, but for some odd reason this calms me." Shrugging my shoulders, I go back to work.

Reed weighs my words. Reaching around me, he grabs the wet wash cloth that's resting on the other side of the sink. Added to the rage inside of my head, this closeness is overwhelming. Thankfully, he moves back and starts cleaning the tables. We barely utter any words to each other as we let the juke box fill the empty bar.

I calm down and get lost in my own world. I begin to hum one of my favorite songs, forgetting that I am not alone. He startles me when he brushes my shoulder as he reaches for the towel draped over it. He begins drying the dishes. "What song are you humming?" he asks when I look up at him.

I shake my head. A few strands of hair had slipped from my elastic ponytail holder and were tickling my face. I try to push them out of my face with my shoulder, but give up quickly, realizing it is useless. I reach for another glass. Reed catches my hand, and, bringing it up to examine it closer, determines "I think the water might be a bit hot."

I gently pull my beet-red hand away, glancing at it, "So… you have to kill germs," I say.

"But you're scalding your hands," he states. I shrug and fidget a little from the touch of his rough hands on my steaming ones. I tuck the loose strands behind my ear, not worrying anymore if my hair gets wet.

"Here, let me wash some dishes so you can put these glasses away." Placing his hands on my hips he guides me out of his way and fills my post. He turns on the cold water to cool it down.

"Pansy," I tease.

His mouth turns up at one corner in a crooked smile, "You know that song you were humming?"

"What about it?" I question, unsure where he is going with this.

"You really shouldn't hum until you get some lessons," he teases. I turn to face him and see he is laughing at my annoyed glare.

"That joke is old."

"It was a joke. Lighten up." He continues washing dishes while I dry and put them away. He begins to hum the same tune I was humming.

"You are an actor; I think you should stick with that job," I comment.

"Hardy-har-har, but I already used that joke, which I think proves you shouldn't do standup comedy either." I couldn't help but crack a smile. He continues, "There we go and she is back, ladies and gentlemen. You know you are much more fun to be around when you are smiling and not on the defensive."

"And you are much more fun when you don't act like you are better than me."

Reed's lips purse as if he is considering my statement. "Point taken, so where does that leave us then?" He speaks to the water, rinsing off the next glass.

"Wherever you want it to leave us." I was feeling exasperated.

"I'll work on my rudeness if you work on loosenin' up a little."

"Loosenin.' I don't think that is a word, but I smell what you are stepping in," I say sarcastically. He grins widely at me.

I nod as I consider the new rules. "I will try."

"As will I," he mocks back. "So…. that song you were humming, what is it?"

"A tune."

"Another joke from our wanna-be comedian," Reed snorts in a playful tone. "I am serious, what song? I recognize it."

"Nothing really. It is just a song that I learned recently on the guitar."

"Will you play it?"

"No. It's kind of private." I feel my cheeks grow warm.

"I wasn't trying to snoop, but I have seen guitars in your house. I work faster with music. So…" he nods toward the stage.

At his mention of music, I realize the juke box has run out of songs and the bar is quiet again. "No. There is a juke box over there that can play music. I doubt it has your favorite band, but it works," I said, moving on as if this was the dead end to the conversation.

"Why not? Is it because of the joke I made earlier?" he pushed.

With a sigh, I explain, "No, it has nothing to do with your joke. I just don't play for people."

"The song you were humming, it had a light sound to it. C'mon, play it!" His eyes grow softer as he gazes down at me. I set the towel down and move towards the stage. Swiping up the guitar, I sit down on stage. I decide to play a different song than the one I was humming. One I am sure he hasn't heard before; therefore, he can't pass any judgment. My fingers quiver as they play the first few measures.

Reed keeps his head down as the lyrics ring out. I'm shaky on the first notes because this is something that I normally do just for me. The song *Paper Doll* by Rosie Thomas makes me reflect on the fights I've had with Milo over the last few years. The words to the second verse sting because I want to break free from what is expected of me concerning Milo, Lance, and my family situation.

I don't want to sit back and just let things happen, but I feel helpless. Like those paper dolls who have no say in how they are perceived or dressed. This line rings truer than anything else in the song, because if I do what I know I should, I fear I'll lose everything I know. I cringe at the thought of how vulnerable I feel in this moment, singing this song for Reed.

The last note is played. I refuse to look up. I sit, stunned by how I feel. It's as if a burden has been lifted, because the words are out there and not trapped inside any more. My eyes sting with tears that have not yet fallen. Milo would think it was just about paper dolls. I only hope that is what Reed thinks too.

I quickly blink my eyes, hoping he won't see how I truly feel when I look up. From his expression, it is clear he understands more than I intended. We are a good twenty feet apart, but I can tell he is seeing the truth. His body is relaxed and all his attention is on me.

I begin to squirm under his heavy gaze, so I start strumming the strings to fill the silence and divert his attention. When I glance up, he is back at work scrubbing the dishes. I play for a while longer. When I am done, I put the guitar back on its stand and connect my iPod to the sound system. Mellow melodies that fit my mood fill the air. Then I return to the task of closing the bar.

6

With the lights off and the door locked, we start our walk back to Bromley. "I liked the song," he says to break the silence.

I tuck my head down, feeling shy and unsure what to say.

"Did you write it?"

I chuckle softly, "No." Feeling very exposed to Reed after that song, I want to gain some privacy. I pull the elastic band out of my hair. It spills down my back with kinks all through it. I feel comforted as some hair tumbles over my shoulder and creates a protective shield between us.

"I really didn't mean to be rude tonight during the game, or to start something between you and Milo."

"Reed, just leave it alone." I push him in the shoulder to let him know it was okay. It really isn't fine, but I want to move past it. He grins with his head down and we continue walking.

Reed tries to be helpful. "You know Milo means well, right?"

"Are you defending him? You just met him," I retort. His shoulders rise to his ears. I do agree with him. "I know his heart is in the right place. This isn't the first fight we've had about this." I huff out a sigh. "Unfortunately, I don't see it being the last, no matter how bad we all want it to be." Despite the temperature outside, we slowly meander our way back to my dad's house.

"Have you guys always been friends?" he asks.

"For as long as I can remember. He and my brother Ben were always together when we were really young. But after my parents divorced, Ben changed and Milo became a better brother to me than my own."

"Which is why you guys have stuck together for so long," Reed pieces together. I nod, reflecting on how grateful I am to have a friend like Milo in my life.

"So what do you do around here when you aren't working?" Reed's voice was soft against the early morning air.

"This," I said, spreading my arms out in front of me. His expression scrunches. "Nothing. We do nothing." I laugh as he gives me a look of boredom. "It's not that bad. At times, it's rather nice. I like nights…well… I guess mornings, like this, when it's calm and quiet, the stars are out, it's cool but not too chilly."

"How do you enjoy a morning like this?" By this time we were walking across the park. I smile widely when I see it.

"I swing."

"Like swap for your neighbor's husband kind of 'swing'?"

"No!" I sound a little shrill. I walk towards the swings. Sitting in one, I begin pumping my legs. "Swing, like you did in grade school."

"I can't remember the last time I played on a playground, let alone did this." He sits next to me, rocking side to side instead of swinging the traditional way of back and forth. Reed eyes the playground and appears deep in thought, like he is truly trying to think of the last time he played on a playground. "It feels childish."

"Just because you are in the adult world doesn't mean you have to give up those childhood games. In fact, I bet you still play some of those childish games yourself."

"Care to elaborate on that theory?" he questioned.

"When I was in school, there was a boy who acted up in class all the time. He did whatever he could to get the class laughing. The teachers would say he was acting out to get attention. As I got older, I understood that life at home wasn't easy for him. Any attention was better than none at all, right? Kind of like walking out with your arms around some other girl that isn't Zoey." I glance over to see Reed staring up at the sky.

Zoey was Reed's Hollywood girlfriend, but getting to know Reed kind of made me feel like Zoey was more of Will's girlfriend. It felt like they were two different people.

"Or what about the classic bully motto," I continue. "You know, 'I am going to make you feel smaller than I feel', or the other classic game of boy pulls girl's hair to let her know he likes her."

"Are you saying guys, adult males, are still pulling your hair, because if you are, you really have some inbred boys around here who haven't grown up."

I laugh but go on to explain, "No, I was just saying that acting as if you don't care about them and ignoring them, or simply giving them the wrong type of attention to show that you like them isn't worth it. All in all, it's giving them a hard time. How did you get Zoey?"

Reed shakes his head in reluctance. I watch his body language as he starts to shift uncomfortably in the swing, "Oh come on!" Giving my best impression of an announcer's voice, I continue, "So tell me William Montgomery, which stunt did you pull to nab the great Zoey Green?"

He looks at my triumphant smile and starts to laugh, "I ignored her so she'd chase me."

"See, you can't make fun of me for wanting to swing when you still play those playground games too." Then it dawns on me, "Is that why you are always so aloof towards girls?"

I can tell Reed wants to move on to another topic and fast. "Bet I can get higher than you!" He begins pumping his legs faster, and rises higher and higher into the sky.

"You're on!" I pump my legs harder, and join him as we giggle like little kids.

"It's fun feeling like a kid again," I say, after we couldn't feel our fingers and Reed couldn't feel his toes due to the improper foot attire. We decide it is time to head back to Bromley.

"Why does everything have a name? Like you have Marcy, your jeep, and then you call your house 'Bromley.' Why?"

Reed's questions take me by surprise because he always seems to ask about the details everyone else ignores.

"Because...I have my reasons." I don't feel like he is the one I want to explain my issues to. He challenges me with a look. His eyebrows narrow and his lip curls up to one side. I cave immediately.

"Because I don't feel like they are mine. The house was my dad's. Ole' Bess, the red truck I picked you up in, belongs to the auto shop. And my jeep was something my dad bought me. How can I call something mine when I didn't have anything to do with it? I mean, do you call the movies you have been in yours or do you call them by their title?"

"I refer to them by their title, but that's because there are so many of them." I catch the cocky smile playing on his lips but his eyes bestowed more of a genuine statement. "I guess I can see what you are saying, but Bromley is *your* home."

"It was my home when my dad was alive." And that is when it settles in for both of us - with my dad gone, nothing feels the same. The house doesn't feel like home; it feels empty, unfilled, and lonely. Nothing like what a home is supposed to feel like.

"How did he die?" I don't look at Reed but I can tell he isn't looking at me either.

"He had pancreatic cancer." I take a slow breath as my chest tightens.

"How did you come up with the name Bromley?" He quizzically looks at me.

"It's an old English name which means 'Where the brushwood grows.' When I look at the house, it seems a little old and run down. I swear if it talked it would have an old English-man accent." I giggle, which causes him to grin.

"What were you going to college for?" His attention to detail, again, surprises me.

"I wanted to be an architect and a photographer." My voice comes out a little shakier than I wanted, but he doesn't say anything about it or look at me with sympathy.

"Ahh, so I do need to be worried that you might be the paparazzi?" Reed lightly pushes me in the shoulder and I laugh. We reach Bromley and I unlock the door. "No, you are lucky. I only got my basics out of the way. I didn't even get to do any fun classes," I answer, stepping into the toasty warm house.

He gave me his winning smile. "Harley, I had fun tonight. It was nice to be normal. And again, sorry I crossed the line about your past."

"I think normal is over rated. And it's okay." Reed laughs softly. I set my bag down and take off my jacket. He stands there like he wants to say more but doesn't know how to start the question. I attempt to fill the awkward silence, "By the way, I had George change your order tonight and the parts should be in next week."

Reed nods. We stand there a little longer and feel the awkwardness growing. I rock back and forth from heel to toe. Reed has his hands shoved deep in his pockets. I couldn't help but stare at his broad shoulders and taut arms. I begin imagining what it would feel like to be held by him. I know what he smells like, but I wonder what it would smell like to be encircled by him. My mind starts down a path I don't intend and I feel my cheeks flush with embarrassment. I quickly turn away.

"I'm going to... go to..." I couldn't get my words to form in my mind, let alone my mouth, so I point to the stairs.

"Bed?" he finishes for me.

"Yeah." I point my finger and thumb in a gun-like motion. I laugh, feeling completely humiliated by my actions. Reed chuckles and gives me an awkward wave as I climb the stairs. At the top, I look down over the railing and see him with his head down, shaking it from side to side. He looks up the stairs and sees me. He smiles weakly at me then takes one large step out of view. I walk away quickly to my room.

Once behind my door, I stand there. I don't know what happened, but I smile at how weird it was.

7

HARLEY

I spring out of bed the next morning, thinking about how Bromley is supposed to be a "Bed and Breakfast" and I should at least try to make breakfast for my guest. With the coffee brewing, I start the toast, crack some eggs in a pan, and start frying bacon strips in another. Feeling proud of myself for multitasking in the kitchen, I run upstairs to grab my laptop so I can check on orders for work while the food is cooking.

Before my feet reach the bottom step, there is a horrible burning smell. The fire alarm starts beeping. I rush around the corner to find my kitchen in a cloud of smoke. Not sure where it is coming from exactly, I reach for the window above the sink and grab the dish towel. I fan the smoke through the open window.

Reed appears in the doorway and mutters a curse. He grabs the pot handles, throws them on the back burners, and then he unplugs the toaster. His hands cover his ears to block the alarm's obnoxious beeps, while his eyes scan the room. Grabbing the towel from my hands, he moves to wave it under the smoke detector. Reaching for the extra towel, I desperately try to wave the remaining smoke outside. Fresh air slowly begins to replace the smoky haze. The alarm finally turns off and leaves a deafening silence in its wake.

"Do me a favor next time you wake up and want breakfast. Just eat cereal and drink orange juice," Reed huffs at me. Clearly he is not a morning person.

I smile sheepishly at him. "I tried to do something nice. Sorry."

He grumbles out a deep, irritated laugh, and then moves to clean up my mess.

"What were you trying to cook?" He attempts to peel off the charred substance. I glance over his shoulder to see if I can answer the question, but I can't remember what I put in that pan. I settle with a shoulder shrug. He gives up and leaves the pan in the sink to soak. "You may know how to open the hood of my car, but I know my way around a kitchen." He places his hands on my hips and shifts me to the crook of the counter top where I am positioned out of the way.

I stand there, feeling helpless, while he digs for the remaining ingredients for what I assume is French toast. Retrieving a bar stool, he brings it into the kitchen and directs me to sit. Once I'm seated and listening to the hum of his hearty voice, I realize he is only wearing gym shorts. His hair is mussed; my fingers twitch to touch it. They want to feel how soft and fluffy it is. His voice is soothing me to the point that I am not paying attention to what he is saying or doing.

He is looking at me and I stare back. It then dawns on me he is waiting for a response but I have no clue what the question was. I blush awkwardly. He smiles his gorgeous smile.

"I swear I wasn't ogling you." The words tumble out hurriedly, sounding like I am trying to hide something. "Your voice is relaxing," I try again, but it doesn't make me sound any better. "What was your question?"

"I was checking to see if you understood what I was saying, but I think I got the answer." I decide to roll with it and will myself to pay attention when he starts re-explaining the process. After the last piece of toast is golden brown, we grab our plates and sit down at the table. The back door swings open and Nikki bounces in, followed by Milo. Our eyes meet but we don't speak to one another. Instead, I address Nikki by offering her a plate.

"We thought we would come see what you guys were up to this morning," Nikki chirps. Reed looks at me with amused brown eyes. Milo catches the look when he walks past us to the sink to wash his hands. He glowers at me, still upset about last night. There seems to be some new irritation brewing as well behind the heated stare, but I have a feeling that isn't geared towards me.

Stuffed, I excuse myself to get ready for work and start to exit the very uncomfortable room. Reed offers to clean the kitchen, so I go upstairs to shower and change. Once my hair is dry, I hear a familiar knock on my door. One I am accustomed to; it's as if someone has spoken my name.

"Come in." I deeply breathe in, gearing up for the long-awaited battle. In the mirror, I see Milo looking back at me and I know all too well what that look means. We've had this same fight ever since the eve of my wedding. "Milo, don't start," I breathe out before he could go any further.

"Why is Lance calling you again?" Lance's name rolls off his tongue like it is a curse word that tastes horrible in his mouth.

"He never stopped calling," I say, exasperated. His eyes flare, indicating that was not the response I should have gone with.

"I thought you said you quit talking to him," he accuses.

"I did, but he still calls. I just don't talk to you about it." I hate having this conversation with him because it always comes back to him demanding a change to a situation I have very little control over.

"But you answer?" Annoyed accusation hangs in his voice.

"No," it came out more like I wasn't sure, "I pick the phone up and hang it right back up. I don't actually talk."

"Why don't you tell him where he can go?"

"Because I can't." I couldn't look at Milo because he only knows part of the story. He knows the part I'm comfortable with everyone else knowing, the part that doesn't show exactly how stupid I was. There is no way he can comprehend how messed up this situation is. To avoid Milo's disappointed glare, I start applying makeup even though I normally don't wear any. Roughly brushing powder on, I'm extremely flustered and I want to keep moving.

"You can't or you won't." We are both exhausted with this conversation.

"Please let it go?" I force though gritted teeth. "I don't need you to fix this."

"Let it go? Harley," Milo uses my full name, which means he is mad at me, "I know he hurt you in more ways than one." He eyes me in the mirror. My heart picks up, thinking I had been found out, but then I remember the truth. "I find it delusional that you are not cutting Lance from your life when he cheated on you. But that's really secondary. Why would you keep him around when he physically harmed you?"

"I don't need this!" My voice is rising. My walls are going up quickly. He is starting to tap the fragile glass that is holding me together.

"It's because of her!" Milo's voice is matching mine now.

"What is that supposed to mean?" My body feels tense and on the verge of snapping.

"You think you can save her," he accuses. "Shelby is an adult. She is choosing to be with him. Newsflash for you Harley, Lance moved on. Lance found someone else to tap. Remember?"

The word "tap" strikes me hard and Milo is yelling at me so loud that his face is red and his voice is starting to strain.

Like a dry twig, I snap, whirling around to face him. "Yeah, I remember. I was there. I caught him in the act thank you very much. And yes, I want to protect Shelby from him. Like you said, you know Lance hit me, why would I not want to protect my sister from him?" I shout back at him.

"But she isn't yours to protect." Milo's voice seethes with frustration.

"I know you think I am wrong for this so you don't need to constantly remind me. So, newsflash Milo, leave it alone." Despite what Milo thinks, I will always try to protect my family. Fortunately for Milo, he will never have to be in this position.

"They don't need you. They never needed you. You think you have to take care of them. All you end up doing is meddling."

"I meddle? What about you? What do you call what you are doing right now?" Anger is pulsing through my veins.

"I'm meddling now because we are friends. You're like my sister, damn it. But just because they are blood family doesn't mean their issues need to become yours."

"They are my family, Milo. I didn't choose them. I am sorry you don't understand. I am glad your family is greeting-card quality, but seriously, not everyone has that. So again, if you don't like how I handle my life, there's the door." Thrusting my hand out, I point for him to leave.

Milo's face is as red as mine feels. He doesn't say another word before turning on his heels and walking out of the room. I hear him and Nikki leave the house with a slam of the door. Glancing out the window, I watch them get in the car and drive off.

Internally, I battle with that fight and every fight we have had about my family. He does have a point that I am too emotionally involved with them. We hardly see each other, or have anything to do with one another, yet they affect the decisions I make for myself. But I don't see a way out. If I set the hard line he wants me to draw, I will lose my family. It's not much of a family, but it's what I have.

I finish getting ready while trying to slow my heart rate. I quickly give up when agitation settles into my stomach. When I get downstairs, I see Reed standing at the sink while drying the last pot. Embarrassment rushes over me as I realize he has been here and heard everything. Not sure what to say, I grab my bag and leave without a word.

The walk to the shop wasn't enough to cool me off. The accusation of being a meddler dug under my skin. If he doesn't want me to meddle then why is he meddling in my personal business, I argue in my head. He came in as if it was his job to take care of me, after he just snapped at me for taking care of family. How hypocritical is that?

Of course he doesn't see the hypocrisy in it at all. This is who I am, and if he doesn't like who I am then I can't change that.

In the safety of my shop, I turn up the radio to drown out my repetitive thoughts. I begin working on Miss Tilly's car, which is never a good task to start when I'm already in a bad mood. Her car can be as stubborn as she is. Luckily, I will have a few hours to work on it before I have to deal with her. She likes asking questions about every line item on the bill, which tests all my patience on a good day. Today, she might just tap me out completely.

I crawl under the car to change the oil. Loosening bolts and filters, I allow the oil to drain from the engine. I am startled when I see a face peering down at me. I jump a little and hit my head on the engine block. I let out a curse before pulling myself out from under the car.

"First, never do that to a person." I gently touch my head with my fingertips and they come away bloody. Reed smiles at me and hands me a rag. I dab my bleeding forehead and move to wash my hands and the cut. "And second, what are you even doing here?" I sound snippy but don't care.

"My car is here, so I thought I would come check on it." He shrugs.

"Yeah, because someone might steal it around here."

"No, I actually thought you might take your anger out on my baby."

Reed eyes me as I march over to the shop sink. "Why were you under the car anyway? You have this nifty car lift in your shop."

I roll my eyes at him. "No scripts to read, so you decide to come pester me?" My annoyance is bubbling out and getting the best of the situation.

"Hey, just because you are mad at Milo doesn't mean I will be your punching bag." His voice is gentle and makes me feel a little guilty. I should apologize for my behavior but I am stubborn and don't want to.

Dabbing my head with a wadded paper towel, I catch a glimpse of him in the smoke-colored mirror. He walks around his car, which I had moved to the next bay over while we waited on parts. There is a somber weight resting on his shoulders as he circles the car.

I make an effort to explain myself. "When I get frustrated, I like to do things the old way." Reed's eyes meet mine in the mirror. He moves back towards me and abandons his car. I go on with my explanation. "A ratchet or a screw driver takes more effort and concentration than a power tool. Helps refocus my mind. That's the answer to your earlier question of why I am not using the lift." He seems satisfied with that answer and bumps the toe of his shoe against the tire.

"Whose car is this?"

"Miss Tilly's." Once the cut is clean enough, I move back to work on the car. Using a ratchet, I start unscrewing the spark plugs.

"What is wrong with it?"

"She has been complaining about a knocking sound." I squint, inspect the part, and deem it unnecessary to replace yet.

"So do you know what is wrong with it?" He must be asking that question again only to pester me.

"Reports keep coming back clear." I inspect another plug and wire. Both seem to be fine. "…so I am working on it."

"Therefore… you don't know," he states, falling back on his old taunt. His arrogant smile lets me know he can see he is poking the bear.

"Do you have to be such a jerk right now? I am sure it is the oil, but while she has it in I thought I would do her a favor and do an overall check." He only responds with his chuckle. He points to the ratchet and the part I am holding in my hand.

"Did your dad teach you everything you know?" I nod, not wanting to talk about my family after the fight I just had.

Reed continues, "I know a little about cars but I pay people like you to do the dirty work."

"The dirty work?" I can't help but laugh as my mind slips in the gutter. It fascinates me that no matter how snippy I am with him, he remains calm and collected. His calm is leaking into my bad attitude.

"Get your mind out of the gutter Anderson. And if I paid for that....it would then be considered prostitution. Something I don't want on my record." He nudges my shoulder playfully.

"Doesn't mean you haven't done it, you just haven't been caught yet." I look up at him to see his reaction. He stands there looking at me with a cocky grin but doesn't comment. "Man whore." I say disgustedly, which results in another chuckle from him. "Do you change your own flat tire or is that considered dirty work?" I ask.

"I haven't had to." He evades the question smoothly.

I poke at him further. "Do you know how to?"

"Nope, and there is roadside service." I laugh at his honesty.

He has moved to lean against the support pillar in the garage. He seems relaxed and I find it hard not to feel dreamy about him.

"You are so spoiled," I sass, trying to clear my head. "Did you really come to check on your car or did you come to annoy me?"

"I came to annoy you." Reed can't stand still long and begins walking around the garage, inspecting the place and seeming to take it all in. "You and Milo..." He left it hanging; I guess he is not sure how he wants to finish the thought.

"Leave it alone," I warn, but politely add, "I am sorry you had to listen to it."

"It was awkward. But don't worry, I didn't hear anything specific, just a lot of yelling." He mutters something under his breath about his childhood but continues on before I can comment on it. "Again, it was awkward but nothing I haven't heard before. Nikki mentioned it is typical for you guys to fight."

"Nikki would know. She's seen and heard it all, but I thought I told you to leave it alone," I retort.

My forehead tickles and I reach up to scratch it. "You're bleeding again," Reed murmurs as I press my grimy hand to my head. "Don't do that," Reed chastises me and takes my hand by the wrist to lead me over to the sink. He begins wiping away the smeared blood and grease from the cut.

"Where is the first-aid kit?" I start to bend down, but he stops me and repeats his question.

I roll my eyes and point to the cabinet under the sink. He retrieves the kit, dabs hydrogen peroxide on some gauze, and gently starts to clean my cut. I wince and jerk back reflexively. He calls me a baby and blows gently on the cut. I can feel the fizzy bubbles as they pop and tickle.

"Better?" Reed looks at me, pleased with his first-aid skills.

"Yeah," I exhale a very embarrassing breathy response.

I try to remember the last time anyone has taken care of me like this. I can't recall that anyone ever did. After my mom left my dad, he had always told me to buck up or reminded me where the Band-Aids were. Even with my mom, there was never the level of tenderness that Reed is showing in taking care of my wound. Not that I was ever mistreated, I was just brought up to take care of myself.

"Reed, why were you in Florida?" I am swooned by his gentleness and want to know how I was graced to have him end up here.

His gaze drops to mine and his whole body stiffens. He must be trying to find the words to answer the question. "I had some stuff to take care of," he answers vaguely.

When the cut is clean enough to his liking, he puts the antibacterial ointment on a Band-Aid and covers my cut. We are standing close and all I can smell is his heavy cologne of musk and woods. Staring straight ahead, I can see how his shirt fits nicely against his torso. My eyes trail up to his Adam's apple, up to his square jaw, and up to his brown eyes. They look warm and inviting and almost depthless. His eyes move from examining my cut and lock on mine.

"That's better." His voice comes out a little husky as our eyes stay magnetized to each other.

A gold metallic Lincoln Navigator pulls up in the drive to break our trance. Ben climbs out, wearing his expensive Rolex and Ray Ban sunglasses. He has his cell phone up to his ear while his kids are yelling in the car. He has an irritated look to his posture.

"Can you take the kids for the night?" he asks, holding the phone away from his ear. I shake my head. The back passenger car doors swing open, spilling out two rascals who turn around and slam them shut. "Quit slamming the doors," he growls at the two kids who barrel into my open arms. He apologizes to the person on the phone and climbs back in his car.

Reed looks at me, confused by what just happened. "This is my niece, Charlotte. Charlie for short. And this is my nephew, Wilbur." I grunt as I sling him up on my hip, "but we call him Caleb. And that would be my brother Ben."

Smirking, he asks the infamous question. "Charlotte and Wilbur? As in Charlotte's Web?"

"My sister-in-law is an English teacher, so she has a thing for story-book characters. Charlotte's Web is one of her favorites," I say, rolling my eyes.

There is a crash in the background and everyone jumps. Charlie is in the corner, where pans of nuts and bolts were sitting on a rolling cart but are now all over the ground. She stands there with her shoulders up by her ears with a half-grin, half-guilty look on her face. Caleb grabs Reed's shirt sleeve and starts playing 20 Questions. "Who are you, why are you here, what do you do for fun…" He is asking questions so fast that Reed can't answer quickly enough, but seems to be handling the barrage of questions pretty well.

"So, are they here to help you?" Reed asks me when Caleb's attention span burns out just as fast as his questions came. I laugh and shake my head. I whisper in Caleb's ear to go help his sister.

He giggles and runs over to her. I redirect my attention to the spark plug and move under the car to replace the plug on the oil pan. I can hear Caleb's questions again, but the attention has changed to Charlie. She is still working on picking up the nuts and bolts she had dropped. Another crash causes me to chuckle as the poor girl drops them all over again.

Ben finally climbs out of his car, grunts a hello in my direction, and heads into the office. I can see part of Reed's face through all the engine parts. He is watching the office window where I can picture Ben going through the filing cabinet, checking the bank accounts, and transferring money. Reed's brows pull together as he tries to understand the circus around him.

My family, like all "normal" families, has its own form of dysfunction. In my father's will, he left the house and the shop to me, and left his financial estate to my mother and three siblings. He trusted that I would know how to support myself and build on what he had left me.

My siblings thought they got the better end of the deal. When my father passed, the three of them, Ben, Shelby, and Elan, made a pact to pool their money and to never touch the principal. However, with Shelby and my mother's spending habits, they chewed up most of the principal. Ben doesn't need the money because he has a successful law firm and Elan's husband supports her. To keep my mother and Shelby afloat, and out of my two other siblings' wallets, Ben comes by twice a month to take money from the shop and transfer it into Shelby's bank account. Shelby will then share the money with my mom. It's one of those things we don't talk about. It's easier to keep my mom and Shelby funded secretly, with Ben's intervention, then it is to have to personally support them by handing over money whenever they run out. Even though I am the one supporting them anyway. I guess Ben just looks at the shop as an entity built by my father rather than my earned income.

Ben comes out of the office and I roll out from under the car. He gives Reed a once over and nods. "You really can't take them for the night?" His voice drips with condescension.

"I work a double tonight," I lie.

I love his kids, but they are the least of my worries at the moment. I have Reed to take care of. Ben grumbles under his breath then hollers at his kids to get in the car. The kids give me a hug and pile back into the car.

Ben looks uncomfortable while eyeing Reed. Normally, no one except me is around when he does the money transfer. He fumbles for some type of pleasantry to ease the situation, but stumbles with simple words like, 'hello' and 'nice to meet you.' I wave him off, granting him permission to leave. With that, he nods but doesn't say anything else. He's in the car faster than I can say "bye" and out of the parking lot before I can even wave.

Reed looks at me, puzzled. I shrug it off and go back to work. Reed helps with a test run and the car is now running perfectly fine.

"I need to work on billing, do you want to hang around for a while or head back to the house?" I question. He asks "Want to put your tools away?"

I can tell the disordered mess is bothering Reed. I shake my head amusingly, "How about I put your organizing skills to use. Would you be willing to fix my main office area?"

He smiles teasingly at me. "I don't know, I never got a 'Thanks' for fixing your house and I get the sense I overstepped my boundary."

I laugh, acknowledging my initial disapproval, but direct him into the office and give him instructions on how I would like everything to be laid out. "It's not that I don't like organization, I just don't make the time for it," I inform him as I move to work on the mound of paperwork on my desk. I feel his eyes twitch at the piles that are scattered around.

We find our quiet groove, with a few interruptions from phone calls to book more appointments; and, of course, the call from Miss Tilly letting me know she wouldn't make it in to get her car today after all. Finished with the last entry, Reed and I lock up and make our way back to Bromley for dinner.

"All your siblings are named after cars, but you got tagged with Harley?"

I laugh, knowing it's ridiculous. "You picked up on that! Most people just assume Ben stands for Benjamin, but yes, Ben is Bentley, and I am the only one not named after a car. Right before I was born, my grandpa, my dad's-dad, passed away."

"Hence, the auto shop is named after him and you." Reed puts the pieces together. "How did your dad get his way with all of his kids being named after transportation?"

"I don't know," I admitted and let my mind reflect on my childhood. My mother's city roots didn't fit in the small town my dad brought her to. She was used to shopping, bar hopping, and walking to all the art galleries - all without needing to drive. Many of my childhood weekends were spent in museums and theatrical shows, and because of that exposure, I donate to a small theater company that my friend operates and runs in the city. It's one of the few good experiences I will acknowledge my mom gave me.

When my mother lived with us, she had the house decorated with fancy paintings and sculptures. It felt like we lived in a museum, but it was home. She hosted a dinner party one time, where she dressed in a fancy dress and accented it with beautiful jewelry. She made us girls put on dresses and Ben wore his suit jacket. When our guests arrived, they came in jeans and nice tops. I remember how uncomfortable everyone looked.

When she left, she took the paintings, the sculptures, and my father's heart. Sadly, he never fully bounced back after that. He dove into his work even more and started helping the community out by doing side jobs in an effort to make the local businesses shine. In order to spend time with him, I dove in with him. At the shop, I would sketch plans for my make-believe town, which I think became my dad's inspiration. He was a jokester and very playful, but his smile lacked the sparkle it once had. I knew he missed my mom and my sisters. Nobody would ever replace them.

I always felt bad for my dad. My mom left, my sisters chose my mom over him and never came to see him, and then Ben declined any interest in the family business. All my dad had ever experienced was abandonment. It hung over our family like a death of a loved one. It feels like a gut punch when I realize why my dad and I bonded. We both felt left behind. I could never be enough to heal that hurt for him. Now he isn't here to feel it anymore.

Overloaded with emotions, I feel raw; and on top of all of that, it feels like so much of my personal life has been puked up on a complete stranger. We finally reach the house to find Milo and Nikki in the living room watching television. "There is a huge snowstorm moving through tonight so you know what that means…" Nikki said, without moving from her spot.

I smile while working on getting my shoes off and respond, "I guess pizzas are in the oven then?"

Milo moves from the couch to join me in the kitchen. "Harley, Seriously… Ben?" He starts in before I get my other shoe off. Milo's tone caught Nikki's attention. She was in the kitchen in a flash.

"Milo! We talked about this," Nikki scolds him.

Milo continues anyway, "I saw Ben peeling out of town like a bat out of Hell. I wish you had a backbone with your family!" Nikki looks past me and nods, following Reed out of the kitchen. I had worked on my temper all afternoon while trying to remind myself why Milo cares so much. I know he is caring, but after he patronizes me, all that work goes out the window. My heart is racing and all I can do is glare at him.

"So let me get this straight, you don't want me to talk to Lance," I count on my fingers, "or my brother, or my sisters," three more fingers, "or my mother? Is there anyone else I need to add to 'Milo's Do Not Talk To' list?"

"That's not what I am saying," Milo attempts to cut me off.

"Really, because you're mad at me for talking to Lance."

"Fine if you're going to call it a list, yes, Lance ranks at number one on that list," Milo interrupts. "I'm not saying you can't talk to your family, but you are letting them take whatever they want from you."

"The business was my fathers. It's theirs…" I start to protest.

"It was never theirs, Harley. Your dad left the business to you and left them a nice-size inheritance. If they burnt through that, then that is their issue to fix."

"I am tired of saying these words, so either accept them or get out, but this is my family. If your family needed money, whether you honestly felt they deserved it or not, you would help them out, right? Because it is family. It's what our dads taught us. It's what feels right."

I breathe in, trying to calm down, but I am so pissed that taking the one breath is not enough.

I am angry at him because this fight has been going on for the last few years, ever since Lance and I separated. Milo has felt the need to protect me. No matter how much I tell him off, he still wants to direct my decisions and tell me how to handle my family. All in the name of "protection."

"So I say again, accept me and who I am, or there is the door." I point my hand, shaking a little as my blood pumps through my veins. Milo's eyes stare me down, weighing the situation out. Seconds tick by with neither one of us moving or speaking, but it feels like minutes.

"I originally came to apologize for this morning but got mad all over again because of Ben. You are right though; it is your family," he spits out. "And if you want to continue to be used by them then that is your prerogative. So… sorry I overstepped the boundary." Milo's apology came out very hard, forced, and cutting. But I know he means well and really does mean it, even if it doesn't sound like it.

We aren't the huggy type of friends. We settle situations with a nod of understanding that the fight is over, but he will need to give me space. He moves to find Nikki and Reed while I check the pizzas. I know this will surface again. He is a very opinionated friend. He once told me that I dressed like a homeless person after my mom left. I went home crying about it and that's when my dad sat me down and explained that the Walker Family (of which Milo is a part) believes that they are helpful when they share their thoughts, whether they are hurtful or not. My dad said sometimes they will be right and sometimes they will be wrong; not only in what they say, but also in how they say it. He tried to teach me that the truest of friends are the ones that are always honest with you. They aren't the ones that will only tell you what you want to hear.

When Milo and I fight, it's those words that I reflect on and they are why I keep Milo around. Plus, Nikki balances us out right now.

8

REED

It sounds like all hell breaking loose inside the kitchen as we escape outside to the front porch. I turn to face Nikki and she starts laughing at my expression. I probably shouldn't be shocked after their fight this morning. I heard how boisterous they can get. I had hoped though, after some space today, that they would have cooled off.

When Harley and I walked in the house tonight and Milo stood up, it was obvious that the fight had only hit an intermission and was about to resume. I wanted to jump in and defend Harley, but Nikki caught my attention before I could intervene.

I cough and try to hide my discomfort. "They fight like cats and dogs."

I lean against the weathered banister, and look out to the open field that rests on the other side of the rough road. The sky is gray and the cold wraps around us. Neither of us dressed for this kind of cold. I huddle into a borrowed fleece jacket I found in the closet and am thankful I put on my running shoes earlier before I left the house.

Nikki sidles up next to me, shivering. We are right next to each other, which should feel weird, but it's comfortable. "They would be pissed to hear you called one of them a cat." Nikki grins, then hesitates for a second, contemplating what she is about to say next. "When

I first met Lee, it took me a while to get comfortable with how close her and Milo were, but if I wanted to be with Milo, I had to get over it. I liked him too much to walk away, so I got over it." She smiles with a small laugh at that memory.

"Once I warmed up to her, I saw Lee for who she was and what she meant to Milo. The three of us had so much fun together. We just clicked. They had their little spats but nothing big. The fights really started after Lance and Lee broke up. It hasn't been the same between any of us. Sure, we still have fun but she became distant. Milo was always protective of her. But she is Independent Lee." Nikki's voice comes out warm and motherly as she speaks about the two people she cares most about.

"How long have they been arguing?" I ask.

"For a few years. Lee's dad passed away during what would have been the start of her junior year of college. That's when the light arguing started, but it got more heated after the broken engagement about two years ago," Nikki explains.

"I get that Lance cheated on Harley, but why does Milo get so worked up about her family and the whole Lance thing? It just doesn't seem like his business." Nikki fidgets, indicating this is a touchy subject and I shouldn't bring it up. Since Nikki seems talkative now, I am hoping to gain an insider's view. "I've watched Milo, George, and some of the other locals, and it feels like everyone is watching out for her, protecting her. But from what?"

"I don't think this story is mine to tell." And just like that she clams up, like the rest of them. Harley Anderson remains a mystery to me.

I respect Nikki for the friendship she has with Harley. Their friendship is very different from Zoey and her staff a.k.a. friends. They all talk about each other and spread rumors with embellished details, but in the end, they would still call each other friends. Zoey defends their actions by stating that airing out the dirty helps clear out the stink and makes everyone become transparent. In reality, I think it makes everyone guarded and even more backstabbing. I avoid Zoey's friends as much as I can to escape the dramatics. Unfortunately, most of what ends up being leaked to the media about me is by their mouths.

We hear silence from the house, finally, and the seconds tick by while we wait to see if it is a cease of fire or the calm before the next storm.

"I take it no camping tonight then?" I ask, not trying to hide my hopefulness that the plans have been canceled.

Nikki smiles and shakes her head. "I think they are done for now." She sighs, looking at the door with relief washing over her small frame. I look at her and try to calculate how she figures they are done.

"Normally, when there is a pause, it's because Milo has run out of points for his arguments," she states matter-of-factly. "Deep down, Milo knows he is wrong for pushing Lee. No one can make her do anything that goes against her true character. Even though Lee may understand she doesn't handle situations in the best way, she won't verbalize she is wrong. They will reach a point to agree to disagree. Lee will forgive him and he will sweep his issues under the rug until he can't take it anymore."

"So you think he was in the wrong? I didn't know wives could so openly talk about their disapproval," I say sarcastically. Even though I haven't known her long, I had previously assumed Nikki wouldn't be the type to talk against Milo in public because of how meek she appears to be.

"I think he is right in what he says and means. Lee needs to make changes, but I don't think Milo handles it right. The problem is how do you tell two stubborn mules how to change their approaches to life and to arguments?" I can tell Nikki is an expert in dealing with her two best friends. We stand outside and take in the air as it gets colder and the storm moves in.

The door creaks open and Milo joins us. His face is a little flushed from the yelling, but he is calming down. We sit in awkward silence for a beat or two. I swear I have had more awkward silent moments with these people than I ever had in Hollywood. Ironically, I feel more a part of them then I do in my own circle of friends. It makes me question if I can really call my Hollywood friends, friends.

These three people are the only ones who have known me as Reed since I left home. Most people don't even know my given name, nor do they care about my background unless it gives them the upper hand in my career. I've worked hard to keep conversations at the surface level, which I like, and wouldn't want it to go any deeper. I haven't opened up to Milo, Nikki, or Harley yet, but I am feeling a stronger connection to them during the last few days than I have felt towards my Hollywood friends, even Zoey.

"I'm going to go help Lee with the pizzas." Nikki slips back inside, leaving Milo and I in our own thoughts.

"So... none of this has been awkward." Milo's attempt to move past the situation makes me chuckle.

"I have had my fair share of public fighting. At least for you it doesn't hit the tabloids," I point out, to help him brush it off.

Milo nods, "Very true." He stretches his arm behind his neck, "I just wish she could cut ties. They only keep her around to use her. Why doesn't she see that?"

Milo talks to me like I know what he is talking about. When I don't agree, or give a reaction, he takes a deep breath and blows it through his teeth to release some of his frustration.

"I don't know her past, and from what I can tell no one is going to tell me details, which is fine, but I have observed and I am making my own assumptions. There is always more to why people stay in their situations," I state. My mind goes back to a few of my own situations. "It is by choice, but it's because they can't seem to see any other options."

Milo starts to cut me off but I keep going, "You might try helping her see another option instead of telling her how to fix her situation." Milo takes a moment to consider and I pause to let him soak that up. "I am not trying to bust your balls, it's just an outsider's opinion."

"You know you have only been here a few days," he states, more as a fact than to be rude.

"I am a passerby and don't know the history. I get it." I concede.

"I have nothing against you... I just forget that you are only here for a few weeks." He walks over to the rickety steps and plops down. Milo isn't a big guy, but the boards creek underneath him. "You do know you're supposed to back me up though, right? Not defend her. Bro Code, you remember?"

"Will try to do better next time," I mock.

We talk a little longer about anything that isn't deep. I learn that his family owns a local business shop and what he does for his dad. We don't get too much more covered before Nikki comes to the door to let us know dinner is ready. By that time, we are chilled to the bone and ready to go in. I am the last to walk through the door. While I am shutting the storm door, I see the snowflakes drifting down in the air.

9

HARLEY

Stuffed with pizza, we rearrange the furniture to accommodate a Milo-friendly game of Spoons. Milo doesn't hold back when it comes to game nights and can be dangerous if you are not prepared for his competitive streak. He has been known to fly across the table reaching for the last spoon, card, or game piece. I have had lamps, chairs, and pictures broken. I can't totally blame him since Nikki and I antagonize him. We are definitely a rough and rowdy group. Reed thinks we are just kidding until he experiences a head-butt from Milo.

"We tried to warn you Reed," Nikki sympathetically consoles, while both boys rub their heads.

"You have to physically watch out for me, but mentally you have to keep an eye on quiet, gentle Nikki." Milo lovingly ruffs up Nikki's hair. "She is pretty good at slipping cards and slighting the deck... She knows how to cheat!"

Since Milo's earlier rant, I have been working on leaving our fight behind us. It's easier as time ticks by. I look at my friends and can't help but notice that even though things seem to be back to normal, with our even flow of jabs and laughter, "normal" is slightly tainted with Milo's disapproval and my defensive attitude.

"What tricks do you play?" Reed looks at me. His forehead is a little red, but he uses his deep voice to ask the question. I can't help but feel my heart kick up a notch.

"You'll have to figure that out on your own," I respond smugly.

A couple hands later, Reed starts toying with Milo and acts like he is going to reach for the spoon. Everyone jumps in. I am laughing so hard my sides hurt and the corners of my eyes are damp. I feel the tension from today slipping away.

We decide to settle down and play poker. Nikki is slighting the hands in favor of me and Reed in attempts to bring Milo down. Milo catches on halfway through the game and flips the cards at us. Reed goads Milo and the boys start throwing verbal cheap shots at each other. I feel a little softer towards Reed. He fits so well in our group that it's easy to forget he hasn't been here all along. He will be leaving when his car is fixed. The warehouse I order from has stated that his car parts will arrive in just a few days.

Reed catches my eye and gives me that famous, panty-dropping smile that cameras love to catch. The boys run out of things to bash each other for and Milo suggest a game of Pictionary since there are four of us. "Guys against girls," Reed calls and puts me in a gentle headlock.

Reed draws first and we learn quickly that Reed can't draw. Milo hates losing and his face is showing it. He is shouting at Reed to draw something different, while Reed is jabbing his finger on the note pad indicating there is nothing left to draw. Nikki and I are in fits of laughter.

Time runs out. The boys get no points. Nikki and I rake in a few points before I can't guess Nikki's drawing of lumber. Milo takes over the drawing. He has his game face on and is in the zone. He looks at Reed and points to his eyes then points to his own. Reed nods, giving Milo the silent signal that they are on the same page. Milo dives into the drawing, which is pretty good, but Reed starts guessing stupid answers. Milo slams the pencil down and shakes his head. The timer runs out.

"Oh, it's a rollerblade," Reed mocks and that's all it takes for Milo to give in and start laughing. Milo flips him the bird and calls him a name. Reed boisterously laughs at him.

"Is this the best you can do then?" Nikki asks, laying down Reed's previous drawing, doubting him now after realizing he was playing around.

"I thought it was good; isn't that how abstract art is supposed to be drawn?" She shakes her head at the drawing, snatches it back from Reed, and puts it in the box while she continues to pack up the rest of the game.

"I think it would be fun to watch one of Reed's movies," Nikki jabs back playfully. I could sense Reed's hesitation but he didn't object.

Soon, the furniture is back in its rightful place, the games are put away, and the movie is selected. We all settle on the couch. The introduction music cues up the movie and Reed begins to fidget. "Are you uncomfortable watching yourself?" I ask teasingly. He nods.

Milo takes the opportunity to rib him since Reed forced him to lose most of his games tonight. I quietly offer to turn off the movie but he shakes his head. I notice Reed never settles in as the movie continues to build the sappy love story.

I turn to Nikki and repeat the next line of the movie in my most dramatic love-story voice. She replies with a dramatic gasp and repeats the next line back. She wraps her arm around my neck, covers my mouth with her hand, and stage kisses me loudly. The boys grin at us but act as if they're too cool to laugh at us. It's enough of a break for Reed to settle in and he starts giving us the behind-the-scenes bloopers and stories. It's fun to have *the* actual commentator in your own living room.

Halfway through the movie we stretch out on the floor to get more comfortable. Nikki and Milo are the first to fall asleep. I am getting restless just laying here. I sit up a little to see out the window. The storm is in full force. I calculate that it's about midnight and the bar will close in a few hours. I start contemplating if I should call Kayden to make sure they close early. "Kayden is a good manager; he will close up when he needs to," Milo grunts in a groggy voice. My head snaps over to him. He continues "I can feel you fidgeting and he knows the drill and the rules. So stop micromanaging."

"I know, but…"

"What are butts for?" Nikki stirs.

"They're for pooping," Milo responds with the punch line from a TV show we watch.

"Gross," I say, hitting her with a pillow. Her giggles are muffled by the pillow.

Milo nudges Nikki up. They call it a night, and head upstairs to the extra bedroom. Reed follows suit and heads towards his designated room. Alone in the living room, I sit back against the couch. The sappy love story builds to the epic fight. I do like being home right now and almost feel relieved from work responsibilities, yet I can't quite shake them completely. Deciding to compromise, I text Kayden instead of calling. At least I think it's a compromise. I don't mind that Kayden never texts back.

I stay up for a while longer and watch Reed's character chase after Zoey's character on the screen. *Typical.* Losing interest, my mind drifts to today's events. It felt like my day started off on the right foot, despite the fact that I almost burnt my kitchen down. I fight my grin while reflecting on Reed scrambling to fix my mistakes.

Even with that small hiccup, I had hopes that today would be fine. The moment Milo came in wanting to dig up all our issues atomic-bombed those hopes. I'm discouraged that Reed learned about Lance yesterday, overheard Milo and I this morning, then met Ben. I feel ashamed of my mess of a life.

At least we were able to salvage part of the day after dinner and end on a good note. Despite the laughter and a snippet of leaving the past in the past, I now sense the clouds closing back in on the reality of the embarrassment and frustration that is nagging me.

The movie ends with Zoey in Reed's arms, which leaves me feeling jealous on top of everything else. I decide to get up and shut off the movie and the remaining dimly lit lamps. I'm still restless as I glance out at the snowstorm.

The house is old and leaky and no amount of heat from the furnace can eliminate the frigidness that has settled throughout

Bromley. Rubbing my arms, I put more wood on the fire in an attempt to keep the chill at bay. Then I make my way upstairs. With everyone in bed, I decide to be selfish and take a long hot shower to warm up. I want to wash away the icky feelings that have buried themselves deep inside as well.

I run the shower till the water cools off, knowing I've wasted enough water for the environmentalists to be busting down my door tomorrow. Steam covers the mirror and I ignore it and begin to dig in the drawer for my comb. A glimmer catches my eye. Moving ponytail holders and hair clips to uncover the source and my shoulders drop as I look at the small diamond gleaming up at me. I pull the ring and comb out of the drawer and set the ring down on the counter. Combing my tangles from my hair, I can't take my gaze from the ring. I am dazed by the innocent symbol. My stomach drops, thinking about Lance and the commitment we once had.

After removing all the tangles, and with a deep breath, I grab the ring. The thought about accidentally dropping it down the drain crosses my mind, but I decide against it. Instead, with the ring in hand, I leave the warmth of the bathroom.

I gaze at my dark bedroom, which screams "black hole of loneliness" to me. My gaze moves over to where Nikki is sleeping in the bedroom on the other end of the hall. She wouldn't mind if I woke her up, although I would end up convincing her that I am fine. Neither option sounds remotely appealing. The fireplace becomes a beacon in my numb brain as it flickers up the stairwell.

Downstairs, I scrunch down into the couch. Pulling a blanket around me, I allow the couch and blanket to embrace me in a cozy hug. I examine the ring with glazed eyes, and distractedly place it on my left hand where it once lived. Seeing it on my hand, my mind drifts back to that day.

"Harley, it's not too late," Milo states, frustrated. He has been trying to get me to walk away from Lance for months.
"Stop," I warn.

"Just because he's been here through your dad's death doesn't make it the right decision." I glare at him because this is not what I need right now. "I'm looking out for you. I don't want you to look back later and think you made a mistake," He counters.

"Why do you think this is a mistake?" I ask. I'm pretty sure I know why, but I just need him to say it out loud.

"I don't want you to ever feel like you are trapped."

"That didn't answer my question. Out of all the years I have known you Milo, you've never been one to hold back your opinion."

"If I told you the truth, would it change how you feel?"

I look at the sincerity in his eyes; and, for the first time, I start to doubt my decision. I quickly shake it off, "Milo, I am getting married tomorrow and you are totally making this last-night hurrah thing miserable for me."

"Ok." His voice is weary and exasperated. "If you feel that Lance is the one then he is the one. Now why don't you go get him so I can do his bachelor party like I am supposed to."

I kiss Milo on the cheek and run up the steps into the lodge to get Lance. The last place I recall seeing him, he was talking to my family, but my mom is in the kitchen talking to the caterer and everyone else has seemed to have scattered. I find Rachel, one of my bridesmaids, and the rest of his family. But still no Lance. I head to the room where our coats are, thinking maybe he had gone to get them, knowing it was time for us to leave. Passing the dressing rooms where we will be getting ready tomorrow, I smile at the thought of what tomorrow holds. I push open the boy's dressing room and freeze in the door way....

Someone grabs my foot, jerking me from my subconscious nightmare and startling me. "Sorry, I didn't mean to scare you." Reed settles onto the couch with me. His hair is roughed from his nap. "You going to share some of that blanket or not?" He is a little grumpy as he shivers from the chill.

I nod, not trusting my voice not to betray me. I was still shook up from the emotions the little ring has drummed up. *I'm emotionally exhausted.* Standing up, I unwrap myself and flip the blanket over both of us. The ring glitters at me again and I thrust my hands under the blanket. I glance over at Reed as he sinks into the couch. His gaze is lost in the fire and it appears he did not notice my rash movement.

The firelight dances across his face. Reed looks over at me, likely sensing my watchful stare. I smile sheepishly at him and avert my gaze. My heart speeds up and I want to think it's because I'm embarrassed by being caught eye groping him for the umpteenth time. Truthfully, I feel the flutters of butterfly wings tickling my insides.

"Like what you see?" he teases me. I can't bring myself to look at him and opt to keep my gaze on the flames. "Can't sleep either?"

"No, but do I ever?" I joke. After staying with me, I assume he has picked up on my non-existent sleep habits. The wind blows the snow against the bay window and catches my attention as the blizzard continues. "Can I ask you a question?" I ask hesitantly.

"You already did," Reed mocks and I nudge him with my shoulder. "What is your question?" He looks at me from the corner of his eye, unsure where I'm going with this.

"Are you happy with where your life has taken you?"

He takes a big breath and slowly lets it out. "That's heavy."

I guess it is but he interrupted my reverie so I'm pulling him into it. My gaze returns to the fire and I allow my mind to contemplate if I am happy with where I am. He takes a minute to think before he answers.

"Life hasn't always been easy for me. Hard to believe, isn't it?" He mocks himself but feels distant.

"You're taking the tortured artist storyline," I tease, hoping this eases his reluctance to talk.

"Maybe." He pauses, possibly letting his mind go. "Sure, there are aspects of my life I would love to trade, but I believe in cause and effect. If certain events in my life hadn't taken place, then I wouldn't be who I am today." I let his theory wash over me and think back to events in my life. Connecting instances and circumstances, I can see how the events were laid out for me to make the decisions I have made.

"Did you always want to be an actor?"

"I don't think so. Most of my childhood was spent in survival mode." His facial expression drops into something somber. "Sure, I daydreamed of happier places, but there was never a future goal I strived for. When I finally started to settle down, I wanted to make something of myself, to make my life mean something. Cities like L.A. and New York always seemed to have the ability to do that. So that's where I went. No plans, no goals, I just… fell into it."

"It has to be pretty cool to be you though. I mean you get to travel all over the world for movie shoots and work with some of the most famous actors and actresses." I glance over to see that he gets my sarcasm at his aloof attitude about his life. He smirks and I continue on, "In the end, I think you accomplished the goal of making yourself into something. You will always be remembered as the teen heart-throb. Your movies from five years ago are still played monthly on cable networks. And these pre-teens that grow up watching you have set their standards of romantic gestures based on your characters," I compliment.

He rewards me with his grin, but his eyes hold questions. Maybe he is wondering if I am making fun of him or if I am being genuinely supportive. He watches me for a beat, and I wonder if he is searching for cracks in my genuine praise. When he doesn't find any, he continues. "I get that, but what have I really accomplished? The heart-throb persona…people expect me to be that all the time. It's like they forget they are movies and I am just playing that character for that brief moment in their life." He appears exasperated with the weight of the expectations that have been held over him.

"Most characters built in books and movies are built from the real lives of multiple people." He continues, "The creator picks personality traits they like from this person or that person. Then they mash the characters with a little drama. The storylines are generated. People are created. When these stories are produced to the masses, they embellish key traits of characters to pull the heartstrings of the audience. That's what they fall for. That's who they remember. Then when fans meet you and you fall short of their expectations, they aren't shy to let you know what they really think of you."

"Is that why you and Zoey are together? There is no expectation between you?" I piece together a small snippet of who Reed really is.

"It's much easier, but we never had more than a theatrical romantic connection. We tried but felt better as friends. I wish I could say it keeps the media at bay, but you know that isn't true."

"Yeah about that, what's this about William getting caught with drugs?"

Reed starts chuckling. "I wish I could say it was all publicity, but that's why I needed to leave for a while. I needed to prep my family so they wouldn't be too hurt, and to reassure them that they raised me the best they could."

"Aw, such a sweet son," I tease. There is sorrow in his eyes.

10

REED

The fire had died down and Harley moves to add more wood. I'm absentmindedly smoothing out the blanket when I feel something in the folds. Peeling them back, I find a ring. "Lance?" I ask, trying to sound curious rather than accusatory. She turns to me and I hold the ring up.

"Yeah, I don't make it a habit to get engaged just to collect engagement rings, so that would be the one and only." Her sarcasm brightens my darkness.

"Why didn't you return it?" I ask.

"I didn't stick around long enough to give it back." She fidgets as she sits back down on the couch.

"Decided you weren't meant for each other?" I grit my teeth at myself for giving her the third degree. It's obvious that there is more to this story. I should leave her personal life alone but I'm like a bug drawn to a flame. With each answer she gives, I have thirty more unanswered questions. I'm used to Zoey answering one question and thirty other unasked questions. Harley is proving time and time again that she is her own breed of female.

She wiggles under the blanket and scrunches down into the warmth, "No… he did. I went to get my coat and walked in on him on top of one of my bridesmaids."

"Ouch," I hiss through my teeth. I've never met Lance, but the mental image would probably be scarring for anyone. It's one thing to be cheated on, but it becomes its own monster when catching them in the act.

"Don't look at me like that. Don't have pity. I am not broken. Hurt deeply at the time, yes, but I'm not broken. And don't psychoanalyze me either," she snips at me.

I laugh, realizing I *was* studying her body language and looking for chinks in her armor. I put my arm around her and give her shoulder a squeeze, which she fights, but giggles as my other arm wraps in front of her. She may not be broken, but she is struggling with her past whether she wants to admit it or not. In this moment, all I want to do is protect her and help to heal her.

"So why did you keep this?" I ask. Once I release her, I turn my attention back to the small ring in my hand and examine it.

"I don't know why I kept it." She laughs, staring into the diamond. Reaching over, she takes it back from me and puts the ring in the pocket of her hoodie.

"I'm done with you knowing about my personal life. You know I had a fiancé, you know I have a dysfunctional family, and that Milo and I don't see eye to eye on how to run my life. I only know you date Zoey for publicity and that you had a rough upbringing," she states matter-of-factly and with a little bit of a huff behind her points.

I would have grinned, but I know where the conversation is leading and knots are forming in the pit of my stomach. Harley does have a point though; doors were unintentionally blown open in front of me, and some very personal details about her were exposed over the last few days. I motion with my hand for her to let the questions roll.

"Tell me what your mother is like." Not the direction I expected, but a question that I still trip over.

"Which one?" This catches her by surprise. "My birthmother or my adoptive mother, or all the foster ones that were in between the two?"

"Birthmother," she says quietly.

"She was kind, very quiet, timid, but she always looked for fun. She loved dancing." My mind takes me back to her taking my hands into hers as she twirled in the kitchen with me. I remember laughing and kicking my legs around, stumbling, but she was always there to catch me. "Her name was Pearl, which suited her because she had gone through a rough background but still brought beauty to the world."

I had blocked most of my earlier childhood years out, but my adoptive mother Lisa had encouraged me to focus on the good times. She and her husband Jerry believed that I needed to know exactly who I was and where I came from. They lived by many mottos, one of them being that history repeated itself, and that we have the power to choose differently. They felt that knowledge was power. If I couldn't remember certain details, I would ask about Lisa or Jerry and they openly told me. Sometimes they might sugarcoat the story and other times they were straightforward with what went on. I eventually learned to read them, and they knew it.

"What about your adoptive mother?" I glance over at her. There was no doubt she picked up on the fact that my mother was no longer living. Instead of asking about what happened, she moves past it. We both understand the loss of a parent.

"She was the opposite but the same. She was loud, protective, loving, but very orderly. It's my adoptive father that brings the fun to the room." Harley smiles warmly at me and a knot loosens in my gut.

"Tell me about him?"

"I feel like you are psychoanalyzing me now," I state.

"Maybe," she teases. "Keep talking."

Jerry was and still is a strong, stable man in my life. There was something about him that drew me in. He is the one I want to be like. The one I don't want to disappoint. When the minor drug scandal hit the news, I desperately wanted him to know the media was blowing it out of proportion.

I admitted that when I had first moved out to LA, I had toyed with some drugs, but knew it wasn't a path I wanted. When I finally was able to talk with him in person, Jerry assured me he could tell the articles and photos had been manipulated.

"I strive to be like him," I admit to her. "I realized when I was in Florida how much his opinion of me matters. Growing up, I didn't have good father figures and so when I went to live with them, I expected him to be the same. I rebelled and fought often with him, but I realized that weekend that I thrive on his approval and that I need his acceptance and support."

Harley sat still, soaking in every word. I tell her how my younger brother, Blaine, and I bounced from foster home to foster home. What I don't share is how the foster parents struggled with agreeing to take us because of my biological father's history. Those are the thoughts and memories I need to keep locked up.

"The car is actually Blaine's." I start to fill Harley in on the sentimental value I have for it. "Every time I acted out or exhausted a set of foster parents, they would move us to a new home. Blaine was uprooted once again. I was so angry and selfish that I didn't realize how much I was affecting him.

"We ended up with Jerry and Lisa when I was about fourteen. Blaine didn't take to Jerry like I did. Even though Jerry and I fought and I pushed his buttons, he stuck with me and could see through all the nonsense I pulled on them. He saw it in Blaine too, but Blaine was so disconnected because of what I had dragged him through growing up. Unfortunately, by that point, Blaine had lost all hope in humanity. After I graduated and left, Blaine sought out approval in all the wrong places.

"He got picked up for drugs, theft, and a few other heinous crimes that I still struggle to stomach. I guess he felt abandoned by our birth parents and the foster program. When I left, he felt the same abandonment all over again. Now he won't be getting out of jail for a long time."

"Did he work on cars?" Harley asks, breezing over the hundred other way more personal questions that could be asked. Her kindness is not lost on me.

"Yeah. It was something he wanted to do ever since we were little. So, in high school, Jerry bought us this junker of a muscle car and Blaine restored it. I sat in the garage and made out with girls, and horsed around, but whenever Blaine needed help with something, I was there." I grin, remembering how he would get mad at me for not understanding the task he needed me to perform, which usually resulted in him kicking me out of the garage.

"Blaine was the mechanic, which is why I only know the basics." I have a nagging thought that won't go away so I say it just to get it out. "Even though I know I didn't abandon him, the car is his and I want to take care of it for when he does get released. It's the least I can do."

"Do you see him often?"

"No, the last time I tried, he turned me away."

Harley never once tries to console me, nor does she offer advice on how to fix anything. She just sits there, wanting to know about me, Reed Montgomery, the orphan. Not William the movie star. Not about a movie. Not about Zoey. Harley wants to know me.

Eventually I run out of stories I'm willing to share and she stops asking questions. Harley had snuggled up against my body at some point while we were talking. The quiet crackle of the fire fills the silence between us. I feel her weight shift and glance over to find she'd fallen asleep. Her head had dropped forward, which will cause a kink in her neck when she wakes up.

She stirs a little as I shift our weight, but her head now rests on my chest. I battle with my arms trying to figure out where I should put them, but to cuddle them around her felt too intimate for our situation. The way we are laying, the couch back doesn't give me much room to put my arms at my side. Sick of the battle, I give up, and wrap them around her. She feels small in my arms and I can't figure out how someone could cheat on a girl like Harley.

I try not to psychoanalyze her but it's a trait I've picked up. It's how I survive the system. Studying her, I realize she is equal parts of my mothers. She is like Lisa: strong, in charge, and loving but she has Pearl's timid personality when it comes to those that matter to her. I saw myself in her as well, as a person seeking approval, as someone who could take a hit but wouldn't stay down. Some hits were harder than others.

"Boys get down here!" Billy yelled at us.

"I told you, you shouldn't have said anything," Blaine hisses at me.

I wish I could listen to him, but I know deep down what Billy does isn't right. I do my best to shield Blaine from what I know, which for the most part just leaves him frustrated with me. But I can shield him from the monster.

However, this time when a school teacher asked about my limp, I decided to say something. When the police showed up, but left, I knew I had made a mistake. Protecting Blaine was all I could do. Billy knew he couldn't hit me hard enough to hurt me, but touching Blaine was a whole other issue.

"Blaine, climb out the window now," I ordered.

"And where am I supposed to go?" His six-year-old body squared up against me.

"To the playground. I'll come find you." I helped him out of the window and watched him scale down the side of the house. The kid would have been a fantastic rock climber for the way his little fingers could support his weight.

"BOYS!" Billy yelled once more. I stayed till I saw his feet hit the ground. He looked up at me, discouraged.

Blaine's little discouraged face haunts me when I wake up a few hours later. Harley is nowhere to be seen, but there is movement in the house. Feeling groggy, I sit up, facing a window which reveals it is still night. Nikki appears at the bottom of the stairs and starts throwing winter clothes in my direction.

"Hurry, we need to get there before sunrise," she urges. Her bubbly personality is like its own perky cup of coffee. I wonder if she drinks coffee and then start wondering if this is her with it or without it. Either variation sounds scary.

For now, I let her excitement pull me out of my slumber state and seep into my bones. I have no idea what is going on, but I better hurry as she and Milo are zipping through the house. The clothes are snug but they will keep me warm. I tie my shoes as Harley races down the stairs. Harley is all smiles, a look that I come to learn is rare. I feel drawn to her and unintentionally step closer to her.

"Ready?" she asks, breathless, when I reach her. I nod and follow them out the door. Harley tosses her keys to Milo and we climb into her jeep. Nikki pulls out her iPod and plugs it into the stereo system.

"Where are we going?" I ask.

"No talking," Nikki snaps, which comes out as tough as a little kitten. I mouth "sorry" and she cranks up Indy rock ballads as the jeep takes us into the mountainous terrain. There aren't many stars out this early because the moon is low and bright, but the sleepy town looks peaceful.

Harley leans my way and my body automatically reciprocates her movement. "Have you skied before?" she asks quietly, to be undetected by Nikki. I answer her with a nod. "When we get to the resort, you can borrow Ben's skies."

"I get we are skiing but what's with all the hype?"

Her eyes twinkle, "You'll see."

A few cars pull onto the road behind us as we ascend the mountain that paints a backdrop to Middleton. At the resort, Milo throws the car in park. The three of them rush out of the car and I follow suit. We reach the locker banks under the lodge and Harley hands me a set of skies and boots. She starts putting on her own gear.

"The boots may not fit, but the shop doesn't open until later and we have to go now. We will get you fitted later." She looks at me standing there and scolds me, "Hurry!"

I rush to get my gear on and we take off for the only lift running. It's been a while since the last time I skied, but I find my groove. Nikki and Milo hop on the first chair lift and Harley and I follow behind them. Once situated, she hands me headphones while she sets up another iPod. The same music from the car ride plays into my personal surround sound. I breathe in the chilly air and watch the stars above me glow in the early twilight sky. It's been forever since I have seen stars this bright. I turn my gaze to the girl beside me who looks so calm and relaxed. It's a side of her that I feel rarely gets to come out.

Last night, I opened myself up to her in a way I've never done for anyone else. She allowed me to open up like no one has ever done. Lisa and Jerry were the only two that I shared with, but even that was surface at times. I never wanted to scare them away with some of the truths about me. They read the reports and knew my history, but it is one thing to read a report and another to be told the demented things I have dealt with. Those secrets still choke me, but at least I was about to let a secret out and some partial truths go. All because of her.

The lift is long and we don't talk. The music is the perfect soundtrack for the moment. The snow glitters under the moon. The trees are washed of their color and stand as tall, black beasts on the ground below us. We are carried over barriers blocking off boulders that have yet to be covered by the season's snow, even after the heavy blizzard. A few stars make their mark, letting us know they won't let the moon drown them out. The air feels crisp and chills my lungs when I breathe it in. It's peaceful, except for the occasional bounce from the pulley system.

We reach the end of the lift and prep to get off the ride. As we come off the slope there is a large gathering of snowboarders and skiers. Milo shouts a crow and everyone joins in, causing Harley and Nikki to giggle. We ski over to a few people huddled together and are greeted with hugs, handshakes, and shoulder bumps. Harley takes the iPod again, pauses the music, and changes it to another soundtrack.

"Wait till you hear three then push play," Harley instructs me. "This is a tradition. The first day the slope is open for skiing we all come here and watch the sunrise as it comes over the peaks. We have done it since college. Most of us know each other from high school, but the group has grown since college," Harley explains.

She introduces me to a few people, calling me Reed. No one seems to catch on to who I really am, thankfully. I chalk it up to the scruff on my face and the ski gear which helps keep me incognito. "How big was your high school?" I ask, taking in the amount of people that are on the mountain.

"Not big, but we hung out with kids from the surrounding schools. The number of attendees has changed from time to time but there is a good core." Harley's voice starts to sound a little distant and I glance at her to see what she is doing. Her eyes are trained in the direction to our right.

"You ok?" I ask, eyeing the guy I assume is Lance.

"Yeah, just someone I don't want to talk to yet." She grabs my hand, leads me over to a large group of people, and quickly gets us involved with their conversation. They are all excited to see her and she starts introducing me to several of the regulars. I see her occasionally scanning the group, but keeps low key, not standing out.

There are a couple of hollers and it gets eerily quiet as everyone turns to face east. I follow suit and remember Harley's instructions. I fumble with the headphones, and get them in place as some guy, I think his name is Brian, counts to three.

I push play and music fills my ears as we all stand in a scattered row. The sky gets brighter. It feels like slow motion but it's going quicker than it appears. The music picks up right when the sun rises over the nearest mountain and everyone greets it with shouts and crows. It's an indescribable feeling of joy, tradition, and comradery that I can't help but join in on. The song changes as more drums are added, and Harley and the band of hooligans break out in little dances. We look like fools and outcasts, but no one cares. She looks so free and happy. I soak up the moment and let it wash over me. The group takes off down the hill. It is official. The slopes are open.

The music continues to play through my headphones, morphing from one genre to a completely different style. The music matches the rhythm of everyone slaloming from one side of the run to the next. It is amazing to watch and even more fun to feel included.

I spot Harley a little ways down the mountain. Her shoulders are relaxed. Her smile is wide. Her cheeks have more color in them than I have seen since I met her. Some would say the color is from the cold wind whipping her face, but this is the kind of color that comes out when you are lit up with life. I have seen her look beautiful, but not like this. She belongs here.

We make it down the hill and I follow Harley over to Milo and Nikki.

"What do you think?" Harley's voice is so chipper that I feel myself feeding off her excitement. I can't stop smiling.

"That was awesome!" I respond. Her giggle is so musical and giddy. "I know, right?" she exclaims.

Out of the corner of my eye, I see the blur of something come right for us. Harley squeals as she is picked up and carried a few feet from us. A loud, gruff laugh erupts from the person holding onto her. Everyone is laughing, but I am watchful of the situation. This is something I learned growing up.

Nikki must have noticed my reaction, because we catch each other's attention and she has a look of awkwardness playing in her eyes.

"I looked for you this morning and wondered if you had missed it again this year," the newcomer said.

"We made it," she says through fits of giggles. "How are you?"

As they make small talk, I realize this is the same guy she was avoiding during the sunrise festivities. My protective mode kicks in as I brace for Lance's introduction.

11

HARLEY

I can feel Reed's eyes watching me. He must be trying to figure out whose arms are around me and weighing the situation for signs that he needs to step in. I twitch, feeling uncomfortable from Reed's stare and from the arms locked around me. As I wiggle free, a hand shoots out past me in Reed's direction.

"I haven't seen you before. I'm Thatcher and this is Jake."

Reed takes Thatcher's hand and gives it a firm shake. Looking him in the eye, he introduces himself. Reed seems at ease with this situation. I feel like I have been caught, but I don't know what I have been caught doing.

"What do you think Lee?" Thatcher asks, jarring me out of my head. I have no clue what the question is but I know the answer. Every question Thatcher asks pretty much ends with the same answer.

"Sure."

Jake and Thatcher lead the pack, because that's what they do. They are natural-born leaders. Wherever they go, most will follow; I do no different, although I follow behind the group in a very clumsy way. I chastise myself for my head being out of sorts, but don't get far into the self-talk before my skis and I run into a wall. Reed and I topple over each other in a tangled mess of legs, poles, and skis. I apologize profusely and try to get untangled, while Reed laughs at my struggle.

His laugh is deep. I feel it reverberating in my bones and my own laughter escapes. Realization dawns on me that the harder I try to right the situation, the worse it is getting. We wave Milo and Nikki on and tell them we will meet them at the top.

"Here, take your skies off. That will help," Reed says, a little more composed, while reaching for a pole.

He leans closer to me and pushes the release lever with his pole. With his nearness, I inhale his scent from yesterday's shower. The body wash is faint with the slightest hint of musk. The ski pops off my boot and I am able to move my leg freely. He pulls back and our eyes meet. I look away, this time knowing I have been caught for something I shouldn't be doing. He clears his throat and we begin untangling from each other.

It takes a few minutes to get us put back together. We make our way over to the lift without another word. The chair scoops us up and ascends the mountain again. It's still quiet, like this morning, but charged with a different feeling. This morning I was charged with excitement from our tradition. Now it's charged with embarrassment, longing, and frustration.

My mind drifts back to last night and the fireside talk I shared with Reed. I miss having someone to talk to at night when I can't sleep. Lance may not have been a great guy, but he was still there. He was someone that I shared a life with. Despite his wrongdoings, he still had shining moments.

Reed can't fill that void for long, but I enjoy his company.

Lost in my thoughts Reed's voice startles me when he starts to speak. Because of my jolt it causes the chair to shimmy a little. Reed's hand tightens around the chair lift bar and his swallows hard. I smile slightly while he lets out a slow breath.

"Thatcher?" His eyebrow quirks up at me. "You're a love'em and leave'em type aren't you?"

"No," I giggle at his jab. "He is a friend. I didn't know you were afraid of heights." I decide not to be nice after all and call him out on what I noticed earlier.

"Just a little. I can do stunts and acrobatics as long as I have a harness on and there is a technician around, but we are simply sitting in a chair with nothing holding us in. Yes, I am a little freaked by it." His voice is getting tighter the higher the chair moves up the mountain.

"A friend with benefits?" he pushes.

I sigh. "Thatcher is Thatcher. He visits here throughout the year doing various mountain excursions, and I see him occasionally when I am in the city."

"Should I be expecting company tonight?" Reed wags his eyes at me, causing me to laugh.

"No. We aren't like that. Not saying he hasn't tried." The pull to be honest about what really happened pulls deeply at me. I'm just not sure I'm ready to verbally admit it.

"The problem is always the same." Those words struggle their way out. My mind blocks the rest. What is left is the lie I have told myself and everyone who ever asks. "This is where I live. This is my life. Not many will give up their lives to live in Middleton. Sure, it's nice to visit and many talk about living here and making this their life, but then their reality sets in. They have jobs, friends, family, and lives they have to return to."

I pause for a moment, letting my thoughts linger on how comfortable I am with him and how empty my house will feel when he is gone. When he leaves to go back to his reality.

"Thatcher and I had a few dates after the breakup. You just can't build much of a relationship on sporadic dates. I run two businesses and help with another; he works for his dad at a high-demand law firm. So…eventually someone has to give up what they have in order to be with the other person."

"And neither of you would sacrifice your current situations to be with each other," Reed states, and I confirm with a nod. Even though this isn't the real reason, there is still a lot of truth to it.

"I mean, isn't that what love is, a sacrifice? A sacrifice for something that you really want?" I glance over at Reed, who acknowledges the rhetorical question. "Problem is, I just don't feel that kind of love for Thatcher, nor do I believe he feels the same for me.

"Is that why you dodged him this morning?"

"You noticed." Reed grins and nods at me. "That's one reason. I settled once for love and got burnt. I'm not about to do it again. I get the feeling he is settling for me because he is comfortable and is ready to take it to the next level to see where it will go. Reason two: the first day of the hill's opening is my moment. It's a moment that I can get lost in, where there are no distractions," I finish as we reach the top of the mountain.

The gang is sitting off to the side waiting for us. With whoops and hollers, they are up and flying down the mountain again.

"They like to crow," Reed comments. I answer with my own crow and laugh as I head down the hill.

For the rest of the morning, Reed and I spend our lift rides apart and I find myself disappointed. I end up riding mostly with Thatcher, who talks about his promotion and the new responsibilities at his job. He knows my routine and avoids asking questions about my family; because of that, we don't talk much about me until he asks about Reed. I evade his real question and explain that I am working on his car.

He asks a few more questions and must have deemed the situation at hand innocent. Quickly bored talking about the shop or Reed, he moves back to topics he likes talking about. He isn't arrogant. He just likes to talk. He shares stories of pranks he and Jake have pulled on co-workers, and the crazy adventures they have had in the past. He is full of life. It's easy to feed off his energy. I know he will find someone who deserves him, it's just not me.

At some point, Reed cut out for a little bit to go rent the proper equipment. As we waited at the top of the mountain for him to join us, the boys got restless and started betting on who could make the best snow angel. Jake deemed Nikki to be an unfair judge because she was married to Milo, which left me in charge. Knowing the losers would argue my decision, I refused and left the boys to verbally battle out their opinions. Tuning their banter out, I watched people exit the lift. I couldn't fight my grin when I heard Thatcher's lawyer voice debate with Milo as to why he made the better snow angel.

I don't notice Reed until he comes off the lift and heads right at Nikki and I as we sit in the snow. He isn't slowing down as he approaches and I start getting nervous. At the last second, he does a quick turn to shower us with snow. I try acting mad until he tackles us. He is laughing and looks more comfortable now, like a male snow bunny model in properly fitting coat and snow pants.

On our last run before lunch, Thatcher and I reach the top and are pelted with snowballs. I duck out of site, pop my skies off, and start making my own arsenal. Looking around the tree while packing the snow tight in my hands, I catch a glimpse of my friends laughing and yelling. I normally would have skipped out by now, feeling like I needed to get back to the shop, but today George told me he has it covered. I feel like he is begging for a chance to show me that he can run the shop by himself. Not that I ever doubted his abilities, I just never want to let the responsibility rest on someone else.

Watching the snowballs fly between my friends, I never realized how much I was missing until this moment. I swallow a big lump in my throat because I missed being a kid. I envy Thatcher for his carefree lifestyle. I envy the love that Milo and Nikki have for each other. I also cherish them all for those reasons. I embrace the moment and let a snowball fly at Reed. I am not going to live vicariously through my friends any more. This is my life.

Reed's face scrunches in surprise as the damp, wet ball hits him in the shoulder. Milo's head whips in my direction. His face shows surprise, warmth, and joy at seeing me participate in the game. I smile back at Milo and am taken off guard as a hailstorm of snow comes flying at me. Squealing and giggling, I duck around the tree. I quickly start making more snowballs when I am tackled from the side. I can't help but burst into another fit of giggles because I can't move and can't breathe with the weight on me. Reed is laughing and throwing snow all over my head. Soon the whole group ends up in a dogpile.

We call the war a draw and head down to the lodge for lunch. Reed and I stay close as we ski down, nudging each other occasionally when opportunities arise.

He is becoming a friend that I know I will miss when he leaves to go back home. I tried my hardest not to get close, but he is charming and sweet, and more real than I ever thought he could be. I know they say never to judge a book by its cover, but I totally did with Reed. He could always be lying, but what would he gain by lying to us?

Before my thoughts can grab hold of the reasons to not trust him, I breathe out and give him one last nudge while we climb the stairs into the lodge. Reed throws his arm around my shoulders and squeezes me before rubbing his knuckles in my hair. I playfully glare up at him but know that is a mistake when our eyes meet. He clears his throat and we get in the lunch line. We grab our food with no more touching or talking.

Lunch isn't quiet because Jake and Thatcher fill it with their stories. What fascinates me about these two is that they never repeat a story. I have known them since college and have wondered if they make these stories up. From spending time with them over those couple of years, I know better.

Everyone breaks out in laughter when Jake hits the punch line. My eyes drift over to Reed. I can tell he is amused, but kind of annoyed with their constant chatter. It is true that Thatcher and Jake can be a bit much. With the duo, you have to train to be around them for hours. It's like a drug. If you take a big hit, you come out coughing and not enjoying it, but in small doses, you can become addicted to them. Reed looks like he took a long drag and isn't quite sure what to do now. I smile out of sympathy for him right as his eyes turn to mine.

I feel my cheeks warm just the slightest. Reed's shoulders do a slight rise as he takes in a deep breath. I wonder if maybe he has to try hard to look so calm and collected. I grin deeper and he rolls his eyes. We are speaking our own language. With a jerk of his head over his shoulder and a slight nod of mine, Reed stands up. "Well, who is ready for more skiing?"

Thatcher looks a little startled to be cut off. With the silent moment, I stand and start clearing my stuff. "Let's hit it." And off we go.

Skis on and ready to go, I listen to the banter. Thatcher and Jake bash each other, while Reed takes notes from Milo and Nikki on which slopes we are running next. I look at my friends and know this is where I belong. I wish this could be all I ever did. But we all have responsibilities that beckon us.

With the plan for our next run set, we head towards the lift that takes us to another side of the mountain. Nikki says my name and I slow down to wait for her. She comes up beside me, moving in a slow pace. She slaps me on the butt and says, "Oh, never mind, I can tell you later." She winks at me and digs her poles into the snow to gain speed to catch up with Milo. Reed comes up next to me and he gives me a questioning look. I shrug my shoulders and we propel ourselves forward to join the group in line.

As we are getting on the chairlift, Nikki turns around in her chair to face me. She has a face-splitting smile and her eyes bounce between Reed and me. The puzzle piece snapped into place. This girl has skill. Milo's shoulders rise and fall with a huff because he knows what his wife is up to. I just shake my head at her but can't help but smile back.

Nikki had set up this chairlift ride up for me to hang out with Reed. Even though we have our evenings together, I am still working the bar most nights. We don't have much time to spend together. Last night was the first time I really got to know Reed.

I can't deny the fact that being around Reed is a nice escape from reality. The need to be near him is growing deeper as we spend more time together. I'm slightly frustrated with myself for letting Thatcher's charisma consume my morning and take me away from Reed, but doubt is setting in that he may not feel the same way I do. Reed hasn't made much of an effort to spend much time with me.

"Ok, so how do you put up with Thatcher for a whole week's worth of camping?" Reed asks. I laugh and we start mocking some of the stuff Thatcher said over lunch.

"Are you saying you don't have any friends that are like that?" I ask accusingly. "He can be a little much to sit and listen to, but when it comes to doing activities, you forget he even talks. You get lost in the experience and so does he," I explain. If anyone were to spend time with us on a regular basis, they'd see how little we talk as a group. We just go and do.

"I get why he's not your type," Reed concludes.

"What makes you think you know my type?" My brows furrow.

He sat there for a moment, thinking with his old man pose. His fingered glove taps his upper lip. "Not Thatcher."

"That's all you can say?" I say incredulously.

"I can't believe you went out with him." He laughs but never answers the question.

"How's Zoey?" I ask to get the attention off Thatcher and me. I kind of meant it to be mean but also because I was curious. I have spent a lot of time with him but never have heard him on the phone with anyone.

"I don't know." He leaves the statement hanging. I never used to ask such imposing questions. Mostly because I knew if I asked them, that meant I was giving them the right to enter my life story and ask the same questions of me. That wasn't a path I wanted to share with anyone. But since Reed entered Middleton, my normal habits and aversions have been changing.

"Not going to elaborate?" I asked coyly.

His shoulders rise ever so slightly, almost in a shrug. "I don't know. When I took my little vacation, I took a break from us. We technically haven't been in a romantic relationship with each other for a while now. We just never called it off because our publicists indicated our 'love story' keeps us popular and relevant. We are comfortable with each other and don't mind keeping up the act. Zoey and I basically use each other for our personal gain and our private needs. The public sees us together because that is how we want it; it protects our real lives."

"What are your needs? 50-Shade-type needs?" I laugh, but my face is red with embarrassment.

Reed's jaw drops and he starts laughing too. "Dang Harley, where is your head at?"

"If the media version isn't real, then what is real?" I try to recover.

He ponders that for a moment. "That was what the break was for. I have portrayed so many characters and changed personality traits to get movie roles. I've become a chameleon, all to make people like me and to boost box-office sales. In a way, Zoey and I are just props in the big scheme of things. I've lost who I am." He takes a breath and looks over at me with a halfcocked smile. "That was deep. Back to your original question, I told her I needed a break from everything and everyone for a while. I haven't talked to her since I left a couple of months ago."

"So much for a little vacation," I say sarcastically.

He smiles gently at me. Back at the top, I breathe a shallow sigh, disappointed that our conversation is being interrupted. I feel like I am getting to know the real him. He glances over at me, with a look like he knows what I am feeling. It might be my imagination.

12

REED

"What's the plan after this?" I ask. We had been skiing pretty much the entire day and I am exhausted.

"Hot tub, anyone?" Milo asks. I am watching everyone's reaction to make sure I didn't seem overly excited at the suggestion. Good news...I think everyone is game.

"I checked in with George around lunch and he has the shop under control. I guess you can count me in." Milo's head whips around to look at Harley straight on.

"You're kidding, right?" he says, his voice oozing with doubt.

"No, why not take a break today? I mean, I jacked around all day with you guys, why not just enjoy the rest of the afternoon before I head over to the bar?" Harley sounds a little irritated with Milo, but I guess that is how my brother and I would talk if we actually talked.

"That's the Harley I know. Can't take a WHOLE day off." Milo rolls his eyes at her but she shoves him in the arm and he ruffles her hat. "I guess hot-tubbing it is, fellas."

"Sounds good to me," I add.

Thatcher and Jake decide to head back to their lodge to take naps, but promise to catch us later tonight at the bar. The group splits and I can't say I am disappointed. I have become very comfortable with our little group of four: Milo, Nikki, Harley, and myself. I chastise myself for thinking this is *my* group, but it feels like home. Like a place I have always belonged to, and a place I desire to belong to. I feel the sense of reality trying to settle in, but I wave it away, refusing to let it take root right now. Soon enough, I know I will have to go back to my life.

A half-hour later, I settle into the hot tub across from Milo. He keeps eyeing me. I lay my head back and try to relax. I can't help but grin.

"What are you grinning at?" Milo asks.

"I am trying not to think that I am taking a communal bubble bath with you right now."

Milo grunts in disgust, "Thanks for pointing that out." Then he hollers, "Nikki and Harley get out here, Reed is freaking me out!" We both start laughing but the girls don't seem to be in a hurry.

Milo's eyes settle back to observation mode. I chide, "You are making this weirder. STOP. Why are you staring at me?"

"I am trying to understand what has gone on between you and Harley," Milo states accusingly.

"And by watching me in the tub, what have you figured out?"

"First, stop calling it a tub, it's gross." He pauses for one last evaluation. "Guy body language would ooze of victory if you had nailed her, but I don't see that. But, at the same time, I feel like something is going on." He pauses for a minute but never takes his eyes off of me. "It's just that Harley has never hung out with us all day like she has today. I mean never. Even when we were in high school, she would ski the slopes a few runs then head home to do homework, or to go to work. In college, she left early to take care of her dad. The only variable to this equation is you. I just haven't figured out what's going on."

I don't really know what to say except, "From guy to guy, nothing has happened. I don't normally respect girls in the old-fashioned way, but Harley is different. I'm not trying anything with her."

Milo nods in approval. "Don't hurt her." His protectiveness bleeds through his voice.

I nod back with respect for someone who has watched his friend suffer enough. I don't want to be another one that is added to the list of people of who have broken Harley's heart.

The girls have impeccable timing, and show up with beers in their hands. Saving us from some more awkward bro-soaking, they join us. As Harley's towel falls away, I clench my jaw just to make sure it doesn't drop. Milo ever so slightly kicks my leg as a reminder to mind myself, but my eyes have a mind of their own.

Harley's hair is piled on top of her head in a messy bun, something I have become accustomed to as part of her normal dress attire. What I am not used to is the sight of her pale winter skin glowing against the low-cut one-piece black swimsuit that hugs the nice curve of her body.

Most swim-suited girls I see are tan, with so very little covered that there is not much mystery to what's underneath. They are also typically adorned with showy accessories like jewelry, sunglasses, and hats, to simply sit at the beach or pool side. I would never complain about what I have seen, but I do have to say this sight is also, and quite possibly more, appealing.

I am used to seeing small, toned muscles that flow down tiny arms and legs. Harley is thin, but her strength is more defined on her small frame. Her work at the shop has made her ability to break a bolt or lift heavy objects evident. As she moves up the stairs of the Jacuzzi, her legs flex with each step, showing the definition of calf and quad muscles working as one.

I notice a few bruises that I assume are from work. The Band-Aid covering the cut on her forehead from yesterday's accident has been removed. It has a little hue of purple behind it, but she still looks perfect. I am mesmerized by her grace and simple beauty. She doesn't seem to pay attention to my gawking; and if she is, she isn't showing it.

The four of us settle into our spots, with the girls sitting on either side of me. Our casual conversation falls into a steady cadence of the plans for the rest of the week and the happenings lately. I learn more about their past, who they are, and what they mean to each other.

Milo is your home-grown country boy who loves his mama and respects his daddy. I am jealous of his upbringing. He makes side comments occasionally about how he used to think about going out and doing great big things for the world, having it all at his fingertips, but knowing his responsibilities were here. Despite the disappointment of not being able to stretch his wings, he takes pride in his work, the shop his family has built, his home, and his wonderful wife.

Nikki is her own creature. She grew up in a large artistic family. I see her eccentric side shine through, which is why she and Milo are a perfect match. They keep each other balanced. I also understand why she is a teacher. She reminds me a lot of Miss Frizzle from the "Magic School Bus" without all the crazy dresses. But who knows? Maybe that is what she wears in her classes. Either way, I can't help but be drawn to her. She is full of energy. Her mind is always ticking. Everyone around her must often decide if they want to follow her or just let her run wild.

Harley is determined, content, and humble. She, like Milo, knows responsibility and doesn't shy away from what has to be done. She might err on the side of gruffness and may be somewhat cut-throat on decisions, but it is necessary to be this way with her busy schedule. As Milo has pointed out, those business practices don't bleed into her personal life, at least not that I have seen. The most intriguing characteristic about Harley is that she doesn't fuss about things that don't go right, or how she wants them done, she just moves.

I am beginning to fall for her. It excites me to feel this way about someone again but it also scares me. I loved Zoey at one time but it was on the surface and out of convenience. Harley makes me feel transparent. Like when she is looking at me, she can read my thoughts. Zoey took me at face value, while Harley can cut through my self-imposed wall and see who I really am. I am just not sure who that is yet. Maybe she can help me figure myself out, but that means exposing the demons from my past that still haunt me.

Nikki makes a goofy childish joke that makes us all laugh at the stupidity of it. I glance over to see a few stray hairs have fallen out of Harley's ponytail. I smirk. In the movies, the romantic thing to do is to sweep them off her shoulder, but I don't know if I should. If Nikki and Milo weren't here, I'd probably lean in, brush the strands aside, and kiss her shoulder as I've done in countless movies. But I thank God that I am not alone with her right now, because I don't want this to be like the movies where everything is planned, evaluated, revised, practiced, and never real.

I hear a phone-alarm chirp in the background. Harley jumps up. "That's my cue. Are you guys coming to the bar tonight?" She asks us, but looks directly at me. I try to shake my wandering thoughts and focus on her face, rather than the curves under that black swimsuit.

"Why wouldn't we? We will see you in a bit," I offer before anyone can say anything else. Her cheeks turn a very light shade of pink and she gives me an awkward nod. She climbs out of the Jacuzzi and heads for the house, leaving me staring in her wake.

"Could you be more obvious?" Nikki's sweet voice drips.

I turn to see them grinning at me. I can't help but laugh because I know I wasn't very suave about my gawking. Milo changes the subject to sports. Surprisingly, Nikki knows her sports trivia and keeps pace with Milo and me.

They are the Hallmark card of super-sweet couples. And great friends too. Through all the time I have spent with them, I have yet to feel like a third wheel. After a while longer, I decide to go back to Bromley and change. We make plans to meet at the bar later that night.

Back at Bromley, I shower, feeling the hot water run down my skin and ease my tired muscles. I force myself out of the shower, thinking of Harley's increasing water bill. Thinking of her makes me smile. I think about how lively she was today. How often she laughed. I noticed her honest laughs with me, versus the polite laughter she offered Thatcher. My ego inflates.

I reach for my toothpaste and realize that I have used all of mine. I feel bad for using Harley's stuff but run upstairs quickly to use her toothpaste. I will replace it before I leave. Digging in the drawers, I come across the diamond ring. I get a good look at it, this time in the bathroom light instead of the firelight from last night. I realize now the diamond is a good size and sparkles brightly. It's what every girl wants, but not what I picture on Harley's mechanic's hand.

I still wonder why she keeps it. I see her as a fighter, someone who would throw a punch before walking out on someone who had cheated on her. In the mirror, I catch a glimpse of the tattoo that covers my past. I wonder how Harley would have handled the people whose stories are locked behind these scars. The very thought makes me sick because I would never want her to feel what I have felt. I hope she never has.

Looking into the mirror, I see the torment from the past etched in my eyes. I touch the scar hidden by the tattoo.

> *After making sure that Blaine is well on his way to the park, I head downstairs to face Billy. He is fuming. First strike, I took longer than he wanted. Second strike, Blaine isn't with me. Third strike, I ratted him out. I knew hell was coming my way. My ten-year-old body braced itself. The belt buckle struck me across my chest repeatedly. I willed myself not to let a tear fall. If it fell, he won. I would not let him win.*

I suppress the emotions threatening to boil over. I breathe a tight sigh as I place the ring back in the drawer, grab the toothpaste, brush my teeth, and head back downstairs to finish getting ready. I try to leave my toxic memory upstairs.

I sit down on the couch to put on my shoes and realize that I have been neglecting my homework for my next movie role. These scripts were the only assignment my agent gave me before I left. He instructed that if I was taking a break from being the "American Heartthrob," (which he thought was a crazy move), then I needed to figure out what role I wanted to take next. He handed me scripts and sent me on my way to self-discovery.

After organizing Harley's house, I had quickly run out of things to do. I've spent most days vegetating and watching reality TV. If I turn the volume up loud enough, I don't have to listen to Harley's house phone ring, followed by an annoying message left by Lance. He is calling four times a day now. I've come extremely close to answering it, but know better. I haven't brought it up to Harley as I'm sure she's aware of how often he is calling. The message light is always off when I get up in the morning so she at least sees the number of voicemails that are left each day. Whether she listened to them is unknown, and I do not want to know.

As I leave to walk to the bar, it's snowing again. The short walk from Bromley to Cheapshots takes the warmth from my shower away. The chill is settling down into my bones. As I enter the bar, I shake the snow out of my hair, ruffling it up then patting it back down. My eyes spot Milo and I am thankful that he and Nikki have settled into a booth by the fire. I also notice that Thatcher and Jake are there. I grumble to myself.

"They can't be that bad," I hear in a low voice right by my ear. The voice chases away the cold I was feeling. A smile splits my face and a soft chuckle comes out instead.

"You keep saying that... and I still don't see how you handle them." I turn to look at her. Her hair is still piled on top of her head, but the one-piece has been replaced with a beer t-shirt and skinny jeans. She is standing there with a pitcher of beer in her hand, looking at me with a coy grin. I miss the bathing suit but she still looks sexy, especially holding that pitcher of beer. Both are making my mouth water.

Harley hands me the pitcher and directs me to take it over to the booth where Nikki, Milo, Jake, and Thatcher are sitting. George is playing pool and stops me to report they got the engine block today despite the snow. He will be checking it out this week before installing it in the Chevelle. No complications thus far. I feel my heart sink a little.

Harley had sauntered over and interrupts, "Well good news, I could use some help. Have you ever worked at a bar before?" I nod. "Good, I am a rule follower but I am willing to look past that you don't have your license with you. We will just keep in mind this is temporary. So, follow me."

The group spots us as I follow Harley to the back. I give them a nod. Nikki's eyes sparkle and Thatcher gives me a good once over. I try to hide my smile and just keep walking. Harley walks me through her system and we set to work.

"Now tonight will be heavier, because of the slopes opening. They pile in here because we have the best bar around," she informs me. "Watch out for fake ID's - that's going to be a big issue tonight. If you have questions on a license, let me know. I am aware of the regulars and can spot them easily."

I nod, trying to take in all the information. She points out some locals and sends me on my way to take their orders. I fumble a little in the beginning, but pick up my rhythm. The locals are becoming familiar with me. Some figured out who I am underneath the scruff on my face, and even fewer were brave enough to ask for autographs. Most have kept to themselves.

Here, no one really cares about my status in Hollywood. They are more concerned about their crops and the local economy or when their next beer will be served, rather than what movie is playing this weekend. Over the course of my stay, however, they still seem to be uncomfortable with me. Eventually, they might loosen up. Tonight, by serving them beer and food, I'm starting to make my way in. They openly talk trash about each other, but I see endearment under it all. They may bash their neighbor or complain about somebody up the road, but they are a large family. Harley had told me that when I first arrived, but now I was witnessing it firsthand.

As Harley mentioned, we kept an eye on those that were known to overdo it. Harley watched them closely and would give me the cut-off sign when she felt like they had been served enough. The bar got louder and louder but Harley watched them all like a mother hen. She would count the drinks, communicate with the drinkers, and bark orders if she needed to. She knew the people and they trusted her.

Even though we are slammed with people, I find myself purposefully making my way behind the bar to be near her. Embarrassingly, I also look for ways to slightly touch her or playfully tug some of her hair that came loose from her bun. She giggles and I recall our first conversation about flirting when we were on the swings.

When closing time comes around, people start heading home, including our group of friends. Thatcher bids us goodnight with the promise of seeing us tomorrow. Walking behind them, Harley shut the door. The sound of the deadbolt sliding into place left the bar feeling very empty. She turns and smiles deviously at me and my heart picks up. I know she isn't looking at me the way I wish, but I can't help but let my mind go there for a second.

"Clean-up time," she says. Her grin is getting more mischievous and she starts telling me what she needs me to do to help her close. I start cleaning up the bar area while she cleans the booths, tables, and the floor. As she moves between tables, I can see her body swaying to the music she had selected from the juke box. Whether her movements are intended to accompany the music or not, she has me hypnotized. I pull myself back to the task at hand, but sneak occasional peeks at her.

Her naturalness is appealing. Not sexy, but attractive. She remains somewhat of a mystery to me, but with each conversation, that mystery fades. There are parts of her that I am not allowed to know yet, and may never know. I don't hold that against her because I have my own secrets.

13

HARLEY

I know he is studying me and has been since this afternoon. I don't mind because I have been doing the same with him. From the corner of my eye, I watch him work. His muscles flex ever so slightly as he extends his arm to pick up glasses and move things around. I see deep thoughts crease his forehead. I want to reach out and smooth the concerned look off his face.

My staring gets in the way of what I am supposed to be doing right now. I bump into a table, rather loudly, which startles him from his task. He looks up at me. I am so embarrassed that I feel my cheeks heating up. I glance away quickly and wipe the already-clean table. I peek up at the cocky grin plastered on his face. I can tell he is trying not to laugh. I relax and continue with cleaning up.

I move to the bar to finish up the night's bookkeeping. Reed finishes his task, grabs us both a beer, and sits next to me. As I spread my papers out to start working the numbers, I can feel his eyes on me.

"Why are you smiling?" he asks.

"I have felt you watching me all day." He shrugs, most definitely proving that he isn't going to deny it. "Am I making you uncomfortable?" he asks hesitantly.

"It should." I look up from the books, realizing that I may have just admitted something I didn't intend. He smiles and kindly reaches over to brush a few stray hairs from my face, gently tucking them behind my ear.

We have become more comfortable since the last night's snowstorm. I am not sure what broke the barrier, but we both have found ways to bump into one another, or nudge each other playfully. My hair has become his thing to tug or to stroke. I think it's his reference to our first conversation on the swings. I haven't minded one bit. I like his playfulness.

"Thanks," I whisper quietly, wondering if he can even hear me. He nods and takes out his phone, busying himself with it. I look back at the books, but I can't focus. I grab my beer and take a big drink, trying to give myself a moment to get back to reality.

"So, George told you your parts came in, but he forgot that we are lacking one. Bad news is, it's on back order and I don't know when it will be in. During that time though, George is going to start working on what he can." Informing him about his car is enough to sober me.

He nods his head and we get back to our task.

"I saw you and Thatcher step outside for a moment tonight." Reed doesn't sound jealous, but he seems a little sour about me being alone with Thatcher.

"So," I state, amusingly.

"Everything okay?" He tries to be nonchalant, but is totally failing at it.

"He just wanted to say bye." He nods like he isn't buying it, but is aware he doesn't have any claim over me.

I reflect on what was said between us, and I feel like Thatcher's goodbye was a little more than that. He normally passes off a *see you next time* or *see you around*, but tonight left me feeling like he wasn't just leaving to go home. It felt a little more like he wouldn't be around anymore. Our friendship would remain, but there was something different about it now. I just can't put my finger on it.

"Earlier today when we were in the hot tub," Reed states, drawing me back to the present, "you mentioned you have an event you are attending next weekend. What event, if I might ask?" I am reminded how attentive Reed is. I can understand being nosy when you don't have many people to talk to. Small-town life.

"The event is for a non-profit organization that helps underprivileged kids gain access to the arts. Whether that be dance, music, sculpture, painting, anything you can think of that deals with personal creativity."

"How did you get involved?" He asks, intrigued.

"In college, one of my roommates watched a movie about a prestigious school that worked with street kids and encouraged them to pursue their artistic talents. She wanted to make the movie a reality, but with her own spin – focusing more on community involvement than strictly school programs. She built the program, getting the city's symphony, acting clubs, local recording studios, and dance companies to volunteer to train and work with these kids," I explain.

I see Reed is grinning wide, knowing I'm referring to one of his movies. "Huh," he cockily chimes in, "I think I'm familiar with that movie."

"Anyways," I smile back and push on, "the kids have to apply and make a real effort, and they can be kicked out by not meeting certain requirements. Each year there is a Graduation/Fundraiser event where scouts from the supporting companies can come in and hire the students, make contracts, give scholarships for future education, or whatever they feel led to do. What makes this event special is the student performances. They show off their own potential. It's their way of saying "Thank you, look at what I have done with the opportunity you have provided." It's very rewarding to see their hard work and dreams come to life on stage."

Reed sits there quietly, with a look of awe on his face. "Would you like to go and see it?" I ask softly. The offer has more emotion in it than I prefer. I want him to see this organization in action, but as the question sits there, I realize I'm actually asking him to go with *me*. His quiet pause is making me more anxious as seconds tick by.

"I would love to." A smile splits my face and I can't wait for the weekend.

"We will need to leave early Saturday afternoon. I had a hotel room booked before you arrived because the event runs rather late into the night. Is that ok with you?" I feel awkward mentioning the hotel room but it's inevitable. "I can call them tomorrow and get you a room too so we will be at the same hotel."

Reed nods. "But why don't I call them tomorrow and take care of it. It will give me something to do for a few minutes." I write down the hotel name for him.

His eyes sparkle with anticipation, which I feel is being reflected in my eyes as well. "After observing me all day what have you discovered Mr. Montgomery?"

"What?" he asked, startled, but his grin grows into a bashful smile.

"You have been caught. I know you have been watching me all day. You weren't very discrete."

He laughs and his cheeks brighten with a touch of heat. "Neither were you," he banters back.

"I just wonder what you are thinking after all that observing." I shake my head as what we were told about boys in middle school pops into my head - that boys think about sex every three seconds. "On second thought, I may not want to know." Now it's my turn to blush at how intrusive and maybe out of line I am to think that he thinks about me that way. I am getting all flustered. He can tell too because he starts laughing.

"I observed that your eyes don't seem as tired and weary as they were when I first met you." He is being nice by not adding to the awkwardness of my question and reaction. I appreciate him for it as he continues, "I observed that you looked utterly happy today. I saw a sparkle in your eye as you flew down the mountain. I saw you relaxed. I saw you smile more than I ever have. I can only imagine what next Saturday will hold because you lit up like a Christmas tree just telling me about the non-profit organization. I've noticed that when you light up, everything and everyone around you shines too."

I am speechless because I can't remember the last time someone gave me such a beautiful compliment. Lance never said anything like that to me. Thatcher just always treated me like a guy friend, even though he has interest, but never compliments like those.

I then remember who I am talking to. This guy has played characters who have repeated lines like that for years. He has made writers' characters come to life over and over. He knows what women like to hear. He has studied us.

"What's wrong?" he asks, and I realize that what I'm thinking must be showing on my face. I stand up, shake my head, and start stacking papers. "Harley?"

I start to say something but can't pull the words together. I stop fidgeting and look at him. I truly look at him, trying to see through the actor facade. Is that what I'm hung up on? That he's an actor? Or is it because I don't fully trust my own judgment since Lance?

Reed's eyes are concerned and soft. His mouth is slightly open as if he were going to try to say something to make me explain. He closes his mouth as I stand there searching for my answer. He moves his hand and gently places it on mine. I contemplate asking him if he is just messing with me, but the look on his face tells me differently. I want to lean in to kiss him but what if I mistake what is going on here? I swallow hard and lean towards him. His body reacts to mine. Our lips touch. My eyes close. I hadn't realized how much I missed this.

My hands drop the papers and slowly make their way to cup his face. His arms move to wrap around me, in an embrace I could only have wished for. Our kissing is soft and slow. I can tell he has had practice and knows how to seduce with his mouth. I easily get sucked into his spell.

A throat clears behind me. Startled, I clumsily twist in Reed's arms to quickly come to a halt. My heart rate quickens and panic settles in.

Lance stands there with a scary-calm expression on his face, a calm that I am all too familiar with. I protectively grip Reed's arm and move to stand in front of him. I can feel Reed's body tense behind me as though he wants to protect me, but I firmly squeeze his arm. Multiple questions bounce in my head and I don't know which question to ask first.

"How did you get in?" I feel like that question isn't the one I should have started with, but it beats the alternative of just standing here while I watch Lance size up Reed.

"Harley, come on its Middleton. The locks around here are easy to open," Lance responds with a taunt.

"Why are you here?" That's the question I should have started with.

"You weren't answering my calls." He feigns concern.

"I've been busy."

"I see that." His sinister response makes me cringe. "Hey, can we talk. Just you and me?"

Lance is lean and lanky, but strong as an ox. Not only can he throw mean punches, he is a master manipulator. I ended up in his trap because he knows how to work angles and is very smooth with words. I could never see where he was coming from and he knew he kept me guessing. Being caught kissing Reed tonight is evidence to him of why I've been avoiding him, which has only angered him more.

I don't want Reed to go, but I also want him away from Lance. I have no doubt that Reed could handle his own against Lance, but I don't want to see it happen. I turn to Reed. His eyes show me the same reluctance that I feel in mine. "Just wait outside, it won't take long." He hesitates, eyeing Lance.

"Harley, I don't think…" he starts, but I cut him off, pleading with my eyes to give me just a minute. I am hopeful I can defuse the situation. Without a nod, Reed simply walks by me while making eye contact with Lance. Oozing confidence in his a purposeful gait, Reed heads outside. This might be a male pissing war, but, in this case, I don't care as long as they don't hit each other.

My decision to walk away from Lance was scary and something other people don't understand. They think discovering your fiancé cheating is enough reason to walk, but that's only what the outsiders know. The real problem is his jealousy. It's moving on from Lance where it gets dangerous for me.

Milo thinks I still have feelings for Lance and that is why I haven't cut him out of my life. In reality, I have entertained Lance's calls and played his games to keep him from showing up like this. I have seen the worst of Lance's temper often enough to know he doesn't like to be ignored and people get hurt when he isn't in control.

The door shuts behind Reed. My lungs only allow me to take shallow breaths and I suddenly regret making Reed leave. Lance's eyes lock on me. I can tell he is angry and he knows I'm spooked. My skin starts to crawl.

"Don't worry, I have been taking anger-management classes. I won't hurt you. I hated hurting you before." He steps closer to me and I back up.

"Regardless, could you still keep some space between us?" I see his eyes flash, which makes me question the sincerity of his admission. He nods like he wants to respect my wishes and doesn't move closer.

"How long has he been in town?" His tone is serious. He hates lies, but the truth might set him off. I have to tread carefully. His jealousy has the ability to cause physical pain, and it is the emotion from him that I fear the most.

"Reed has been here a few weeks."

"Right around the time you stopped answering my calls," Lance says more to himself than to me. Something in me wakes up. I am getting tired of being on his leash and square my shoulders. "I stopped answering them long before he arrived."

"Oh, but see that isn't exactly true." He steps closer, forgetting our agreement. I continue moving backwards and bump into the bar. "See, before him, you would pick up the phone. You may not have said anything, but I at least knew you were there. But then you weren't picking up at all. It scared me." It scared him because that meant I was gaining a backbone. Last time I stood up to him, I had major hell to pay.

"I thought that there might be something wrong," he continued. "I mean, you are all by yourself on the edge of the woods." His reference to my living situation sends chills up my spine. He is close enough that he reaches his hand out to stroke my cheek, but I pull away. The ever-present anger flares to the next level. I have two more chances before he turns on me.

"So, I came to check on you. I ran into Kayden and he informed me that you picked some random guy up off the side of the road. I mean really, how stupid are you?"

Another tick. I have one more chance to defuse the situation before he snaps.

He smirks at me. "Come to find out he is staying with you too. You were always a slut, weren't you?" The last chance to calm him down is gone. As Lance's face twists into rage, he must be recalling the kiss he interrupted. No matter what I say, I am done for.

His hand lashes out and grabs my face. He pulls me directly against him. "You are a fucking slut. You just like to make everyone believe you smell like roses, but you are a dirty whore." He throws me back against the bar. "Did you already forget what we used to do? How much fun we had? Am I so easily replaced?"

I am tired of these questions. I want him to swing and get it over with. I am tired, fed up, and I just want him gone. I straighten my back and level my eyes with his. "You replaced me. You found a new slut. What we used to have was miserable. I thank God that we are over. I wish daily I could forget, and I wish daily that you were dead!"

That did it. I said my peace. I feel strong and invincible, even when his fist strikes my stomach, followed with a blow to my ribs. I lose my balance. On my way down, my head hits the bar top. I know I will survive this. Lance is one of those smart abusers. He knows where to hit you so no one will know. He screams at me and kicks me in the thigh. I wonder where Reed is and how I can get his attention for help.

Lance moves to stand above me. This move is what haunts me and alarms roar in my head. I could take his hits and the words, but this was the final, vicious level. The level I had always tried to stay away from. His words started seeping in.

"You want to forget... I will make sure you never forget this." He starts grappling with my shirt. His knuckles brush my stomach, which churns with fear. I start fighting back. He gives me one hard fist across the face and my head starts swimming. Through my fogginess, I see him undo his belt and unbutton his jeans. I put my hands up to push him off, but he just laughs and swats my hands away like they are annoying flies.

I hear a clatter, but can't see anything but Lance above me. His head is turned as if someone had punched him. His head hits a bar-stool. I scramble away from him as he is knocked off me. My head is throbbing and my eyes are blurry. Lance's attention is on the intruder that interrupted his rage-filled conquest.

I glance over to see Reed with his shoulders squared, ready for Lance. His eyes never leave his target. That cool, calm anger indicates that this probably isn't the first time Reed has beat someone to a pulp.

Lance knows how to fight, but it's a dirty way of fighting. Anger is what powers his punch. Reed, on the other hand, looks skilled and quick. Reed has a scarier calm than Lance will ever have. I scoot back more trying to distance myself.

For each punch Lance throws, Reed gets two. Each hit knocks Lance more off his game. The door to the bar is still open and I see red and blue lights flashing. I feel myself slipping away.

14

REED

I sit off to the side and watch the paramedics tend to Harley's cuts. She must have hit the back of her head on something because she has a gash that the paramedics had to staple shut. The cut can be concealed by her hair, but her other injuries are way too extensive to conceal. The bastard knew how to hit her so that most of her injuries wouldn't be as noticeable; however, the blow to her cheek cannot be missed. Exterior wounds can heal, but what has me worried is the damage done inside her mind.

I hate myself right now. I have experience with the level of anger I saw in Lance's eyes and should not have left her side. Another huge regret of mine is that I had gone to the car to warm up. The distance caused me that much longer to get to her.

I had spent too much of my life witnessing the pure evil in some human beings. When my fist met Lance's skin, all I saw was red. My rage elevated as I felt a bone crunch under my knuckles.

Seething about my actions, I reflect on the fact that I had left her inside the bar with him. I made the right decision to call Milo about Lance. I dropped my phone when I heard a crash. I had felt like I couldn't get to her fast enough. Milo had called the police and their quick arrival is the only reason Lance is still alive right now.

"I can't let you go yet. They still have to talk to her and get her statement. And you need to calm down." Officer Meeks says to me.

He had directed me to the back of a squad car. I sat stewing and re-gretting my delay to get to her.

I glance over at the other squad car to see Lance sitting in the back. Officer Meeks breaks through my remorse, "We have all wanted to lock up that asshole for a really long time."

"You guys knew about him?" A little shocked, my head whips to glare up at him.

"He has a reputation, but he is slippery," he says, giving me my an-swer. "Harley never talks about it, if you can imagine that." He laughs without humor at his own joke, but keeps going. "Milo told us what he knew, which wasn't much, but I knew enough to fill in the missing de-tails. This line of work shows you the darkest people society has to offer."

He pauses as his knowing gaze settles on me. I clear a knot that has formed in my throat, which I instantly regret. It confirms what he was assuming about me. He may not know exactly who I am or what had happened in my past, but I feel like it is written all over me. Officer Meeks acts as if he doesn't pick up on it though. "Unfortunately, we can't do anything about tonight if she doesn't press charges."

"Think she will?" My eyes wander back to where she is sitting. Her eyes, wide and wild from the adrenaline rush, have now glazed over and locked on the pavement in front of her feet.

"You better hope she does. Otherwise, he has a right to press charges against you," Officer Meeks informs me.

When most people hear the threat of charges, their stomachs drop, but not mine. Tonight hasn't been my first experience dealing with this, so I sit there watching her. I hope she doesn't feel like any of this is her fault. She is not responsible. She needs to press charges for her safety, but I know that she needs to decide that on her own. She pauses in her statement. Her gaze finds mine and it bores deep. I'm a little unnerved at how exposed I feel. Between Officer Meeks' statement, and Harley's fear-filled eyes, I sense they are uncovering the parts of me that I have strived for years to keep hidden.

She doesn't look away, but inclines her head to continue to talk to Officer Kane. He asks her a question. She sits there and continues staring at me. Tears begin to fill her eyes and she nods. A tear slips down her cheek. Officer Kane nods, gives her arm a squeeze, and walks away.

Officer Kane makes his way over to us and quietly talks to Officer Meeks. My eyes never leave Harley's. Tear after tear falls down her face but she stays frozen, never wiping them, never moving, never breaking down entirely. I am screaming in my head, *What are you thinking? Are you okay? Will you be safe?* But all I get is the sight of her tears. I have no idea what is going on in that beautiful, bruised head.

Officer Meeks steps in front of me and squats down to my eye level. He is old enough to be my dad. With him in front of me like this, I feel like he is about to talk to me like he does with his kids.

"She is pressing charges. Lance may try to press charges against you as well so be ready for whatever. He isn't saying anything right now, but just hang around for a while until we get through some of the paperwork. In the meantime..." He pauses and glances behind him to look at Harley, then levels his gaze back on me. "Please keep an eye on her and take care of her."

I meet his gaze; in that moment, it's obvious. He knows my horrible secrets and expects me to protect her from the monsters we both know live and breathe in this world. I realize that's all I want to do. I want to take care of her.

I stand, shake both officers' hands, and make my way over to Harley. The squad car holding Lance pulls away, leaving a strange calm over the invisible circle the officers had made while they were taking statements. Milo and Nikki had been held on the outside of that invisible line until all parties had been released. Now that it is over, they come rushing in to meet us. Both sets of arms wrap around Harley and she winces. Knowing her pain, I bite back the warning bark of *careful* that wants to escape. Her friends check out her cuts and bruises, needing reassurance that she will be fine.

They fire several questions at her while she numbly gives them short answers. She is fighting to keep it together for them, but her eyes aren't focused. She must be fighting the replays in her mind. I hate that I know these signs and these situations. I am fighting my own recollections of tonight and several other nights.

I can still hear the whimpers and stifled cries of my past that haunt me at night. They are clawing their way to the surface again. I want to take Harley and run. I want to escape the horror of this night. I want it to disappear as if it never happened. My memories threaten to overpower me and I force a dry heave down. Trying to pull myself together, I focus on her deep, fearful eyes, which remind me to stay in the present. Harley is stronger than most girls I know. She will fight back, because time has already proven that. However, no matter how much you fight, those internal scars never heal or go away.

The flashing lights are gone and the four of us are left alone in the quiet morning. Nikki uses her motherly voice, "I don't want you out of my sight. Will you come home with us?" Harley is wobbly as she walks to her car.

"I'll be fine. Reed is here." She gazes up at me, seeming to plead for help. I have learned that Harley enjoys her space. She thrives in being left alone. After tonight's events, she needs to be alone to process what took place. It took Harley and I several attempts to reassure Nikki and Milo that she would be fine. They finally give in and part ways with us.

Harley breathes a deep sigh of relief. "After everything that has happened, their leaving is what you consider a relief?" I tease. She gives me a half smile, but it feels off. I attempt to take the keys from her since the medical team had informed me that they gave her heavy-duty painkillers. She pushes against me and stumbles to the car. Knowing it is a short drive to the house, I give up, help her in, and get in the car.

We make a few turns and come to the T in the road that faces Bromley. The jeep idles and I hear Harley's breath quicken. She steps on the gas, takes a hard left, and the car barrels down the road. The city is north but we are heading south.

Middleton is getting smaller and smaller as Harley picks up speed. The road inclines as it begins to work its way through the mountains.

At some point, the road will wrap around a mountain. I don't know if Harley can manage that in the dark, at this speed, with where her head might be right now.

"Let's bring it back down a little." My voice is the only calm part of me. I see the road slightly curving ahead. I reach for the side-door armrest as she accelerates around the curve. "Harley, seriously, we need to slow down. It's foggy and it has been snowing on and off today. The roads will be slick," I try reasoning with her. Staying calm is hard and my control is slipping away.

"Why couldn't he just leave me alone?" Her voice is wavering and is thick with unshed tears. "I didn't want you to see that."

"It's ok," I reassure as she continues to talk. I need to defuse the situation before it gets out of hand.

"No, it's not!" she shouts, taking her eyes off the road to glare at me.

"Watch the road," I snap as panic rises in my voice.

"Want to know what's really sick? He cheated on me with my sister," she yells at me.

Stunned into silence, I don't say anything.

"Yeah, that's right, this is how twisted it all is. She thinks that I lied about the abuse. She thinks he is a real charmer. She doesn't see that he charmed himself right into her pants. They had been sleeping around together behind my back for months. Months! While I was taking care of my dad, he was screwing her. Somehow they have made me to be the scum."

"Harley..." My voice is a little calmer, but I see movement off to the side of the road.

"No, don't say it. Don't say sorry, don't say anything."

Before my mouth can get more words out, a deer jumps out in front of us. She slams on the brakes, jerking us hard against our seatbelts. The car slides towards the guardrail, which is the only protection we have to keep us from careening off the side of the mountain. Luckily, the car stops inches away from it. The deer scampers off.

15

HARLEY

My heart is pounding hard against my rib cage. Reed fumbles with his seatbelt and clambers out of the car. The cold winter air swirls through the cab of the jeep, along with my recklessness. Humiliation washes over me, from what I have allowed Lance to do to me in the past, and from what he attempted to do tonight. I almost got us killed all because of him. I am humiliated that Reed witnessed my inability to protect myself. Panic rises against my rib cage and I can't breathe. I feel as if the car is resting on my chest.

I climb out and try to hold myself up with shaky limbs. I breathe as deep as I can to let the air refill my lungs and relax my body. I take a few steps away from the car. I take another deep breath and try to slow my heart rate. The images of tonight, and of past incidents with Lance, replay like a movie reel. Bile rises in my throat and I lose it. I feel like such a mess but I want the feelings to get out. Tears stream down my face as dry heaves rack my body. I feel a hand rubbing my back as Reed tries to help me regain control.

My breathing slows to shallow breaths rather than gasps. I peer over the railing in front of me into the vast abyss that almost swallowed us up. I am shivering from the cold as I regain control.

"Come on," Reed says quietly as he gently lifts me to my feet. He helps me get in the jeep, on the passenger side this time, and I don't argue with him. Reed attends to my seatbelt, making sure I am secure and safe. His hair is wet from the snow that is falling again, which makes his cologne strong in my nose. I feel myself melt towards him. Cranking the heat up, he moves all the vents to blow warm air on me. Before shutting the passenger door, he looks me in the eye, swipes my hair behind my ear, and lets his knuckles linger on my face. "You ok?"

I nod because I don't know what else to do. A few hours ago, the nearness of him spurred longing for him to touch me. Now that he is, I am reminded of how broken I am and how much of a mess my life is. *I don't want him mixed up in this.* Once he feels comfortable with my position, he pulls away, shuts the door, and walks around to the driver side. I watch him take one big breath and blow it out forcefully before he climbs into the car.

"Where to?" he asks. I shrug. "Where were you heading?"

"Away." My voice is hoarse and quiet.

"Away we go then." He heads south in the same direction I started us on.

The quiet lingers between us as the miles stretch into the empty night. The silence feels a little familiar with its hint of awkwardness, but with a whole new meaning of why it feels awkward. There are so many questions he could ask me, but none are asked.

"I remember walking home from school to find police outside my house. My father was crying like a baby." His voice startles me and my head jerks to watch him. His eyes are distant as he recounts a story I can only assume is full of tragedy and few people know.

"He apologized repeatedly. I was ten. It wasn't until Blaine and I had been removed from the home that I learned he hit my mom too hard and she never got back up. He killed my mom."

"He hit my mom a lot when I was little. As I got bigger, he decided to make a man out of me. I started taking his lashings and eventually Blaine got to be big enough as well." He shakes his head as if he is trying to shake off the oncoming memories. "I always tried to protect Blaine from him. My father is now in prison. All my money from my first movie went to the media to keep that piece of gossip out of the tabloids. I bounced around from foster home to foster home after that. Not many homes wanted to take two kids that belong to 'Billy, the wife killer.' It didn't take long for me to be labeled as a troubled kid." He says this with mock humor. My heart sinks.

"Why are you telling me this?" I whisper.

"Because I know what abuse feels like. My dad wasn't the only one to have laid a hand on me though. I had a few foster homes that wouldn't have passed any inspections if there had been any. I'm telling you this because I know what angry looks look like. Not the type of anger that is just mad or upset, but the type with fury behind it. I understand the broken trust of those who are supposed to love and protect you. I know the feeling of keeping secrets." He takes his eyes off the road to look pointedly at me. My gaze immediately drops.

He guides the car over to the shoulder. Shifting in his seat, he faces me. "Harley, I also know a smart abuser when I see one. He hit you where you could hide the bruises, except this one." Reed's fingers lightly run over the bruise on my cheek, then move under my chin, lifting my gaze to meet his. I want to shy away but I fight the urge to hide.

"I tried to protect so many people from being hurt. I felt so guilty when I couldn't, and still feel the guilt for the past from time to time." He pauses. "I'm sorry I left you. I saw it in his eyes. I basically gave him permission to do what he did when I walked out."

My voice is weak but I need him to know I don't blame him. "It's not your fault. I blame myself for not asking you to stay." If Reed hadn't come back in for me, this night would have wound up completely different.

"I know you don't blame me, but you need to place the blame where it belongs, and that is on Lance. He chose his path. I just feel that I owe you an apology because I know what it's like. Of all people, I should have known better."

Milo and I have rarely talked about Lance. He had witnessed some of the verbal abuse, but I never talked about what went on behind closed doors. I am sure Milo has his assumptions. I had kept the truth bottled up, but I couldn't hold back any longer. The urge to finally talk about it burns as my tears are hot against my eyes again. One slips out and Reed reaches over to brush it away. His attentiveness to me only makes them fall more quickly to the point that he couldn't catch them all. He pulls me into his chest while I sob. I let my hurt, shame, embarrassment, and anger pour out of me through tears.

"C'mon let's go back to Bromley," Reed whispers after my sobs turn into small hiccups.

He makes a U-turn and we head back home. He reaches over the console and searches for my hand. I take his and hold on tight. His knuckles are split, jarring my mind to recall the sound of his fists hitting their mark. Reed said he understood fury. In that moment, Reed's face was black fury. It leaves me wondering how much of his abusive past has bled into him. If we are a product of our environment and he carries that kind of anger, how does he deal with it? I've never felt unsafe with him, but the question is still there.

Reed pulls the jeep into the driveway and sits there looking at the old worn house. "Stay here for a second, please." His request sounds off, but I do as he asks. He gets out of the car and disappears into the house for a minute. Lights quickly flip on in the rooms and he comes back out looking a little more relaxed.

"Sorry, just after tonight... I am a little on edge." His eyes are unsteady but his body is calm. "I am just waiting for him to be around the corner."

"I know that feeling. You just want to throw something or hit something?"

"Yes." His eyes are still swirling with anxiety.

"Look at me." He levels his eyes with mine. I am feeling stronger now and want him to know it. "I am ok all because of you." I breathe in deeply before I continue on. "You do terrify me though. I have seen anger, but tonight I saw hate in your face. I understand now where the hate is coming from. I am sorry, just like you are, that we both know this situation. At the same time, I am grateful that you were there tonight." He smiles gently at me in the moonlight.

I rest my hands on his shoulders and lean in to gently kiss him. His hands move to my rib cage as he deepens the kiss. It becomes an urgent need to be closer. Subconsciously, I know we are both trying to work through the adrenaline from tonight, but I am comfortable with what is happening right now.

One hand slides up my back and settles between my shoulder blades. Guiding me out of the jeep, we back against the door, shutting it. I feel aches shoot through my body but I don't care. Clumsily, we find our way across the lawn and into the house. Pulling each other's jackets off, we barely miss a beat with our kissing. We kick off our shoes and leaving a trail in our wake to the couch. My hands at his stomach, I work his shirt up.

The way he has taken care of me today, and the way he studies me with pure interest, overwhelms my thoughts and I want to be close to him. I want to explore this feeling to its depths. I saw his strong arms in action tonight and I want them on me and around me.

He helps me work his shirt over his head and guides me down to the couch. Hovering above me, he pauses. "Are you ok with this?"

It's enough of a pause to realize what is happening. My breathing is erratic. My head is swimming. I look up at him and shake my head "no."

16

REED

I back off and sit down next to her. "It's ok." My voice sounds shaky. We both lean back against the couch and try to calm ourselves down. "I'm not sure if I was ready for that either." Her head whips to look at me and I can see she is eased by my admission.

I still want to be close to her. I put my arm around her shoulder and pull her into my side. Her arms naturally wrap around my middle. She keeps adjusting and re-adjusting against me, all the while her fingers twitch on my stomach. "You're really fidgety."

"I keep thinking about tonight and I desperately need a shower."

"I'll start a fire and we can meet back here." She nods with her brow puckered but doesn't move. "What's wrong?"

She is acting shy; something that I can assume is a rarity. "I'm not sure I am ready to be by myself yet." Her voice is quiet and small. I rub her upper arm. I am not ready for her to be out of my reach either.

Reaching for her hand, I take it and lead us up the stairs. In the bathroom, I let go of her hand. She leans against the counter, refusing to look at herself in the mirror. I start the shower and grab fresh towels.

Studying her in the moonlight outside of the bar, the bruise on her cheek looked like a light gray splotch against her washed-out snowy skin. \ In the incandescent light of the bathroom, I see a completely different picture. I try to mask my horror but her expression shows I failed. She is completely tattered. I thought her hair was just a mess but it is matted in blood. Her t-shirt is stained, torn, and dirty. Guilt creeps in as I am suddenly aware that earlier I let my sexual desires take precedence over what has happened to her.

I inch closer to her and gently fold her into my arms. Her body sinks into mine while she inhales deeply. "I must look as bad as I feel." I give a weary smile at her comment and she lets a small cynical chuckle escape.

"Do you need help?" When she glances up at me, her eyes are kind of wide, which makes me laugh. "Harley, I have seen what girls look like naked, and multiple times nothing has happened. I won't try anything or do anything that makes you uncomfortable. Think of me as a male nurse." She shyly grins at me. There is a little bit of pink staining her cheeks.

"Fine, I could use some help. He got me pretty good." She reaches for the hem of her shirt and winces hard.

"Does this shirt mean anything to you?"

She looks down at the image of a band's album cover and frowns. "It used to but it's been tainted now." I grasp the neckline and rip it open all the way down.

"I figured this would make it easier than pulling it over your head." As I help her slide her arms out of the shirt, I can see he did get her good. There are bruises on her stomach, shoulders, and back. I move to her jeans and pull them down gently to expose the black splotches on her thighs. I am getting sick with anger all over again because I am shocked at how many blows she took before I got to her. She takes in sharp breaths periodically as she moves.

Down to her underwear, we make eye contact and my breath is shallow.

"I can step outside if you want to do this part."

"Just unhook.... I will do the rest." Her eyes are averted when she turns around and she still refuses to look in the mirror. My fingers graze her back and I feel her lungs take in a deep breath and slowly let it out. I glance up to make sure she isn't in pain, but the mirror reflects her steadiness. Her arms are up covering her chest as she waits for the tension of the band to be released.

I have unhooked countless bras, but my hands tremble with nervous energy. It's almost like I am back in high school trying to take off Elizabeth Cramer's bra for the first time in the back of my beat-up Honda.

"Haven't had much practice in taking these off?" she teases.

"No, they typically just fall off when I come into the room," I retort back, easing my nerves. It's enough distraction to finally allow my fingers to unhook the band. I step outside to give her the privacy she deserves and to give me space to gather my thoughts.

I feel erratic. I swing from wanting to hit something to get rid of my anger at Lance, then back to my aroused self. Both have the same end result: I need to calm down. I rest my head against the door frame and take a deep breath.

The image of her bruised body is stuck in my head. She shouldn't have to put up with this. I walk into her room for something to do and decide to hunt for some clean clothes. I stand in her room, which is small, but plain and slightly cluttered. Just like Harley. A few posters decorate the walls. Clothes, that I assume are dirty, are piled in a chair. The small desk is piled high with CDs, which I thought had stopped being produced. When I pick up a few, I see bands that are a decade old. I smile. Her collection confirms she has always had a passion for music, even if it is in poor taste.

I sit down on her bed and let the dark quietness of the room seep in. I will my tired muscles to relax. But the memories I kept fighting all night start flooding back into my twisted head. Memories of past foster sisters who took hits for me; while, in turn, I took hits for others. Memories of little whimpers down the hallway. I gag at those memories.

When I saw Harley on the floor of the bar with him over her, it unlocked the rage I had as a kid. As I threw the punches, I lost sight of Harley and only saw the abusers from my life. Now Lance has been added to that list. I wanted to murder Lance. I knew he didn't deserve to live and I wanted to see him take his last breath. The thought chills me and I have goosebumps on my arms. I glance down and realize my shirt is still downstairs.

The shower shuts off. I pull myself together and head towards the bathroom. "I have clean clothes for you."

"You can come in," she hollers at me. She is still concealed by the shower curtain. "Let me get dressed, but I need some help with my hair." The steam in the room prickles my bare chest, but also eases my tension.

Her hand is sticking out of the shower curtain and I hand her the clothes. I hear her wince as she moves to get dressed. "Be careful, it's wet in there and you don't need to fall," I warn protectively. She mock laughs at me but opens the shower curtain. Clothed in the sweats and t-shirt I found, she looks a little better, like she washed some of the bad away.

Using the sink, I gently help her wash the blood out of her hair. My stomach turns each time she winces when water nears the staples. My knuckles are starting to swell, making my movements a little less than tender. Her shoulders are taut and rigid as she tries to hold still. I do my best by taking the washcloth to sponge out the blood to avoid getting too close to the wound.

Once the task is done, I help her to her feet. Her face is pale from pain, which I'm sure is from rinsing her hair. Rummaging through the drawer, I take out a comb. The ring sparkles up at me. My jaw clenches, but I move as though I know nothing about it. I shouldn't be surprised she still has it. I just saw the ring yesterday, yet I still do a mental double take to make sure it's what I thought I saw. I start to close the drawer, halting when she reaches for my hand to stop me. I glance over at her. Her skin pales and her eyes grow hard.

"I kept it because our relationship wasn't always bad. Plus, it's pretty," she explains, snatching the ring out of the drawer. She looks like she is going to be sick and storms over to the toilet. I start to move to her side, but she surprises me when she throws it in the toilet. Flushing it down, she slams the seat cover closed. Her eyes lock on me while she takes a few deep breaths. "Let's go." Her voice sounds stronger.

Her shoulders are back and the woman I have grown to admire is ready to put tonight behind her. She wants to move on. The strong Harley I met is back.

Downstairs, I grab my shirt off the floor and pull it over my head I am thankful for some shield against the drafty air. Working on the fire, I instruct her to sit on the floor. She wraps herself in a blanket and hunkers down, likely trying to warm up. The fire is roaring while the heat leaks out into the room. I position myself on the couch to where I have Harley between my legs and begin slowly working out the tangles in her hair. I remember where the cut is and avoid hitting it. The staples make my stomach sour each time the firelight flickers off of them.

"There," I say in a hushed voice as I pull the comb through the last chunk of hair. My eyes zone in on the flames as I recline back against the couch. My mind wanders over the last twenty-four hours with Harley. Yesterday, sitting on this couch, I talked about my adoptive family. We so casually talked about Lance and avoided talking about my real father. We talked around the two men in our lives that did the most damage and caused the most change in both of us, as if they were nothing.

"What's the story behind your tattoo?" Her question pulls me back to where I am sitting.

"Come here." She moves to sit beside me on the couch. I pull my shirt up a little to expose the tribal lines that run down my side. Taking her hand, I place over it over the area. She feels the four puckered scars that are masked by the lines. "I fell on an old board that had nails sticking out of it."

"I take it you didn't just trip and fall." She eyes me.

"Nope, that fall was courtesy of one of my foster dads. I was only at the house for a few months. They removed all of us from the home shortly after that event." Her eyes fill with sadness. "My story might be a sad one but I thankful for it because that's how I met the Montgomerys."

"Aw, you look all gooey with love for them." She playfully nudges me. My lips twitch into a half smile as my gaze settles back on the fire.

"They already had kids, but they made us feel like we belonged in their family. It took me a while to warm up though." I pause to remember how much trouble I had been in the beginning. "Both of my adoptive parents had been in the system and were broken from their past. It gave them an edge on how to wrangle my brother and me. They helped me channel my energy by getting me involved with sports and art programs, and helped me to see the brighter side of life."

Her fingers linger a bit longer on the scars. She leans forward into me. I allow her mouth to settle on mine.

17

HARLEY

I want to chase away the sadness in his eyes. He leans into my kiss. Fire shoots through my ribs and reminds us both of my injuries. He pulls back and gently scans me. He probably wants to reassure himself I am still in one piece. "Are you okay?" His hands skim my cheek.

"The pain is dull, but I don't know if the painkillers are wearing off or if the adrenaline has finally subsided enough that I can feel everything."

Getting up, Reed retrieves a bottle from the kitchen and shakes a painkiller into his hand. "Where did those come from?" I ask wearily.

"The medics thought you might need them."

"Isn't that against the rules?" I eye him as I take the offered pill from his hand. "I didn't think paramedics could hand out medication."

"It's Middleton. Don't they operate by their own rules?"

"Look at you! You sound like you've lived here your whole life," I tease.

We settle back into the couch and aim to have a lighter conversation by choosing to talk about music and the love we have for it. Reed grabs our iPods and we start taking turns trying to stump each other on bands and song titles. We swap stories of songs that struck a nerve with us. We share funny memories and woes, but steer clear of the dark times.

Eventually, we tire out and decide to go to our separate sides of the house. Alone in my room, the pressure of exhaustion and medication take over and I finally fall asleep as the morning sun lightens the midnight sky.

> *He is above me, with a sinister grin on his face. His unbuck-led belt tickles my bare skin making me squirm. I am immo-bile. My arms are pinned at my side as he straddles my body. I try to scream out, but his hand on my throat captures my last effort to seek help.*

I jerk awake and feel trapped by something around me. I fight against arms, but they tighten their hold on me and secure me against a torso. As my senses zero in on where I am, my ears finally register his calming voice beside me. He is reassuring me that I am safe. I turn to see Reed lying next to me.

Terror still fizzles my nerves and I start to get up. I need to chase the bad away somehow. Reed pulls me gently back to him. "He can't get to you," he reassures me.

He places my palm to his chest. "Just breathe." My chest rises and falls with his. His hand leaves mine and moves to stroke my hair out of my face. Flexing my fingers against his chest, I revel in his security. With each deep breath, my heart rate settles down and returns to a normal pace. He smiles kindly at me and must sense that I have relaxed. His arm is still draped over me and grows heavier as he falls back asleep.

Unlike Reed, I am wide awake. I glance over to observe him. His soft facial lines contrast the scruffiness of his jaw line. His hair lays floppy against his ear. I am a little shy as I admit to myself how much I have studied him. When he is awake, his body carries a toughness that comes across rude and sometimes abrasive. I now understand it comes from his life experience. While he is sleeping, I wonder where his gentle protective side comes from.

I recap Reed's childhood stories from this morning and under-stand that he and I are more alike than we originally thought. With all he has been through, why doesn't he seem more broken? I feel like I can barely breathe. He seems pretty normal on the outside. Then I realize I have just begun my healing process.

"I feel you watching me," he grumps.

"How did you end up in my bed?"

"You had several nightmares throughout the night," he huffs, rolling up on his side to look at me. "I got tired of going up and down the stairs. So... I crawled in bed with you."

I grin at his nonchalant answer. It has been years since I shared a bed with someone. I feel bad for waking him up throughout the night. He must have read my embarrassment in my eyes. "It's not a big deal. Unfortunately, I have had experience with nightmares." He eyes me closely. "Look that bad?" I ask.

"Not bad, but definitely beat up." His honesty takes me back to what happened last night.

Looking for a distraction, I ask, "What time is it?" I move to sit up and wince, feeling extremely "beaten up." I reach for my phone. "That's another day of work I've missed," I comment as I realize I have slept most of the day away.

"Do you really want to go to work?" He skeptically eyes me.

I look at my reflection in the dresser mirror. "Nope," I answer resolutely. It is one thing to know what happened and for the whole town to hear about it, but it's another for them to see it. My mind feels too raw now to deal with everyone's reactions. Still tired from last night, I decide one more day off from dealing with reality will be nice.

Reed questions, "What's the plan for today?"

"I guess everyone is operating fine without me." The statement turns sour in my mouth. He smiles kindly at me. I know I am replaceable but that doesn't mean I like the feeling. "If it's ok with you, I would like to hide out today with everything that happened."

"Harley..." he pauses and lays his hand on mine. My heart picks up in pace. "I...", his pauses are making me nervous.

A knock on the front door interrupts our conversation.

"Hold on," I say, holding up a finger. My body screams at me as I make an effort to get out of the bed. Before hitting the bottom of the stairs, I stop dead in my tracks. Ben is closing the door behind him. He gives me a once over.

"What are you doing here?" My voice is as deadpan as I feel.

"Elan and Shelby called." He says that as though it should be reason enough. Elan only calls when she has no choice but to deal with us. I shrug and sit down on the bottom step. I do my best not to show how much pain I am in.

"Your point?" I ask curtly.

"You need to remove the charges." Again, like that should be reason enough. Ben is the perfect blend of the worst sides of my parents. My dad was a great businessman but that also meant he was stubborn. He always said what he meant. My mother believes she is superior to everyone. Stubborn and superior attitudes, rolled into one person like Ben, makes for a very unpleasant, intolerable human being.

"You know I can't."

"Stop being childish. So Lance got jealous and was a little out of line." He rests his hands on his hips and peers down at me.

"Why are you defending him?"

"As long as Lance has charges against him, I am being pushed to represent him." I should have known that's how this would have rolled out. "I like living my life without interruptions, but right now, that means I have to deal with you two while you squabble over that white trash."

"You think I still want him?" I laugh without humor. I have been Lance's play toy for years and I'm ready to be done with it. Everyone fails to understand that my actions have consequences and they are either taken out on Shelby or me. I used to answer Lance's calls to try to keep tabs on Shelby. I was always scheming ways to get her away from him. But recently I have learned that I am only hurting myself. Enough is enough.

Ben shrugs as if he doesn't care what my motive is or was. I always figured Ben didn't care for Lance, but like he said, he doesn't like to be bothered.

"I'm not backing off my charges. I want him out of my life. I am sorry that it affects Shelby, and in turn annoys you and Elan, but I can't do this anymore." I stand and ruck my shirt up to show my marred ribs. My eyes stay on Ben's while his eyes take in the black and purple splotches. His eyes reveal what his heart feels but his mouth repeats what his brain thinks.

"I know it sucks, but there are other avenues and ways to get him to back off. I'm not going to let you make a debacle of this family in my social circle or theirs."

"A debacle…" I smirk at him. "Their lives are already a debacle. The inheritance is gone. You know that. I know it too. When you take money from the shop, I keep them from further collapse. I can handle the financial burden. Heck, I can handle their emotional issues too, but I cannot live any longer with Lance hovering over me. Unfortunately for you, I am not paying for their lawyer fees, so it looks like you will be doing your work pro-bono."

Ben just stands there, likely trying to figure out what to say next. He's not used to someone else having the last word. But the truth is that there isn't anything he can say. "You did what Elan asked you to do. You came to try and reason with me. You can report back to everyone that I am unreasonable," I say, giving him permission to leave.

He nods and walks out the door.

I sit back down on the step with a huff. I don't cry. I am not frustrated. I am just numb. I lay back against the stairs. It hurts, but it feels good to feel something when I feel so empty inside.

I see Reed sitting at the top of the stairs. I know he has heard everything, but his eyes still search my face. He must be looking for confirmation that I am okay.

I nod at him and he nods back at me.

"So… what now?" I ask.

18

REED

"Lunch?" I suggest. She nods, stands up, and heads toward the kitchen. "But I am cooking," I throw out there as I follow behind her. "We don't need any more catastrophes for a while." She turns to glare, but her lips turn up just a little. I place my hands on her shoulders and steer her towards the living room.

Harley makes her way slowly to the couch. I know she must be in pain. I want to make her better. Because I can't fix her pain, I feel like today I am going to be spending most of my time feeling irritated by it. Ben's visit doesn't help my irritation.

When I heard a deep voice rumbling up the stairs, my stomach had knotted up. I prepared myself to attack again if it was him. I made my way to the stairs to see who it was. I recognized him from the shop. Per their conversation, I remembered it was her brother Ben.

Harley's body language looked stiff, but I wasn't sure if it was due to her injuries or if it was because she was dealing with Ben. They don't exactly have the smoothest relationship. As they talked, it sounded like they were conducting a business meeting. Very little emotion passed between them and they spoke with a purpose. Harley held her own as her brother called her childish. I wanted to stand up for her by telling him where he could go. I knew, however, if I made my presence known, it would only make her look worse.

He continued to push her to back down, but she showed him proof for why she wouldn't. I could see where a boot came in contact with her back. The marks on her back have turned dark, almost black, against her pale skin. The sight of the marks made my blood boil.

I couldn't see Ben's face, but his pauses indicated that he didn't know how to react. Her brother's attitude changed the minute the money talk started. Pieces of arguments between Milo and Harley are now starting to click into place for me. Milo has been upset with Harley for giving money to a family he feels doesn't care about her wellbeing; and in a way, she has been finically supporting her ex by doing so. I can't really say I disagree with Milo, but it's not always easy to draw those hard lines when it comes to family.

I understand the situation a little better now and all I want to do is hit a punching bag. I wonder if Middleton has a gym. I doubt it. Being a farming community, there is enough muscle-building work on the farms that a gym would be unnecessary. Instead, I take my frustration out on the food in front of me. I especially enjoy using the knife on the chicken. I imagine being a butcher for the mafia, slicing and dicing anyone up who hurts those I care for or have done me wrong. I shake my head at the disturbing image, but it makes me feel a little better.

When everything is simmering, I find the painkillers resting on the table from last night and check to see how Harley is doing. She is stretched out on the couch, zoned out on a movie that is playing on the TV. When I nudge her, she jumps a little and winces from the pain. She looks pallid and uneasy. I ask if she is okay and she distractedly nods her head, but it's obvious something is up. I continue to study her.

"I got a call," she surrenders. "Lance's bail has been paid." She pauses, but her gaze doesn't leave the TV. She works through something in her head in silence. My body tenses as I anticipate a few possible scenarios leading to Lance's release. "Shelby doesn't have money nor does my mom, as I am sure you heard from Ben. Therefore, the money he put in the account for them went to cover his bail. I basically paid for Lance to be released." Her eyes never meet mine.

Milo and Harley have fought so much about this issue. She must be ashamed of the situation and can barely look at me.

"Do they know where he is, or are there any stipulations for his release?" I try to ask gently, but I fail. It comes out ridged and harsh. I glare at the couch and try to fight my urge to go find him myself.

"The Police said they know where he is supposed to be, but keeping tabs on him will be hard. They live in a city two hours away. There is no guarantee he will stay there or that anyone will be able to tell me if he comes back here." She reclines back against the couch. When I look up, she is watching me. "Officer Meeks said they will do everything they can and I believe him. There is the restraining order. I just don't know how effective it will be. Lance is a loose cannon."

I know what she means. I watched him and understood the look in his eyes too well. "Have you thought about taking some kind of self-defense class?" I ask, realizing that someone may not always be around when she needs help.

"I know how to punch; I just didn't think about it at the time."

"Harley, it's not about knowing how to punch. Self-defense is about how to hold your own and knowing how to get away to find help." Her shoulders square defensively. "It's not that you are weak," I try to recover "… it's just overpowering a guy twice your size can only last so long. You need to know how to maneuver yourself to get away." Thoughts of Lance straddling Harley make bile roll up my stomach.

She looks deep into me. "How do you know so much about this?"

"I took karate classes when I lived with the Montgomerys. I ended up working for the gym and helped with some of their classes." I was eager to help them with the self-defense program because it made me feel like I was giving back to those I could not protect growing up. It was a super-hero complex in a way, but it felt good.

"I'll let you think about it. I need to check the food." When I move around the couch, I see her rest her head against the arm rest and zone out again. She seems defeated, but not willing to give in.

19

HARLEY

His suggestion of self-defense training sounds like a good idea. I know he won't always be around to protect me. I am going to have to know what to do for myself. I don't like the idea of being weak, but the truth is I am weaker than Lance.

My mom is very manipulative. Once she learns I've cut their funding off, the brokenness in our relationship will be sealed. Shelby is blind to her situation. Lance has her brainwashed and she will defend him no matter what, which means I can't rely on either of them to protect me from Lance. My family will be family by blood only from this point forward.

Just in case I need a reminder of how un-brotherly Ben is, he barely showed any compassion when I showed him my injuries. However, I did catch a flicker of concern in his eyes - a reaction he tried to hide - as I showed him my bruised and beaten torso. I know he wouldn't represent Lance except that he can't say "no" to our mom.

Reed brings me a plate of food and starts a movie to fill the silence. My mind is everywhere but on the movie. Anger burns my stomach and causes me to lose my appetite. I glance over at Reed and I see that he isn't eating much either. Hyper–awareness that Lance is on the "loose" and I have no one from my family in my corner makes us both very uncomfortable.

Startling Reed, I drop my fork on my plate. "I *have* to get out of here and do something. Want to go to the gym with me? Maybe go over some of those self-defense techniques?"

"Sure. Where is the gym?" he asks skeptically.

"It's in the next town. A small one but it's nice," I say, getting up from the couch.

In my room, I strip down and catch a glimpse of myself in the dresser mirror. My jaw drops in awe of how bad my body looks. I know it is bruised and I am sore, but still, the images are shocking. I get dressed and allow the shock to wear off. Now I am back to anger.

Meeting Reed downstairs, I grab the keys off the hook. I meet his eyes. I remember how I almost took us over the railing. "I'm sorry about last night, but I know where we are going so are you ok if I just drive us?"

He smiles gently at me and puts his arm around my shoulder. Pulling me into a goofy hug, he kisses the top of my head. "We will be fine, just drive us there at the correct speed."

"Deal," I say. We hurry out the door in gym clothes which are not winter-weather appropriate. On the road, we settle into our comfortable quiet even though pent-up energy is bouncing between us.

"What are your plans when you get back home?" I ask him.

"By the time I get home, I will have to start on the next Zoey-William movie." He makes a disgusted face.

"If it's that bad why do you keep doing them?"

"I have auditioned to do other movie roles but producers don't see me as a fit. I can't seem to shake the typecast I am in." I glance over at him. He does have that hot-boy-next-door look down pat. If he would have been my neighbor growing up, I probably would have sat at my window just waiting to catch a glimpse of him. I feel stalker-ish thinking that thought. I smile to myself, which he sees but doesn't ask me about.

"I read some of the new scripts that were left on the table." I pause my sentence when his facial expression makes me feel like I crossed a line. "Did I do something wrong?"

"You weren't supposed to read those. They are confidential and it is a very big deal." His tone is factual, but his lopsided grin makes an appearance. "It's a good thing you are a 'nobody,' in that world anyway."

"I won't tell if you won't tell," I say playfully.

"I've got your back." He winks. "So what did you think?"

"Well…" I hesitate, because what I am about to say will bring up his past and I am not sure how he will handle it. "I think you would be good at playing Drew in Single Rose." I turn my head just in time to see his face pale. "I hope I didn't cross another line."

He shakes his head but doesn't say anything else. I park the jeep in the very empty lot. We jump out and rush inside. Entering through the gate, Reed follows me down a hall to where they keep the punching bags.

"Do you know how to kick-box?" Reed's eyebrows rise at me. He is returning back to his normal casualness with me, but there is still a small edge in his voice.

"I told you I know how to throw a punch," I retort back. "Milo taught me how to fight and I did a kick-boxing class in college. But like you said, I need to know how to get away, not just fight." His smile graces me with an appearance but doesn't reach his eyes.

After our hands are taped up and the dummies are in place, Reed finds the stereo system. With his phone hooked up, Offspring's "You're Gonna Go Far Kid" pours through the speakers. I feel my blood pulse to the beat. I throw out my fist and it collides with the dummy. I turn my hips to kick. My body cries out in pain. I wince and let the pain radiate for a minute.

Reed stands to the side and watches me closely. "Harley, take it easy," he gently warns. The pain ignites my rage and I throw my right fist out with a quick jab followed by my left, then my right again. My body sings through the pain, but my head is clouded with images from last night and many others.

Lance's finger stroking my cheek – my fist goes for an upper cut. *Hearing his talk about the lack of commonsense* – a quick jab to the throat.

His knuckles grazing my stomach – kick to the ribs. The image of his belt unbuckled is my undoing. I bring my knee up and slam it against the dummy. Punches and kicks rage out of my body.

Songs have changed. Time is passing. My body is drenched and my fists are slowing as I lose energy. When I hear labored breathing beside me, I glance over and see Reed's red face. His muscles glisten with sweat and each is taut with tension. His focus is beyond the dummy before him. I can only imagine he is fighting his own demons and nightmares, just like I was.

His jaw is set and sweat rolls down his face. Each punch is followed with a breath. He knows how to fight. His endurance is rhythmic. I glance back at my dummy and the thought of lifting another arm is too much for me.

The rock songs continue to pour out of the speakers, fueling Reed as punch after punch lands its mark. I leave him to go grab us some bottles of water. I feel more relaxed since I left my jitters and rage on the dummy. When I walk back into the room, Reed isn't quite done yet but he is coming back to earth. I stretch out on the mat and let the rhythmic sounds of his work out and the music wash over me.

With one final punch, he leaves the dummy swaying. He breathes heavily in, exhausted, but seems to be relieved. He sits beside me and rests his hand on my knee. Our eyes meet as he gives it a gentle squeeze.

"Feel better?" I ask. His mouth turns into a cocky grin. "You really wailed on that thing. And I thought I was angry." I offer him water and he takes it, pulling in long gulps. I recline back and stare up at the ceiling.

We settle down from our rage binge and let the minutes tick by. When his breathing is normal, he leans back and stares at the ceiling with me. "Are you hurting?" he asks.

"Not too bad. I will definitely pay for it later but my brain thanks me for the release of energy," I muse. He smiles kindly over at me.

"Do you think you have enough energy to go through some self-defense?"

I consider my state of mind. My body is asking for a break, but I also know my time with Reed is limited. "I can try."

"Stay on your back like you are, but bend your knees up," he instructs while he gets on all fours. He crawls over to rest on his knees in front of mine. "This will be awkward but you need to know what to do." He takes a shaky breath. "Last night, he had you in this position when I came in. I know you took a beating before that, but if he gets you in this position again, you will know what to do."

I swallow at the thought of last night, but also because the way Reed is looking at me is making me very anxious. His eyes are tender and full of concern. "Harley," he says my name, which scares me because I know it's about to get serious. He places a hand on each knee. "I need you to communicate with me. If you get uncomfortable, you need to tell me. If you are uncomfortable, you won't learn anything."

My breathing sounds loud in my ears. "I am going to position myself between your legs." He talks me through what he is doing as his hands gently push my knees apart. My heart is racing, but it's not because of how uncomfortable I am.

"Are you ok?" His eyes are intense and study my face. I can't speak but I nod. "Now, to be honest, we need to be closer. We will work on that, but for now I am going to stay here." He reaches for my arm and places it on his shoulder, teaching me that my arms need to be stiff. He emphasizes the importance of my hands striking his shoulder instead of his chest.

"When I come in for the attack," he rocks forward, placing his hands on either side of my body, "your hands need to hit my shoulders and brace me, keeping your distance. I won't put my whole weight on you, yet." The impending threat brings shy smiles to our faces. "But do you feel how when I move you can feel which direction I am going?" I nod, breathing in deeply, feeling his muscles shift beneath my palms. "Now move your hands to my chest." As I do, he leans to the side and I feel my arms crash. This demonstrates why my hands need to be on his shoulders.

"Again, I won't put my whole-body weight on you to test your arms." He grins at me. "So I just want you to know the basics and we will practice these moves later." We move on to the next step, which is foot placement. He explains what a planter foot is and where my heels need to end up. "Remember, you aren't trying to win the fight, you are trying to get away." His eyes drill into mine. "I know you are a fighter, but in this case, don't fight, just get away." He sounds like he is pleading with me and all I can do is nod.

After a few more rounds of practice, we finish and call it good for the afternoon. I grab the keys and our jackets. Reed is standing with the door open for me. I haven't realized it until now that it has been a long time since someone did something so gentlemanly for me. I don't expect it, nor do I care, but it does feel nice to feel cared for.

"Will you drive?" I ask as I feel exhaustion settling in. The thought of driving and holding a steering wheel makes my arms scream. His stares at me, shocked I would ask for the passenger seat. I giggle at his expression and throw the keys at him. It had started snowing again so the ground is mushy and slick. He helps me into the jeep, again surprising me with his chivalry. I rest against the seat as he pulls us back on the road to take us home.

20

REED

I should feel better after pummeling the boxing dummy, but something is still nagging at me as I pull the car back on the two-lane highway. When she suggested coming to the gym, I thought she was a little crazy due to how sore she should be from yesterday's beating. But I needed the outlet and the determination in her eyes told me she needed it too. I figured she would just walk it out on an elliptical like all the other prissy girls I know. I should have known better than to think of Harley as "prissy."

She surprised me when she started wailing on the dummy. Observing her form and sheer will, I worried that she would fall back into fight-to-win mode instead of fighting to get away. Still, her fists and legs made contact with each strike.

As I drive, I continue to examine what might be bothering me. When I was boxing, I had been thinking about what I have had to deal with in the last couple of months. I recall my brother's hateful words that "I made him into what he is." It frustrates me that I feel he is better behind bars. He told me once that I was like our mother and he was an exact replica of our father. The words always turn my stomach.

I think of what my father did to our life. I normally handled that anger fairly well because if it wasn't for his actions, and for Lisa and Jerry taking us in, who knows who I would be. At the same time, I am angry at the pain he caused me and those around us. I am angry that my mom is gone because of him.

The tabloid writers keep blackmailing me with threats of spreading the story of my father all over their moronic gossip publications. I decided a month ago to stop buying people off, but that meant they could spread the rumors, true or false. I was simply waiting for it to be public. It was keeping me on edge. The worst part came the day after I left. I learned that my publicist started collecting payments for leaking details about my family.

After that, I started questioning my publicist and wondered if she was part of the reason I was being rejected for other roles. Most actors would be appreciative of the chance to be in any movie, but as humans, we also strive for the next challenge - the next level. I continued to be denied role after role. I used to refuse to blame anyone but myself for the rejection. Now, there is a seed that tries to plant and take root. I want to cast some of the blame on her.

Then it clicks. I figure out what is currently putting me on edge. I want to know why Harley would think that Drew Moore should be my next character. The villain. He is everything I hate, but that is the part she thinks I should go for. Now that I have my question, it is time for me to ask and get her answer. I assume Harley has good reasons and will be willing to share them with me. I decide that I am ready for her answers.

"Harley, why did you suggest that I play Drew?" This question digs hard under my skin.

She turns her shoulders to face me. She pauses, likely considering her words. My irritation flares as I wait for her explanation. "First, I need you to know that I read the scripts a while ago and came to my conclusion before I knew anything about your past. In the short time we've had together, I thought his character would show a more diverse side of you. Plus, it goes against the typecast of what everyone expects of you."

"Yes, but he is beyond evil." My voice comes out harsh. "A version of men like Lance and every kind of man I hate. Drew Moore is a guy who lurks at fraternity parties looking for girls he can prey on. Broken by his father, his only outlet is taking his own frustrations and anger out on girls he claims want to be with him. His character is a smooth-talking, manipulating son of a bitch." I realized my voice had risen with disgust.

"But think about it." She remains calm. "Not only do you know your father, but all your asshole foster-father figures who have done that crap. You know them. You can tap into that character better than most. In a way, you can use this as a P.R. stance. Bring awareness to people that the fraternity-produced, spoiled, rich kids are just as dangerous as the scumbags we all expect to do the horrific actions." She says gently, "you can do so much more with this role than anyone else. You are the pretty boy no one expects. That's why they are considering you for the role."

I know she's right. It would be a great opportunity. Though a good decision for my career, Drew is everything I am against. It makes me sick to think I would be portraying someone I have spent years running from.

She settles back against the seat and continues, "you aren't anything like your father nor would you turn into him just by playing this role."

My head snaps to her. It's almost like she read my thoughts before they even surfaced in my head. It startles me a little, but she is right. I fear becoming him.

Time and miles pass, with talk strictly focusing on "are you cold, warm, or comfortable?" Harley's very slight nods and shakes of the head continue our one-syllable answer style conversation. I am unsure if the uneasy energy is from what we talked about, or if Harley has slipped away into dealing with her own secrets.

My mind wanders to my tattoo. Zoey knows I have scars and often asks why I just don't have my scars surgically fixed. That answer is easy for me, but it's an answer that's hard for someone to understand that has not been in my shoes. I leave the scars and cover them as a reminder of who I was, who I am, and who I can be. But after Harley called me out about my reluctance to play Drew Moore, I see now that it's my reminder of who I don't want to become. Will I be able to stay me? Is Harley right that I won't turn into my father if I tap into that psychosis?

"How are you holding up?" I ask her, just trying to get out of my own head.

She ponders that thought a moment. "Right now, I think I am holding on, rather than holding up."

"That sounds like a fair statement." I pause for a moment and consider if I want to make my next statement. I decide I need to say it. "You know you are doing the right thing with pressing charges against Lance, right?"

"Yeah." She sounds hesitant. I glance over and am about to say something more, but can tell she is chewing on her own thoughts. "I know it's the right thing, but I am losing my whole family over it. Now that I've called Ben out on what's going on, I won't see him anymore. My older sister Elan walked away from the family when she graduated."

"And Shelby and my mom, they are like Ben. Only need you when they need something. It's not like I kept giving them money to keep them around, which is what Milo thinks. I don't particularly like being used, but it is family. Aren't we supposed to take care of each other?" I assume she's asking a rhetorical question so I just stay quiet and pull the jeep into the driveway.

"That's why Milo and I always fight." She pauses while staring at the vacant house. I hear her take a shaky breath before she turns her body to face me. "Sitting in that ambulance, Officer Kane told me that if I didn't press charges, there would be a good chance you could be sent to jail instead of Lance. I was afraid of Lance being released, but not as afraid as I was to not have you next to me. I could tell in your eyes that you wanted to murder him. The longer I watched you, I knew your fate rested on me. You knew it too, didn't you?" She asks me a question she wanted an answer to. I nod and remember the exact moment that I realized I cared more for what happened to her than I did for myself.

I drop my gaze from her intense stare. I think back to all the times I took someone else's beating. Last night, however, was the first time that I actually wanted to fight *for* someone. Everyone always deserves better than they get, but I actually want to change it for Harley.

Her hand rests on my arm. "The last person who genuinely cared for me was my dad." She eyes me intently as she continues. "Last night did me in. I am done with trying to make sure everyone else is happy. I'm going to start taking care of those who value me like I value them. I love my family, but it's time they learn to swim without me. Thank you for helping me see that."

"It wasn't my intension." I grin at her.

"I am sure of that," she says pointedly. "But it's a result of your actions."

"I know the pain of letting go is scary, but it's the first step to healing, Harley," I say, hoping it comforts her. She brushes the statement off and I smirk, thinking back to who told me that once. "I had the same reaction the first time I heard that. But it is true. I understand now that I am the one watching someone let go of their burdens, those words are fitting."

"What are you smirking at?" Her voice is filled with self-doubt.

"I thought that therapist was full of it. Now look at me. A few years later I am repeating the same line he gave me." I look over to see her smiling. It doesn't fully reach her eyes but I know she is coming back to me.

She settles back into her seat and her eyes seem heavy. I lay my hand on her knee. Her fingers find my hand and gently find their way between my fingers.

"Come on, let's go inside," I nudge.

A couple of days pass since the attack. Harley's cheek is turning back to its normal color. She is hoping that, by the weekend, her makeup will cover the evidence that something happened. Nikki has reassured her over the last few days not to worry about it because she can do wonders with makeup. I had laughed at Harley's disgusted face when Nikki first mentioned makeup.

It feels almost like everything is going back to the way it was before the attack, but Harley still hasn't been out of the house much. No one is pushing her, though concern is starting to rise in those who are closest to her.

I am sitting at the table reading over the script that Harley recommended. I read over the lines in my head. I try hard to immerse myself into this vile character. As I get lost in the storyline, I realize that Drew's character comes natural to me. This is unsettling but I'm fascinated. When the storyline gets too overwhelming, I look up to see Harley and I'm reminded again that Drew is just a character. He is not me.

In one of my moments of doubt about the decision to do the role, I look up, wanting to be distracted by Harley. She is zoned out in front of the TV again. Since she has been home, she has managed the books and done paperwork for both businesses, so it's not like she hasn't done anything, but this is also the girl who used to work until 3 a.m. to avoid this house as much as possible.

"Lee, I need a distraction." Her head leans back, barely peeking over the back of the couch. Her eyes sparkle as she notices I've adopted her nickname.

"I'm not ready to go out yet," she states.

"That's not what I had in mind." I'm assuming she won't leave because she is afraid of Lance, but also because she doesn't want people to gawk at her. It's enough to have everyone know about what happened, but it's another to see their reactions to you.

"I was thinking we should go over the self-defense move I taught you, and maybe a few others." I am hoping this will help her regain her confidence. Last time we ran over the move, she had just finished a workout after a major beating. She said she was up to learning but I am not sure how much she really retained.

She reluctantly nods, gets up, turns the TV off, and replaces the silence with some Ben Howard music. "This is what you choose for your training?" I tease while I move the couch and coffee table out of the way to give us some room.

"My nerves are already a mess; I thought I would try something to soothe me." She draws the word 'soothe' out in a weird, dramatic way that makes me chuckle.

I instruct her to sit on the floor with her knees bent like I did at the gym. In the past, when I was helping with classes, I was always cocky with my looks, but we were taught to make sure the girls were comfortable. As much as I flirted and played, I was adamant that they knew exactly how to get out of these situations.

I always made sure to remind them that guys like me are just as evil, if not more so, than your average Joe. It is the guys that know they are attractive to women, and are rarely turned down, that are the ones to be watched. I realize again exactly why Harley suggested Drew Moore.

Staring down at Harley, I am unnerved. I'm thrown off my game with the image of her on her back in front of me. The same self-defense moves I have taught for years poof out of my brain in an instant. I try shaking it off. I remind myself that I have practiced the same positions more times than I can count, and have been close to girls like this before, but she has me completely unraveled.

Most of my past students took the classes for general knowledge, while some were victims. Harley looks so vulnerable. It's a reminder that I could tell which girls feared this position. Some admitted they had been in that position before. There is a difference though; knowing that fact, versus seeing the actual situation, has made me more sensitive to this. Harley, on the other hand, seems to be calm and ready.

I move between her legs again. Like last time, I don't move as close as I am supposed to but we will get there before tonight is over. I start by asking her what she is supposed to do. She keeps her arms up by her chest, and the moment I lean forward she thrusts her arms out straight and against my chest. I rest more weight on her than I did the other day, sway to the side, break her hold, and gently collapse on her.

"What did you do wrong?" I inquire to see if she can identify the mistake.

"I didn't lock my arms?" she asks, unsure.

I shake my head, "Your hands need to strike my shoulders, not my chest. Your arms were straight like they were supposed to be, but if you have my shoulders, you can keep me at a distance. You can feel where I am going and keep that restraint present. But in my chest, I just rocked to one side, breaking your arm balance." I can tell she understands and I am glad she's now aware of her first reaction. "Let's try again."

I rock back on my knees then move forward again. This time her palms strike against my shoulders and hold me there. My hands rest on either side of her body, but there is a distance between us enforced by her arms.

I lean to left and her arms don't budge. "See, your arms aren't collapsing." My praise is rewarded with a very pleased smile. "Now what do you do?" She plants her right foot and rolls her body slightly to the left and pushes, allowing her to place her left foot on my hip. She moves her hands down to my elbows then she moves her right foot up to my hip. "Excellent," I praise again.

As I pull back, she moves her hands to my wrist, hiking her knees up so she can kick the attacker anywhere from the crotch to the core to the chin. "Always aim for the crotch and the chin. Hit the crotch first to weaken the attacker then give a good solid kick to the chin. A good kick can knock them out, but remember…"

"Fight to get away, not to win," she cuts me off. I smile from ear to ear because I know she gets it.

I do one more run through with her at the safe distance. She excels again and I take a deep breath. "Now, I am going to move closer." My voice is calm but serious. Again, I watch for any signs of panic. I inch further between her legs. I see her take in a deep breath and she looks up at the ceiling. "Harley, talk to me." It's important that she doesn't panic, especially with me. She needs to feels safe with me. If she panics, it won't be good if someone like Lance, or Lance himself, does this again.

"I'm ok, just fighting back the memory," she reassures. I continue to watch her and see no sign of panic as she gains control.

"I'm going to scoop closer again," I tell her. As I inch closer, I pray to God that something won't decide to pop up. Once our bodies are smashed together, I can see her panic rising. Thankfully, this takes away the sexual tension.

Again, her eyes move to the ceiling. "Harley, look at me," I coax her gaze back to mine. "It's just me. You're safe, nothing's going to happen." Her breathing is still erratic. "You know what to do to get out of this." Her eyes are wild but I know her strength. I have seen it. Most of the time I would back off, but I know she can push through. I want her to be uncomfortable so she can fight it.

"How do you get out of it?" I coach harshly. I lean forward and her hands again strike my chest. I break her hold and collapse on her. She pushes against me and I spring up on my arms and pull back from her. Tears are pooled in her eyes and I feel like a jackass.

"I'm sorry, Harley." I pull her up into a sitting position and sit down beside her. "I shouldn't have pushed you like that."

"No, you should have. You did the right thing." Her voice is shaky but she is confident. "That's exactly what would happen. Let's go again."

I hesitate but she snaps at me to go again. She is on her back with her knees bent. Since I know she is expecting it, I know she knows what to do. So instead of easing into her, I grab her knees and move fast between them, butting our bodies up against one another. Panic rises again at the speed, but when I come down on my hands this time, her palms hit my shoulder and hold me back. She pauses for a moment and tests my weight. She shouldn't do this but I'm glad she is getting this part down. She moves her hips, places her feet and hands in the correct spots, and kicks out hard past my head.

Her breathing is shallow and her eyes are wide. Her skin looks pale. Then she sits up and looks at me with a triumphant smile. "Again?" she asks.

I let her lay back again. Looking down at her, I want to stroke her hair back and kiss her. I want to protect her and everything she is to me. I am not sure exactly what she means to me, although I have an idea. I'm just unsure if I want to admit it to myself yet.

Her knees are bent. I grip her knees and push them aside with my hips. I pull her up against me and I bite back a sharp breath. Her eyes connect with mine. I see her shoulders relax and how unafraid she is with me. I move to be above her.

My hands are placed on either side of her body. She breathes in deeply under the cage I have created over her. Her hands come to shoulders, softly, not as strong as she should. I start to pull away but she slides her hands to my elbows, then to my wrist, and pulls me to her.

Our lips collide and I lose all control. My hands start to fist in her hair, but I remember her cut and force myself to be mindful of her healing injuries. Her kisses drive us deeper into want. The little self-control I have left starts to slip away.

I don't want to reject her but we have to stop. After witnessing everything she has been through, I want to respect her space. Ever since I have met her, Harley has been controlled by circumstances and sometimes people. I have concerns that sex might complicate the situation as it always does. Plus, I'm falling for her and want to take our relationship at a slower pace than I usually do. Still kissing her, I start to pull back, and then pull her into a sitting position. Our lips are still insistent, but we are both able to think a little more clearly in this position than the other.

"Sorry, I didn't mean to do that," she informs me between kisses. I smile at her and kiss her cheek as I pull her into my chest.

"It's ok. I wanted it too."

We move apart with no more words, sharing only sheepish looks and grins. We move on to a few more defense moves while making sure to avoid all intimate positions.

21

HARLEY

I haven't been out of the house much in the last few days. Reed has entertained me by renting movies and we have been critiquing the films like we are award-winning critics. I have helped him run lines for his audition for the part of Drew. As much as I fight to keep the dark reality of my relationship with Lance from settling in, I find myself losing the battle often.

The phone rings and I jump. Reed picks the phone up and screens the call before he hands it to me. Officer Meeks has been checking with me almost daily to see if there is anything he can do for me. He makes sure I haven't heard from or seen Lance.

I find it amusing that he asks if I have seen Lance because the truth is that I haven't seen anyone. I catch a glimpse of myself in the living room mirror. My cheek is healing, proof that time can heal a broken body, but I am still really shook up.

I hang up the phone and fall back against the couch, and allow my mind to check out of our current movie. My thoughts race over everything going on. Life hasn't returned to normal since that day. Milo isn't talking to me again. The thought that the money taken from the shop was used to release Lance pissed him off.

Milo and I have always fought about my family. Now he has more ammo against me. Since the incident, or *attack* as Reed calls it, I have closed my bank accounts. My family has been cut off and frequently unleashes their fury at my voicemail. Reed helped me unplug the answering machine so they couldn't leave their angry messages.

I find myself avoiding everyone except Reed. If it weren't for the fact that he is a guest in my home, I would probably avoid him as well. Nikki stops by every other day to check up on me. I reassure her but can see that she is very worried about me. Reed is too.

During my absence from the shop, I check in with George regularly about Reed's car parts. He informed me they will be arriving with a delay on one or two items. For the most part, George can fix his car and I know my time with Reed is dwindling rapidly. I wonder if I will ever get back to a normal routine after he leaves.

"I'm going to get ready for work," I say. "Nikki should be here in a little bit to help me with my makeup." Reed looks at me with concern and I dismiss it. Nikki and Reed have been hounding me to stay home and take it easy, but as much as I want to avoid everyone, I can't handle their watchful eyes any more.

Upstairs in the bathroom, I strip down. My bruises catch my eye in the mirror. Like the bruises on my face, these have also faded in color. Because the injuries went deeper, these will take longer to heal, but I can tell the black is turning more blue and the edges are green. *It's just lovely*, I think to myself.

I quickly shower and continue to be careful while washing my hair. I got my staples removed yesterday but the cut is still very tender. I get dressed and head downstairs. It feels nice to get some independence back. Reed had been so helpful during the last few days by helping me wash my hair and comb it out. I felt like a child but it's nice to be taken care of. But I like feeling like I can take care of myself again.

However, with the staples only being removed yesterday, I'm not comfortable blindly combing my hair yet. I settle between his legs. We don't talk much but it is a comfortable silence. As he strokes the comb through my hair, I try to remember the last time anyone combed my hair. All I can recall is my mom doing it when I was young. The thought of my mom crashes into my chest.

To my mother, my choice to stay with my dad meant her daughter was rejecting her. Our relationship was never the same after that. She blames me for the distance between us. Not only did she feel rejected personally, she was embarrassed and struggled to explain my absence in her social circles. My "failed" relationship with Lance was treated as a scandal by her friends, and she no doubt blamed me for that mess too. Now, my restraining order against Lance is interfering with Shelby's life. My mother will see it as another embarrassment by me for her to explain away to her friends. My heart starts to fracture with each breath.

Tears slip through my eyes. I coach myself as I have over the years. I remind my brain that it isn't my fault. At thirteen-years-old, I only wanted my parents to be happy and together. I remind myself that Lance is evil and Shelby is a child who doesn't want to grow up. No matter what my thoughts are, my heart still aches.

A sob slips through my chest and Reed jumps back. "I'm sorry," I apologize. "You didn't hurt me, I swear. It's all just hitting me."

"Do you want to talk?" I shake my head but he presses on. "Harley, you haven't said more than a few words since you closed your accounts. It's perfectly normal not to be okay in this situation."

"This only makes me feel weak," I say through my tears.

"Lee," he moves to sit on the floor beside me. The sound of my nickname rolling from his lips comforts me. "Not only have you been attacked, you lost so much more in the last couple of days. Your answering machine doesn't only record, but it plays the messages out loud. We have unplugged the machine but you can't unhear what you have heard. Your family is upset with you but you have to protect yourself. You've had to make a very tough decision by cutting your family off and standing up against Lance. No one would be fine or ok after what you have gone through."

Reed tries his best to console me. What he is saying is right, but it feels wrong. It feels like a salt scrub against an open wound. Out of everyone in my life, Reed is the only one who understands exactly what I am feeling. I take comfort in him. He pulls me against his side and I rest my head on his shoulder.

When Nikki arrives, Reed and I are still sitting on the floor in front of the couch. My tears have dried up and my emotions have been packed away again in their little box. Nikki and I head back upstairs to finish getting ready.

I dry my hair and she helps me curl it. Then she helps me cover up my exposed bruises. "Lee, I've been talking to Milo," Nikki says, while applying makeup to my face.

"Don't." I am cold and sharp with her. I feel a little guilty for snapping because it's not her fault that Milo is being a jerk. "I don't want to talk about him."

"I know you don't, but I do." She sets the makeup brush down and looks me in the eye. "We've been fighting because I think he is being a total dick about this."

"That's a strong word for your little mouth." I cough out my surprise.

"Nothing as bad as what has come out of yours." She gives me her teacher look and I feel my shoulders slump from her chastising. I now get why her students respect her. Nikki is gentle and kind, but stern when she needs to be.

"I normally don't pick sides when it comes to you two, and you both know that, but right now you don't need another family member to cast you out. I guess what I really want you to know is that I am sorry he isn't speaking to you right now. Just know I am here for you even if he may not be." Nikki reaches for the next makeup product and a different brush.

"It's not your place to apologize."

"I know, but I just wanted you to know that I am here and his actions or attitude doesn't mean that's how I feel." She brushes the blush on my cheeks. "How are you doing over all?"

"Reed has been really helpful by teaching me some self-defense moves." My cheeks warm at the thought of Reed and our closeness.

"I'm feeling more confident in myself," I continue, "and it's helping me gain some courage to face the outside world again. So by going to the bar tonight, I'm trying to get back into my groove." Even though Reed and I have continued to practice to make sure I am comfortable and correctly repeating the defensive actions every time, I still feel shaken.

Nikki pulls way from applying mascara to my eyes and looks at me, apparently sensing the unease. Her eyes are shadowed with sadness. "You'll get there," she encourages and moves to finish the mascara on my other eye. We sit in silence while Nikki finishes covering what is left of my marks on my face and neck.

After making the short drive, I sit in the jeep and wait as long as I can before I go into the bar. Reed and Nikki have already gone inside to allow me space to get my nerve up. When I finally enter right before closing, everyone asks me how I am doing. I assure them that I am fine. In return, they all pass along their hatred towards Lance.

Kayden shows me the panic button that was installed under the countertop by the sink. "It's a bar Harley, the panic button isn't just for you. It's in case we ever need to call for help," he continues to explain when I glare at him.

Eventually the crowd winds down and I close the bar. I see Milo kiss Nikki then give her a loving swat on the rear. Reed and Nikki leave the bar with a wave, leaving Milo alone with me. He hasn't spoken to me in over a week.

"Reed told me you locked the accounts," Milo states. He sounds hesitant and treads lightly with his words. It's likely his attempt not to spark another fight.

"I did." I wonder if he is only speaking to me because of Reed. I'm starting to resent Milo for avoiding me until now. I move to clean the bar. "I'm not giving into the conditional love thing you do. You can be mad at me, but I am not apologizing for anything. I've made my decisions. They were mine to make," I say, defending myself.

He raises his hands in surrender. "I know. I just wanted to save you the heartache." He walks up to the bar and leans against it. He is deep in thought, which is not normal for Milo. He normally says whatever comes to his mind. I stop washing dishes during one of his pauses.

"Harley, for as long as I have known you, your mom, sisters, and brother walked all over your dad. They took advantage of him and he allowed it. It was your mom who walked out on you guys and yet he still loved her. I never understood and still don't. I realize she was never my mom, but our families were close enough that she felt like a second mom to me. I know it's crazy. After all the years of watching them and then to see you take up the burden of supporting them, I couldn't watch it. Lance just added fuel to my aggravation when he got involved with Shelby."

I never knew Milo had emotional ties to my family other than anger. I just thought he was angry at them for what they did to me. Now I realize there are more layers to this situation. He has been angry, not only on my behalf, but also because he felt like my mom walked out on him too. Milo is angry at my mom for hurting my dad, someone he loved deeply. It isn't until this moment that I realize exactly how much Milo is a part of my family. He's been here all along. Then a random thought hits me.

"Milo, did you know Lance when we were in high school? You played sports and hung out with kids from neighboring towns. Fairfield wasn't far. Did you know him or of him?" I ask.

"I had heard rumors about him, which was why I was apprehensive of him when you two started dating. I assumed it was high-school drama and tried to push my concerns aside. Our relationship changed when your dad died though. You pulled back and away from me. I assumed you were grieving, but then we went on a double date."

I remember that night and I know where he is going with it.

"You leaned in to give me a hug goodbye, and I gave you a side hug that was more of a pat." I say filling in the story. "I was trying to avoid any squeezing because Lance had punched me in the ribs over some stupid phone call from Thatcher. You eyed me pretty good after that," I finished.

"It was clear to me that the rumors I heard were probably true. We were always close and a side hug from you was a definite warning flag that something was wrong." Milo's voice carries a sense of regret.

"So you spent the next several weeks trying to talk me out of getting married," I responded. I really wish I would have listened to him right away and I hope he doesn't hold himself responsible for not doing more.

"I knew he was cheating on you but I didn't know who the girl was," Milo filled me in.

"I knew it too. Like you, I didn't know who she was. I stayed because I felt trapped and nothing you could have said would have changed the outcome. My mom and I were never close. With my dad gone, she was the only parent I had. Remember, the wedding was an event for all her friends. It was like her social status was tied to me walking down that hideously decorated aisle."

"Yeah, that wedding was over the top! Nothing reminded me of you and that dress was huge." Milo smirked, remembering how gaudy the spectacle was supposed to be.

"She told lies to her friends about why I was now coming around and how we were on better terms. It was clear to me that if I ended the engagement, I could lose my mom again. But when I found out he was with Shelby, I knew I had to get rid of him. I thought if I broke the engagement that he would leave us all alone. But then he proposed to her and there wasn't anything I could do. I know this doesn't explain exactly why I didn't walk away from my family right then and there. One day I will tell you why, but I'm not really ready to admit it to myself just yet."

He bobs his head and stretches his hand out, "Hand me a towel, I'll go wipe those tables down."

I hand him a dishtowel and he smiles at me. We are lost in our own thoughts as we work on cleaning the bar. Milo and I are far from where we used to be as friends, but we are also far from who we used to be individually. Life has changed us. Some were changes for the better, and some for the worse. However, for the first time in the few years that Milo and I have been at odds, we are finally reaching a new level of understanding of one another. We still have a ways to go, but it's now up to us to figure out how to remain friends after we get to the other side of the curve balls life will continue to throw at us.

"You're healing up pretty good," he says after a while. "How was your first night out?"

"Good." It feels like a lie but I want to be able to move forward.

"Reed also told me he is teaching you self-defense. How is that going?"

I blush a little thinking about him being between my legs as we practice. "It's going good." Milo stops scrubbing the bar top and looks at me.

"You've got a thing for him, don't you?" I can tell he isn't really asking a question.

"He is nice." My blush is deepening the longer he studies me. I glance back down at the bottles as I take inventory of what we have left.

"Has something happened?" Milo's taunting voice sounds intrigued.

"No," I lie. He can see through it. Like a good friend, he lets it go, knowing I will tell him when I'm ready. "Fine!" I finally snap, unable to handle his intense staring, "we kissed but it's not what you think." Milos continues to stare. "When we got back to the house last week after the attack... we kissed. It was more adrenalin-driven."

I hide the second offense because it was intimate and I don't know how I feel about it yet. I also don't want to explain to Milo the situation we were in, nor do I think he would want to know.

"How does he feel about it?" Milo asks awkwardly, but the years of experience in our relationship tells me he's only asking because he wants to know Reed's intentions.

"Well, he put the brakes on a little to see where my head was. It was enough to wake me up and realize what I was doing." He had basically saved my life that night. I was feeling drawn to my hero. Reed is overwhelmingly attractive and I would love to have him as my own, but he is a guest in my world. I know he will be leaving as soon as the last car part is delivered.

Milo fires another playful accusation at me. "You guys haven't talked about it, have you?"

"No," I answer. "Milo, let it go. I am fine with not having this conversation with Reed. I like where we are. Reed and I understand each other." I like not having a label on it.

After the closing checklist has been completed, Milo takes me home. Our friendship is back in step and we feel better. It may not be smooth as glass, but it's headed in the right direction. Even though we fight often, he is one of the few that sticks around after a fight for those that mean something to him.

22

REED

The weekend is finally here. Our bags are loaded and we are ready to go to the fundraiser event. Harley is locking the door while I wait for her by the driver's side door. She grins at me and eyes my hand. Her eyes glimmer with playfulness and show no indication of what she has gone through. I noticed some of the weight on her shoulders had lifted when Milo finally started talking to her again. Neither will admit how stubborn they are, nor will they admit that they need one another. That must be how they have been able to stay friends for all these years.

Her mouth is set in a stubborn pout that I can't resist. She tries to stand her ground. "I'm not giving you the keys." I lean down close, wanting to kiss her softly, but hesitate because we haven't determined what we are to each other yet. She is distracted by my initial move so I enfold her key-holding hand in mine. Catching on to my game, she nips at my nose playfully and giggles, but releases the keys to me.

Still holding her hand, I lead her around to the passenger side of the car. Opening the door like a good-ole'-country-boy should do, I help her in. Before shutting the door, I steal one last glance at her. I let my hand glide against her cheek. Taking in the softness of her chilled skin, I can feel the warmth spreading through it the longer I stand there looking at her. She is beautiful.

"Ready?" My voice is husky. She does something I have become very familiar with when she's speechless, she nods.

I shut the door and sprint around to the driver side. I feel the cool mountain air as it swirls around me. Jumping into the jeep quickly, I start it and off we head to the city.

The two-hour drive is a beautiful one. The last time I drove this route was the day my car broke down. I was so discouraged that I neglected to take in the how peaceful the valley looks being protected by the surrounding mountains. I glance over to make a comment but notice Harley is asleep. She is snuggled into the seat with her mouth slightly open. *If it weren't for that stupid car, I'd have missed out on meeting her.*

When the valet opens our doors, they startle Harley. "Where are we?" She sounds groggy and grouchy. I chuckle and am rewarded with her glare.

"At the hotel. I changed our reservations to a nicer hotel. My treat. This is my 'thank you' for letting me crash at your place."

We climb out of her jeep, hand the valet the keys, and watch the doorman grab our bags. I notice that Harley appears disoriented as she stands there watching everything happening. Her face is set in a scowl that I am sure is from the fact that her car is being driven away by someone she doesn't know. Despite her scowl, I notice the bags under her eyes are lighter. Her eyes shine brighter. She still hasn't been sleeping well during the night. I wake up often to hear her fighting dreams in the middle of the night. Over the last few days, I have ended up crawling into bed with her to keep the nightmares at bay.

I rub her upper arms to warm her. "Your car will be well taken care of," I reassure her. She grins and nudges me in the side. "Let's go see what they have in store for us, shall we?" I offer my elbow to her and slightly bow like they used to in old movies. She beams at me, curtsies, and weaves her arm through the crook of mine.

Inside, there is a sculptured fountain running in the middle of the lobby. Tan painted walls, light-cream marble flooring, and giant marble pillars compliment the two-story sculpture. A large, elegant staircase with a glass railing leaves the room very open and modern. I breathe in the faint hint of chlorinated air.

I walk over to check us in as Harley lags behind me. I give the check-in clerk my cover name as she stands a little taller and makes subtle adjustments to her appearance. In the past, I would have indulged her by being polite and flirting a little just so her efforts didn't go to waste.

But not today. Today, all I see is Harley. Her wide eyes take in the hotel's atmosphere as she studies the details of the architecture. My smile never seems to leave my face when I am watching her. The clerk clears her throat to get my attention. I glance back and instead of sneering at me like some hosts do because I'm wasting their time, she giggles slightly at me.

"Haven't been together long, I take it?" the clerk comments.

"What makes you say that?" I say, finally tearing my gaze away from Harley.

"There are only three reasons people study one another like that. One, when they are honeymooning," she points to my ring finger, "and that isn't the case. Reason two, the relationship status is very new." She winks at me and I grin.

"What's reason three?" I ask since she didn't finish her list.

"You're a cheating bastard," she states pointedly, but there is still kindness in her expression. I laugh at her forwardness. "But, I will go ahead and assume that isn't the case. She is too lovely for that. Be kind to her." That grabs my attention.

I look at the clerk. "I can't imagine being anything less than kind to her." I thank the clerk and leave to join Harley. Our bags are waiting on the cart next to her. I place my hand on her lower back and guide us to the elevators. She looks over at me and seems a little surprised but she doesn't pull away. The closer to the elevators we get, the closer her body moves towards mine.

Reaching our room, I tip the bellhop and we enter the penthouse suite. There are large windows displaying the downtown skyscrapers. The mid-afternoon sun is glinting off the steel structures. In the middle of the seating area is bottle of champagne chilling. Harley smirks when she sees that the name on the attached note doesn't reflect either name she knows me by.

"Another alias Mr. Jonathan Cooper?"

"One of many."

"How many do you have?"

"I don't know. I just make them up whenever I feel like it."

"But Jonathan Cooper isn't made up by you. It was a character from one of your movies."

I grin and shrug. "So I am not always creative. It works when I need it to. You can take that room." I point to the left side of the suite, grab her bags, and carry them into her room.

She rolls her eyes playfully back at me and flops down on the couch in front of the big windows. I find two glasses and pour us each a glass. I have a good side profile of her. She works her long hair into a messy bun, revealing that the once-tense jaw that I had grown used to has now relaxed into the soft curve of her face. *She is lovely*, I agree with the clerk. Her head swivels over to me.

"Thanks for the room." Her voice is humble.

"Have you ever been here before?" I ask, joining her on the couch.

She smiles, takes the drink from my hand, and takes a sip. "Yes." She is coy with her answer, which makes me want to know more.

"With...?" I press.

"You don't want to know," she giggles out.

"Lance?" I spit out.

"No... he never spent more than ten dollars on me. I paid for most of everything when we were together. Sign number one." She rolls her eyes when she realizes I am waiting for the correct answer. But it hits me. "Thatcher brought you here."

I don't even try to hide my distaste. She starts to laugh at my expression. "I thought you said nothing went on between you two," I tease.

"I also said I knew he had intentions but I wasn't interested in him in that way." She draws lazy circles on the back of my hand that rests on the back of the couch. "We went out one night after my dad passed. Nikki and Milo were busy. Lance was off, probably with Shelby, and I was lonely and needed company. It was supposed to be a group of us but it ended up being an unexpected date. He was trying to impress me and brought me here. Money never has impressed me. One of many things Thatcher has yet to learn about me, so I again drew the friendship line and left."

"Ouch!" As bad as that would suck, I do kind of feel for the guy. I couldn't help but be a little gleeful that he got burnt. "I am still surprised you two are friends."

"Me too." Harley laughs. "But he has always been a good friend. He probably thinks that one day I will wake up and realize I am supposed to be with him."

"Have you ever wondered?"

Her eyes go heavy and she studies my response and my body language before she answers. It's almost like she is asking me why I want to know and what the answer will mean to me. I stare back while I ask the same questions of myself.

"I have from time to time when I see him. Truth be told, I wish I would just give him a chance, but its way more complicated than that." She pauses, considering her next thought. "Lance somehow found out that Thatcher brought me here. To this day, I still don't know how he knew, but that was the first time he 'taught me a lesson.'"

It's not lost on me that she never brings herself to call what happened to her by its correct name, *rape*. It's too harsh for her or anyone to digest.

"I should have left Lance as soon as I found out he was cheating on me. But I was preoccupied in dealing with the death of my dad. I just didn't want to deal with a breakup at the same time. Looking back, if I would have tried to leave Lance for Thatcher, Lance would have hunted me down like he did the night at the bar. Thatcher would have protected me, but..." She stops talking. Her eyes look haunted. "There's more to this but I'm still having trouble dealing with the facts."

"So why did he let you go after you ended the engagement?" I ask, still wanting to understand more but trying for a different angle.

"Shelby is way more submissive then I am." She scoots closer to me and kisses me on the cheek. "I'm done talking about the past and Lance and all that other drama. Right now, I need to go get ready for tonight."

With her close, I gently grab her upper arm and lean in to kiss her lips slowly. Our lips melt together. My body is hyperaware of her mouth, which tastes of champagne. Her lips feel soft against mine and vanilla fragrance is wafting with every breath I take.

I start to pull back ever so slightly, but her body moves with mine and follows me. Our lips quicken their pace. My hand slides up her shoulder to cradle the back of her neck. Her hands press my torso and slide around my back. I lay her back gently on the couch. Our kisses become more passionate and full of desire.

23

HARLEY

The girl in the mirror stares back at me with puffy lips and glazed eyes. I am having a hard time remembering if I have ever seen her before. I smile at myself and examine my eyes. They look less troubled. Some of the weight is gone from them. My hair fluffs from the shower steam, I feel completely content to stay in this carefree moment.

I am hyper-aware that Reed is sitting on the other side of the door that connects to my suite. My cheeks flush a little at the thought of his nearness and my skin tingles remembering where his hands were resting not too long ago. My fingers move over my ribs, tracing the path of his hands and touching the fading bruises. I feel victorious over my past. I used to shy away from any touch after Lance, but Reed gave me back my freedom.

The hot water pricks my sensitive skin and coxes me to relax as I step into the shower. I'm amused by thinking about how the desk clerk looked Reed up and down today. I saw the lingering stares from those around us but he paid no attention to them. I pretended to be in awe of the building but I was in awe of him. I sensed he wasn't aware that I was watching him so I took the time to ogle him too.

Emotions and feelings are bouncing around in my head and I want to talk about this situation. But the one person I have shared everything with is the one I want to talk about. I love Nikki, but I stopped talking to her about my relationships a long time ago. She gets too girly on me. She would take my interest in Reed to start planning a wedding and the timing of my children.

Milo is a typical guy and would give me brotherly love doused with reality. Most of the time it is very helpful, but I don't want this to be solved just yet. I like the blissful state I am in.

Reed has entered the messy world I live in and appears to have passed very little judgment. He does want to fix the situation with Lance, which is evident in the way he has taught me self-defense. What I appreciate about him is that he has been able to support me without ridiculing me. I will miss him when he is gone. As I turn the water off, it moves to cooler temperatures and shakes my hormones back to reality. Our paths were only meant to touch. Not join.

I towel off. Shoving my feelings aside, I start to get ready for tonight's events.

Feeling like this is the best I can do, I glance one last time in the mirror and smooth out my already smooth dress. Nikki spent some time over the last few days teaching me how to hide any unwanted, exposed discoloring. My nerves are a wreck. I throw my shoulders back, hold my chin high, and try to gain some of my confidence back. I force myself out of the bathroom.

Reed's back is to me. "Where did you get a suit?" It's tailored nicely against his shoulders and accentuates his athletic build.

He turns to answer me with a cocky grin but the grin fades into shock. The little confidence I had disappears. The dress isn't revealing. Its plum pleated bodice cuts close to my neck and exposes my shoulders. The collar wraps around, still hugging close to my neck in the back, but a deep split in the back allows a sliver of skin to be exposed. I begin to fidget and smooth my hair and my dress. Something must be exposed in a way I didn't realize.

He saunters over towards me while eyeing me up and down. When he stops in front of me, his cologne wraps around me and fills my head. *Damn, I love the way he smells.* My cheeks flush at how giddy I feel.

He brushes a flyaway hair behind my ear and smiles. "There. Perfect."

My eyes drop to the floor. I'm not normally shy, but it is very rare for someone to stare at me the way he is. His finger runs the length of my jaw to my chin and pulls my head up gently to look him in the eye. Our eyes lock. Butterflies grow into birds in my stomach as his gaze bores into mine. "You are beautiful."

"Cheesy," I tease, because I don't know what else to say. His gaze is so intimate that my head feels at a loss and I am unsure how I should feel. But deep down, I am very aware of how I do feel and am just waiting for my brain to catch up to my heart.

I want him to be the guy that chooses me and stays for me. I want him to wrap his arms around me and carry me off to bed. I wish we'd never leave each other's side. But, that's not reality.

"Cheesy," he shrugs, "but still very true."

My chest tightens with his sincerity. "You still didn't answer the question... where did the suit come from?" I try changing the subject. A simple "thank you" would have been better, but it didn't tumble out of my mouth first.

"I called a shop the day I changed the hotel reservation and they delivered it here for me." He smiles kindly at me, and I see a glimmer of embarrassment rolling over his shoulders.

"Thank you for the compliment," I say self-consciously. I feel as though this is the strangest moment we have encountered to date, and that's a lot considering what we have been through together. "You look nice. I like the suit." My thoughts are so random and sporadic that there is no rhyme or reason to them and they keep spilling out.

Reed chuckles, leans in, and kisses me softly on the cheek. "Relax. It's just you and me."

Looking at him, I see him for who he really is - one of my best friends. I take a slow, deep breath, relax my shoulders, and nod. "Sorry."

"No need to apologize." He hesitates for a moment but continues before my curiosity runs rampant. "I was nervous as well when

I was getting ready. Lee, I want you to know, we may be in the same hotel suite, but I don't expect anything to happen." He watches me to make sure I understand. "I realize we have made out a few times, but we haven't said much about it. I haven't *just* made out with anyone since high school and most of the time even that led to something. I respect you, and after everything you have been through, I don't want to make you feel like you are another conquest."

His admission unraveled some of my nervousness that I had not connected to this situation yet. I smile up at him.

"I was also nervous that things might have changed since we have started kissing, but when you opened that door and you stepped through..." He pauses.

My stomach jumps to conclusions. *Is he going to tell me he's not interested? Will I be able handle those words leaving his mouth?* As much as it would crush me for him to say it, I need him to say it. Reed could leave at any moment and if he turns me down, then that will be it. I at least will know exactly where we stand. He will go back to his life and I will resume my new reality. If he doesn't put me at an emotional distance, I don't want to try to piece that kind of broken heart back together when it ends. But the truth is that I've crossed the line where I can no longer be the one to turn away from him. Reed has to be the one to do it.

"I knew things had changed. Lee, you are feisty, strong-willed, stubborn..."

How many more negatives can he throw at me? I think.

"But, I am attracted to every part of you. You are sexy as hell, and I am not sure I will be ready to leave when my car is fixed."

My cheeks are fully flushed now. His sincerity is refreshing. Reed, *the* William Montgomery, the most practiced seducer out there with an arsenal of one-liners to choose from, chose to use words that describe who I really am. My heart skips a beat.

"I'm not sure I will want you to leave either," I stammer as I realize he has no intention of pushing me away.

Like a gentleman, he takes my hand and places it around his arm. His eyes never leave mine. "Shall we then?"

Speechless, I nod.

At the Performing Arts Center, the small gathering area is packed full of donors. I recognize most of them and exchange pleasantries with some. Reed stays by my side and shows off the kind smile that is found in all the tabloids. He isn't stand-offish, yet he doesn't speak. He is in his observation mode and simply watches the idle chatter, polite soft chuckles, and quiet murmurs of those around us.

Since Reed has cleaned up the beard he has been sporting for a while now, he's a little more recognizable. People are slightly thrown off when I introduce him as Reed Cooper. A few point out how similar he looks to the famous William Montgomery, but Reed bats the comments off as compliments and acts as if they are two different people.

"This isn't where you normally hang out when you come to these events," Reed states when we finally find a break in the conversations around us.

"What makes you say that?" A coy smile plays on my lips.

"Everyone seems to be surprised by your appearance, which tells me you must hide elsewhere until the show starts."

"I think they are surprised because I have a date," I throw back. "I think most people thought I was the spinster with thirty cats. I could still be a closet cat lady for all they know."

He laughs and gently kisses my temple. I find it endearing and I melt against him. He offers to get us drinks.

As he walks away, it is fascinating to watch the crowd part as he meanders over to the bar. No one watches for him. It's as if his presence commands them to move. He places our order and I can see him scanning the crowd.

His ability to be a chameleon enthralls me. He is undeniably an exact replica of his famous alter-ego. His years spent hiding the identity of his past, and convincing audiences of the different characters he plays, aid him tonight. People seem to only see who Reed chooses them to see.

Not wanting to be caught watching him, I duck behind a pillar. I am a little embarrassed by the way I feel towards him and would like to explore my feelings without him knowing I have an obsession for watching him.

We are the classic case of two worlds thrown together that can never merge. He is a prince and I am the peasant. I just don't see how our two worlds can manage to stay as one.

My phone chirps in my clutch and I glance at the screen. There is a message from George and my heart saddens. My time in this fairy-tale world is ending. We may not want to part, but our worlds will call our names and we will be forced to run back like kids edging closer to their curfews.

I breathe in deep and try to let the sadness go for tonight. No matter how short-lived it may be, I am going to enjoy what my fairy tale has brought me. I see Reed walking to where he last left me. His shoulders are back, showing confidence and swagger like a college boy, only better. Reed's swagger oozes sexuality in a private, low-key way.

I step out from behind the pillar. His eyes immediately find me and seem to be drawn to me like a magnet. He makes his way over to where I'm standing against the pillar. I throw caution to the wind and lean up to kiss Reed before another word is passed between us.

24

REED

She is stunning. The purple dress hugs her body in the right places and highlights her auburn hair. Her long curls drape against her bare shoulders. The soft white of her skin glows and radiates with life. When she leans up to kiss me, I revel in the fact that I am here with her.

I am used to being strategically placed next to Zocy with kisses only being passed when the cameras are around. Harley's lips feel like a stolen kiss and we are lost in our world. We are alone in a place where reality doesn't exist except for this moment. Her perfume is intoxicating and her curls are soft in my hand.

I move to set the drinks down on a nearby table. She pulls me gently behind the pillar she appeared from so we are concealed. I take a large step and pull her closer to me. I want her body against mine.

There is a loud clanging of glass as someone is trying to get everyone's attention. I feel an irritated rumble rip through my chest. Harley giggles as she pulls away slowly. I stroke her flushed cheeks. We realize we aren't as concealed as we thought when a few Cheshire grins are thrown our way. I can't help but smile and give Harley one last kiss. I brush my knuckles down her neck and over her shoulder to trace a path until I can grasp her hand. Our eyes never break away.

Our breathing slows as the music hall quiets down and people begin to shuffle into the auditorium. "Shall we?" I pull her hand through the crook of my arm and escort her to our seats.

The auditorium is dimmed. Clattered music fills the air from the orchestra pit. Once we are seated, the heat buzzes between us. Her fingers play tiny circles on the back of my hand. I never knew that a small touch could create this intense connection. It feels very intimate and sensual, but extremely public. My desire deepens for her to explore me more.

I am so distracted by her that I hear the announcer's voice but can't focus on what he is announcing. The timpani drums rumble, lights flash, cymbals clash, and dancers fill the stage. I pick up the beat of the song "Crystals" by "Of Monsters and Men." My head is filled with the sights and sounds before me. My head feels swept away by the performance, but my body is tied directly to Harley.

Needing a change from her finger tracing, I roll her hand over so her palm is facing up. . I stifle my chuckle when I realize my reaction to someone just holding my hand has made me an adolescent again.

With Harley's hand resting on her thigh palm facing up, my thumb circles the middle of her palm. I see her from the corner of my eye as she takes a slow, deep breath and slowly releases it. A celebratory smile spreads across my face. I thank the gods above that I am not the only one affected by such a minuscule movement. It feels childish, but that doesn't stop us from our cat and mouse game.

Lights dance off her face and her mouth pops open ever so slightly when my fingers stroke along hers and onto her thigh. She continues to breathe in and out. If it weren't for the music, I could probably hear her. Her eyes slowly close and her fingers wrap around mine. She grins and peers at me under hooded eyes. *Whoa* she mouths. My smile turns cocky and she gives me a playful, chastising glare. To give herself some space, she places my hand back on my lap. We both fight to calm down and try to focus on the show.

The event showcases the raw talent of the students. They are mesmerizing with their fluid movements, pop beats, and collaborations intertwined with the City's Symphony. I am carried away by everything around me. The local ballet studio is involved, as well as several other organizations and clubs. They all have had a part in training the students, introducing them to different styles of dancing, and incorporating ethnic cultures and heritages. I had thought these kinds of skills were only meant for *Dancing with the Stars*. Tonight, I have learned otherwise, after meeting different club leaders and discussing their outreaches.

I notice heads around me bobbing with the beat and I see college scouts making notes for potential scholarship receivers. I am exhilarated to be witnessing someone's dream coming true. I glance over at Harley. She looks proud of what her friend and these kids are accomplishing. She wants to see them succeed. As I watch them all, the whole experience is truly inspiring.

The show ends and everyone is on their feet. Applause, whistles, and cheers ring out to affirm the students for a job well done. The students beam with pride as they take their bow. The program director, Harley's old college roommate, steps forward and takes her bow. The students fill in around her, giving her huge hugs and appreciation. She takes the microphone, thanks everyone for coming, and invites us to stick around and meet with the cast. The house lights are turned on for everyone to file out of the auditorium.

"Lee, I'm so glad you made it!" The program director takes Harley into a tight hug. I see Harley wince, but she composes herself quickly as the woman releases her.

"Of course I would make it!" I haven't ever seen Harley this enthusiastic. She turns to me. Her eyes buzz with excitement. "Bree, I want you to meet Reed…" She stumbles for the fake last name we have used for me tonight. "Reed, this is my college roommate Bree Arnold." Harley looks stunned and unsure if our cover is blown. Bree eyes me closely and makes sure to check out every inch of me. "Well, it is nice to meet you," she says, shaking my hand with a grin.

"What a wonderful program you have built," I compliment, trying to move past Harley's worries. Bree's cheeks warm a little. Harley sparkles with happiness and takes my lead to abandon her concerns.

"He is very polite, and a keeper Lee. If you ever set him free, you better let me know." Bree coyly plays with Harley. The dynamics between the two friends are fun to watch. Harley is a straightforward businesswoman, while Bree is a go-getter. Neither holds back on what they want, but they handle themselves very differently. Despite their differences, they chit-chat excitedly.

"You have to come celebrate with the other supporters," Bree offers.

Harley glances at me with a torn expression. "You bet. Where are you going?" I ask, deciding for her.

Bree gives me the name of the pub they have reserved.

"We will see you there."

I take Harley's hand, placing it on the crook of my arm once again. Bree smiles big at us, while Harley shakes her head at Bree. They share a knowing grin and giggle. Watching Harley, I am again thankful my car broke down and she is the one who found me.

At the pub, I am introduced to more donors and supporters. Shots are flowing freely and help to ensure that no one pays attention to me. Keeping an eye on Harley, I see that she passes most of her drinks off to those around her in a discrete manner.

"So are you screwing my friend?" Bree asks, a little slurred, as she settles into the empty bar stool next to me.

"No." My voice has a little edge because her direct question was very crass.

"She's been hurt enough and I don't know you, but you are major eye candy, and that always makes me leery."

"But weren't you just eye groping me earlier?"

"Oh yeah," she responds confidently. "But I see people for who they really are. Lee likes to take the broken boys and fix them. Yet she doesn't realize she is the one left broken. So if you break her heart…" She warns me.

It's obvious to me that even though Harley thought she was keeping the abuse a secret, those around her knew what was going on. It must have been very hard for her friends to know they couldn't stop it. From my experience, it takes something drastic to stop abuse, and most people don't know how.

"And you do what with broken guys like me?"

"Kick their ass into next Tuesday."

I can't help smiling at her.

With a polite giggle, she returns, "I'm not kidding."

It hits me that Bree, Milo, and even the whole town of Middleton, are all working in prevention mode for Harley. They will do whatever they can to keep the bad apples away from her.

"I know you aren't kidding. Rest assured, I was broken but I have been on the mend for a while now and that has nothing to do with her." I tip my beer bottle in Harley's direction. "As I have told several of Harley's other protective friends, I would never hurt Harley and you have my permission to kick my ass if I even come close." I hold Bree's gaze.

She studies me for a moment then thrusts her arms around my neck. "I approve, Mr. William Montgomery." She smirks before bouncing off to join the rest of the group.

More shots are brought to the table. I see Harley slip out of the crowd and make her way over to me.

"What were you and Bree talking about?" she questions. She hands me the shot she swiped from the table.

"You," I state. Her head cocks to one side.

"This is for you."

I offer the shot back to her. She shakes her head to decline the offer. "Are you okay?" I ask, throwing the drink back, and allowing it to burn down my throat.

"Yeah, but I'm about ready to go." She is still buzzing with excitement, but it is dimming. I nod and grab our coats while she tells all her friends goodbye.

Soon, we are out the door and into the cold. We climb into a cab which whisks us away from the bar. Sliding my arm around her shoulder, I pull her against my side. She lounges against me and stares out the window. The snow has been piled in heaps at the corners of the intersection and reflects the downtown city lights. The snow reminds me of the thrilling mountain-top experience with Harley and her friends. If my car hadn't broken down, I'd have missed that experience and missed tonight's impressive student performances. Harley acts as if her lifestyle is insignificant but she's slightly blinded. She doesn't realize how many people around her care about her wellbeing. She doesn't seem to fully appreciate the adventures she is having now. I guess we all tend to be blinded by the monotony of our life.

The cab pulls up in front of the hotel as Harley uncurls herself from my side. The door opens and a cold blast of air rushes into the cab. The evening is coming to an end and I'm not sure I'm ready for it to.

"I'm still a little hungry," I mention, noticing the small lounge off to the side of the lobby. Soft piano music plays and I hope to extend the evening a little more.

She takes my cue and heads towards the lounge. "I could use some food. I'm not quite ready to call it a night."

Taking a seat in a corner booth, we watch the jazz singer sing her sultry heart out. The music is beautiful and creates the perfect ambiance. We order some food and glasses of wine.

We talk about what we thought we wanted to be when we were kids. I admit that I wanted to be Walker Texas Ranger. She knew early on that she wanted to be an auto mechanic. Harley shares about her relationship with her sisters. She said they often ganged up on her brother, but she would pass a few secrets of the planned attacks along to give him a slight advantage because she always felt guilty. Harley focuses on the good stories from her childhood.

We both knew our pasts weren't rosy, but we both seem tired of rehashing the bad moments. As Harley shared some happy stories, it was easier for me to find my own good recollections. I share about how my brother followed me around like little brothers do. I talk about watching my parents in their moments of love and how they would dance like they do in the movies. Although those moments were few and far between, they did exist. I knew they loved each other, but it was a twisted kind of love.

"Do you feel like you missed out on anything growing up since you bounced around from home to home?" Her question veers towards the heavier side but I don't mind.

"I am sure there is a lot I missed out on, but overall I am thankful for what I experienced. I learned a lot about myself through all of it. It did take some time to understand how those experiences shaped my life, but I see it now. I stopped feeling sorry for myself once I got my first acting job."

"Is there anything you would do over again?"

I smirk because there are always things to do over again, but why waste the time on the "could have been's"? On this trip, I have learned that the only thing I can do is to try to do better in the circumstances I'm faced with going forward. To answer Harley's simple question, I choose a light-hearted answer, "I guess if I really could, I would go back to high school and attend a prom."

"You never went? That was all anyone looked forward to when I was in high school."

I laugh at her expression of awe over something so high-school driven. "Everyone at my high school wanted to go to dances too. It's not like I refused to go, I just never went... I was the bad boy that no one messed with or hung out with. Let me put it this way... I was the "behind the scenes" action for every popular girl with a boyfriend. There weren't a lot of girls willing to be seen in public with me."

"You little man whore," she chides me with a grin. "I'll bet every one of them would think differently now."

I give her a cocky smile because it's true. I was wild growing up. My adoptive parents didn't know what to do with me. In the beginning, they tried to wrangle me in and teach me obedience and self-worth. Towards the middle of my freshman year of high school they gave up, not on me, but on the teachings. Instead, they worked on being a support team. They worked on just talking. Talking felt strange and uncomfortable to me.

I remember the first time I opened up to Jerry. I was seventeen and thought I might have gotten a girl pregnant. I had a temper and

I knew if I wasn't careful, I could turn into my dad. That idea scared me more than anything. Kickboxing and karate lessons taught me how to fight better and helped calm me down a little, but the anger still resided in me. Jerry was in his office reading. He spent his free time there. He knew I was coming to talk to him before I did. I still don't know how, but he told me he sensed it. That night was where everything started changing for me. Realizing I might have to take care of someone besides myself made me grow up. Jerry coaxed me to talk about my fear of my dad's genetics, and asked me about what I wanted to do with my life. He helped me to understand that if I didn't value myself then no one would.

The baby thing ended up being a false alarm and Jerry and Lisa thought I would revert back to my old ways. I still didn't care about school or life but I was calmer after that talk with Jerry. I started to come home at descent hours and tried to eat dinner with them. I wasn't perfect but they always told me they never expected perfection.

"Where did you go?" Harley's voice dips into my head.

"Just thinking about you. How wonderful it is that I have been given the chance to know you." Her head drops humbly at the compliment. Humility is uncommon in my world and refreshing to witness. At the same time, it is sad that she hasn't been given as many compliments as she deserves.

"When we met, were you scared to pick up a stranger on the side of the road?" This has concerned me because something could happen to her if she isn't careful about strangers. I reminded myself that she was attacked by a non-stranger so being careful isn't always a guarantee of safety.

She snorts a laugh. "Nah. Remember, I told you I don't travel alone."

I nod, but my concern for her is still very real and apparently obvious. "Don't worry." She pauses as she thinks about what she is about to say. "I normally don't pick people up. I normally call for George to come pick them up and tell the stranded people that help is on the way."

"What made me different?"

"I don't know." She smiles, apparently mystified herself. "It was like something bigger was guiding me to you," she mocks. "It's not like I believe in love at first sight, or *the one*, because I think you meet people when you need to. People are brought into your world for reasons we don't always understand or grasp, but they make impacts in our lives." She eyes me closely. "So I don't know what made you different."

"Well, I'm glad you took a chance on me then." She sheepishly grins. Biting her thumb nail, she gazes back at the stage.

"Let's go," she offers, tugging on my arm. "It's time you had a prom dance."

She guides me out of the booth, onto the small dance floor, and starts swaying to the music.

25

HARLEY

He follows me, smiling the entire way, and doesn't put up any resistance. It's clear he is comfortable with dancing. The bass of the music thrums in our bones as we are drawn closer together. A giggle bubbles up. I haven't felt this alive in years.

Several songs come and go but we are locked in our world. I stare deeply at him and study his features closely. The full beard that he had when I picked him up has now been trimmed close into sexy stubble. I pick up on faint scar right by his ear that must have come from his childhood. I memorize the angle of his jaw, his straight model nose, and heavy brow line. It won't be long before we part ways.

He senses my weighted stare and gives me the famous grin. He gently pulls away from me and starts doing the electric slide in slow motion. His moves match the beat of the sultry song that should be danced with a swaying partner. It is random, odd, and out of place. It is exactly something my group of friends used to do in college. Other dancers with confused expressions stop to watch what is going on. He extends his hand for me to join him and I smile as I take his hand.

When the song ends, we gather our belongings and leave the bar. Everyone appears bewildered in our wake.

"Where did this Harley come from?" Reed takes me under his arm and kisses me on the top of my head as he pulls me into the empty elevator.

"She has been in here for a while but just wasn't sure how to get out." I look up at him. His eyes sparkle with joy and endearment. I start humming Abba's "Take a Chance On Me," referring back to our conversation about taking a chance on picking him up. He laughs and sings the first few lines of the song.

"What do you see in me? Why am I allowed to be the one who gets to see that look in your eyes, and the one who gets to know your secrets?" I ask.

"If I told you, you wouldn't believe me because of the hurt you have experienced and the doubt you have in people." He pauses but never breaks eye contact. "But can you trust me when I say I have never met anyone like you?"

My body flushes just like it did at the theater when he was assaulting my hand. I never knew a simple touch could feel that intimate. A smile spreads across my face and Reed looks at me inquisitively.

"And what is it about elevators being so charged with sexual tension?" I press up against him and start kissing him deep. The elevator dings and interrupts us. Reluctantly, we exit on the suite floor. From this height, the city looks amazing through the large windows. The staff had reset our room while we were out. The room glows in low lighting and soft music plays in the background.

I set my clutch down on the entry table and reach for his hand. I walk us into the living room portion of the suite and begin swaying to the music. I am not ready to let him go.

"We didn't get to slow dance at your prom downstairs," he playfully adds and pulls me closer to drape his arms around me. I feel secure and melt into his embrace.

"Lee," His voice is husky and I love the way my nickname falls from his mouth. I glance up and desire fills me.

We draw near to each other and our lips touch softly, gently, but they turn heavy quickly. I know it's too soon but I love the way he makes me feel. The little voice in my head keeps whispering reminders that this is temporary. That he will be leaving.

I pull away almost immediately when I remember the text I got earlier tonight.

"Are you ok?" Reed seems a little alarmed, but not afraid as if he has done something wrong.

"I... I got a message from George that your last car part arrived today and he finished it."

Reed's shoulders slump ever so slightly and his gaze is locked on the windows. "Lee, what do you see when you look at me?"

"I see someone who is strong-willed, kind, but can be arrogant at times with his swagger." My grin makes him smile. "But what I know is different than what I see. You had a rough past, which made you strong-willed. And that past made you have a confidence in yourself that no one can touch, because you know nothing more can break you."

"See that last part isn't true..." He pauses, looking for words, "you can break me."

"I really, really like you Reed."

"But..."

"I've always understood we are just temporary. I have a hard time convincing myself just how temporary we are, but we are." Those words hang between us. Reed's mouth opens slightly, maybe to argue differently, but he is cut off when his cell phone buzzes.

An annoyed curse comes out of Reed. "I'm really sorry, but I have to take this."

There is so much left unsaid between us in this moment. I should be frustrated but the call solidifies my point. We are only temporary and it kills me to admit that. Reed is the first person who has known me in this way. I didn't think I kept walls up until he smashed through them. I find myself hiding nothing from him.

He has helped me find my voice, but what if he is my voice? I have become very dependent on him. I have leaned on him for strength, protection, and acceptance. When he leaves, will I be able to stand up for myself on my own? I thought I was doing fine before but now I know differently. The question now becomes: *am I weak without him or am I stronger because of him?*

I have never wanted to be the girl who depends on a man. I want someone to stand beside me, not in front or behind. If I am depending on him for everything, does that mean I'm standing behind him? Will I follow him blindly? The truth is that if he were to ask me to go with him, I don't feel like I would say no.

On the other hand, is that really a bad decision? Maybe I am still independent but he makes me feel stronger. Maybe I am evaluating it wrong. What if he only brings out the best in me? I feel safe, understood, cherished, and at home when I'm around him. He has protected me. I feel like I found my soulmate. I shake my head at the cliché as Reed hangs up the phone. He turns to face me and looks a little weary.

"Yes, we are temporary." As the words leave his mouth, the glimmer in his eyes dims to reflect the dread we both feel. "So why not enjoy the time we have together? Why are we trying to figure this out tonight?"

I look at him. His lips are in a slight curve. His suggestion is full of double meanings. I throw my arms around his neck and kiss him deeply while pushing my rampant thoughts aside.

26

REED

All alone, as I lay wide awake in bed staring at the ceiling, my mind works on this complicated puzzle Harley and I are in. We want to be together but can't figure out how. While we were dancing tonight in the hotel room, I had been trying to figure out a way to keep us together. However, when she called us temporary, I felt like a bucket of cold water had been poured on me.

I have to keep reminding myself that *Harley's life is in Middleton*. She has two businesses that are thriving and friends that care deeply about her. It wouldn't be right to ask her to go with me. But I can't stay here either because I'm not done with acting yet. I haven't done everything I've set out to do.

My heart sinks as I realize that Harley has been right since that day on the mountain. People have to make sacrifices to make relationships work. It's not fair to ask her to sacrifice everything when I'm not sure that I can make the same sacrifice for her. How do we keep a relationship strong with that many obstacles and miles between us?

Messages from Kyle, my manager, and Zoey's assistant play over and over in my head. Kyle called earlier to let me know one of the movies I had auditioned for before my vacation came through and it was time to start filming. I ignore the one from Zoey's assistant for now. Zoey needs me to return and her team is using my past as blackmail to get me on the next plane. I just don't want to deal with these problems tonight.

I had messaged Kyle earlier in the week that I wanted to audition for *A Single Rose*. He was shocked when I revealed that I wanted the role of Drew instead of the detective. With the next movie starting production, I start mapping out my movie schedule in my head. I am searching for the spaces I can come back and spend time with Harley. I want to make her a part of my life, but I am finding the empty spaces are few and far between. There just aren't enough of them to sustain a decent relationship.

I feel like it is too soon to have her enter my world completely. Our friendship blurs a little more each time we kiss. With each kiss, my desire grows for her. But just as she has stated multiple times, we are from different worlds. I have come to realize that she states this to remind herself as well.

I dread going back to my world without her though. I selfishly want Harley there to keep me grounded to the real me. Having to play the part of William Montgomery in my real life means I have to continue pretending that Zoey and I have the forever kind of love that we show the world. I will have to continue the lies we tell in interviews, to talk about the fake stories of my fake family, and relay the sugar-coated memories that are partially true. I don't just want Harley there. I need her there.

Harley knows the truth. I let her into my deep thoughts, feelings, and my real story. The more I share with her, the more liberated I feel. It is freeing. But the thought of going back to the secrets fills me with so much emptiness. *How can I have the best of both worlds?*

Adding Harley to my world also means that Zoey has to go. Breaking up with her publicly means my father's criminal background, my brother's history, my foster life, and everything that follows my real name will be leaked to the tabloids. *Would it be so bad? Would it be the worst thing to have to stop hiding?*

As much as Zoey can be dramatic, she isn't the real issue. Sure, she is frustrated at me for walking out on her when I started this "vacation." But our problem is really with our acting agency and our publicists. Zoey has her own personal story at stake here too. As long as we play by their rules, our lives will remain as we know them. Zoey and I are just pawns of the media who overanalyze celebrity's lives. We are treated as a brand and not as humans.

I have been grateful for the spotty cell service in the area because it has made ignoring all of them easier. I fear for Harley though. The wrath of Zoey's entourage, along with both of our money-driven agencies, can be brutal and very hurtful. I know Harley has dealt with conniving antics from her family, but I don't want to drag her through the mud because everyone is pissed at me.

I get up and start pacing my room. I just want one more night with Harley before I leave. I need more reassurance of who I am and she's the only one who can do that for me. I also want to make sure that she will be okay. I want to make sure that she knows how to defend herself. I need reassurance that she will be fine before I leave her.

Walking quietly over to my closed door, I hesitate and wonder what I will say when I knock on her door. I try a few explanations out in my head. Each attempt feels extremely lame. I give up and decide to go with whatever happens.

I open my door and startle a wide-eyed Harley. She is standing just outside my door. I pull her to me and kiss her with an aching desire I didn't know existed until this moment.

27

HARLEY

Between kisses, he reassures me that I am the one in control. However, everything inside of me screams that I am definitely out of control. I let my body follow his pull towards the bed. Reed's strong hands against my shoulder blades keep my body pressed up against his. His body heat chases all my doubts and loneliness away.

I wasn't sure what I wanted when I came to his room, but this is better than anything I could have imagined. My desire deepens and so does our kissing. My body craves this nearness to him. A small sigh slips out of me and I feel his lips curve into a smile. Not breaking our kiss, we stumble over one another. Through snickers and kissing, we settle into the bed.

He is above me and looks down to make sure I am comfortable with this position. I take the moment to breathe and study him. The subtle look of joy he gave me when he opened his door is still very present. My shy smile must have reassured him of what he was searching for because he leans down and kisses me softly.

Pulling back, he asks, "How would you get out of this hold?" He pulls my hips against his. Fire shoots through my thighs as they hug his hips.

"I wouldn't," I respond back playfully as I try to pull him back to me. His arms are locked and won't budge.

"Okay Mr. Mood Killer." I frown. "I would shift my hip, get my feet onto your hips, move to grab your wrist, and kick hard. In this case, I kind of want to kick you in the balls right now for making me wait."

He chuckles and moves to put his weight on me. "And this position?"

"I would head butt you in the face, then use my whole body to roll you off and run." I realize what he is doing. This is his goodbye to me. My heart seizes as the reality I hoped would never happen is coming true. It is time for us to go our separate ways.

"Reed, you have taught me well. I will keep working on the techniques. I promise that you have taken care of me. I will be fine."

He moves back to kissing me. Gently and softly, he absorbs every detail of me. My hands explore his body as I try to memorize it. I feel his biceps pull and push with the movement against my body. My hands travel to the hem of his shirt and linger up against his rib cage. I can feel every inhale he takes in of me.

My fingertips touch his back and travel down to his hips. I lightly drag my nails against his exposed skin and inch his shirt up higher and higher. I giggle inside to know I am doing something right to get this breathy reaction from him. He ducks his head and pulls his shoulder to remove his shirt.

My breath catches at the sight of him. I have seen him without his shirt before, but taking it off him might mean there is an expectation for mine to be off as well. With him leaving, is this what I want?

He props himself up on his elbows to peer down at me. His eyes are kind and study my face. His fingers softly trace my jaw line. I feel my heart beating quickly as I enjoy his fingertips against my skin. His hips grind pleasurably into mine and a soft groan slips between my lips. I feel him chuckle right underneath my ear. My hips develop a mind of their own as they press upwards. I crave his nearness.

Both of our breaths catch in shock at the intensity we are creating. I feel his hand move down my side until it reaches my hip. His fingers dig in and draw me closer again. Capturing his lips with mine, our need drives us deeper. Our hips move with the rhythm of our kisses and our breathing becomes more labored. I feel his hand move to my bare stomach.

I haven't made a move to go further. I can tell that Reed knows we have reached my limit. I know he is ready and willing to be intimate. In a movie, that's how this scene would end. It would be our parting gift to one another - our goodbye. However, I don't just want to go there because it's what happens in the movies.

I feel deeply for Reed but I don't want parting gifts. I want more with him, but realize more just isn't in our cards. Taking my cue, Reed backs off gently but continues kissing me. He gently removes his hand from my stomach and moves it back up to my face. He shifts his weight so he is no longer on top of me but our bodies are still close. This small action drives me crazy because I want his closeness, but not a good-bye sex session. I relax into his embrace.

He breathes against my neck, which sends chills down my spine. "Are you leaving tomorrow?" I ask in a whisper to confirm my dread.

"I don't want to think about it right now. Just be with me." He coaxes me back to him.

Later, I wake up to an annoying telephone ring. Reed's voice is rough and sexy with sleep. I roll over to see him sitting on the side of the bed. He is hunched over with his feet planted on the floor. He is scrubbing sleep out of his face and trying to wake up.

It dawns on me that it's time to head home. Sadness settles over my chest. When he hangs up, I crawl over to him and place my arms over his shoulders to pull his body against mine one last time. He chuckles and I feel it in my chest.

"Morning," He says.

"Morning," I say, kissing his neck. He sighs heavily, grunts, and follows with a playful reprimand. "You're going to have to stop. You are tempting me way too much right now."

I giggle and climb off the bed. "Let me pack so we can hit the road." I try to keep my tone light but his reaction shows me that I'm not doing very well.

"Lee." His tone sounds off and I brace myself for what comes next.

"I got a message last night that I have to get back to L.A. today." My stomach drops as the details continue to roll out. "I need you to drop me off at the airport."

"What about your car, your stuff?" I knew he was leaving but I thought I would get a little more time with him. He looks just as disappointed as I feel.

"I'll arrange for the car to be transported back, as for the stuff... you can sell it on eBay." He tries joking with me by bringing up a comment I made from what feels like forever ago. The joke is overshadowed by the pain I feel as a piece of my heart breaks.

28

Harley lets me drive the car to the airport and we make our way to the private jet area. Dread is building in my heart as I face dealing with what is going on back in L.A. When I left, Zoey and I had a big fight. She was moody and had become extremely hateful. It wasn't the first time, but I was dealing with my own personal problems and wasn't interested in also dealing with hers. Despite the tension Zoey and I had for one another a few months ago, I know she still has my back. We can be mad at each other, but when you boil it all down, she's one of my closest friends in our backwards contractual way.

Zoey's staff, however, is a different story. They tend to be the culprit of most of the fights between Zoey and me. I have ignored her persistent staff over the last several weeks and that probably put a bigger target on my back. I have seen them ruin lives of people they once considered friends.

The last message from Zoey's personal assistant has me counting days in my head. I've been gone for almost two months now so there is no way Zoey's pregnancy could be connected to me. But I don't have enough information to stand my ground against the accusation. I replay Kyle's phone call last night in my head, trying to understand how I could be the father when Zoey has been with her current boyfriend Isaac for several months.

Harley and I hit the tarmac and the plane is sitting there. The open staircase is waiting for me. Neither of us moves. We are lost in our own thoughts. This will be our goodbye and I don't know when or if we will ever see each other again. I lean over the console to pull her closer to me for one more kiss. I feel a tear slip down her cheek onto my fingers.

"I'm thankful your brother's car broke down," she says against my lips.

"Me too." I pull away from her and we both exit the car. I head towards the back to get the only bag I brought with me. She climbs into the driver's seat. The flight attendant takes my bag and loads it onto the jet for me. I make my way to where Harley sits. Her head is resting against the side of the car.

"I'll get your car scheduled for a pick up and get your stuff that is still at my house shipped back to you," she says softly. I nod as a response because words won't form in my mouth. I reach for her and pull her out of the car. My chest tightens as I wrap my arms tight around her.

"Keep practicing your escape routes," I instruct. "Please stay safe." I pull back to see tears pouring down her cheeks. I kiss each side. I walk away without saying anymore because it's not going to get easier.

I follow the pilot up the stairs and stop halfway to look back at her. She is standing on the jeep's side rails with an arm resting on the top of the car. Her other arm is on the open car door. When I first met Harley, she looked sad and unkempt. I understand now that it was because she never slept and had poor eating habits. Looking at her now, I see that her eyes are brighter than they were when I first met her. She has color in her cheeks and she radiates beauty. We exchange weak smiles, faint waves, and I head into the plane.

I once thought Harley was a little rude and rough on the edges but I had her all wrong. She was only harsh when it came to the auto shop. She's had to fight for respect as a female mechanic. Over the time I spent with her, I have learned that she is playful, optimistic, and a dreamer.

As our plane lines up for take-off, I see the jeep still sitting there. My thoughts linger towards what is ahead of me. I have to face Zoey when I get back. It's not that I am afraid of her, but that I am afraid of the unknown. I force myself to think of something else, but thinking of Harley only makes me dread leaving that much more. Instead, I force myself to zone in on nothing. When we finally land, I know the dream of Middleton has finally come to an end. I climb off the plane and stretch my legs and back. I take a breath and move forward like I have done for years.

I grab my luggage and head towards the car that Kyle had arranged for me. They already have a meeting scheduled with my team and Zoey's team to get this whole calamity of a story under wraps. Kyle is already in the car and hands me a file with pictures of Zoey's latest scandals to catch me up to speed. Never once does he ask where I have been the last two months, nor does he comment on my well-being. I used to like that because it meant nobody went poking around in my past. Now, I find it very rude that he isn't even concerned that I have been missing for several months.

I realize how much two months have changed me. How Nikki, Milo, and Harley have shown light on the holes in my life. "How are you Kyle?" I ask, interrupting him. He glares back at me to let me know now is not the time for pleasantries.

I smirk. I am definitely *no longer in Middleton.* Resting against the seat, I let his words wash over me and stare out at the sunlit palm trees. My mind wanders to Harley. Wondering if she'd enjoy the palm trees as much as the pine trees that tower over Middleton. Along our drive, there is no shortage of expensive cars, skimpy bikinis, and short shorts. This city breathes extravagance and judgment of those who don't fit the L.A. stereotypes. I long for the backwoods and snowy mountains. Realizing my fondness for the mountains, I know Harley would never adjust here.

We finally reach our destination. At the Canton and Webb Talent Agency, cameras are everywhere because news is leaking out that Zoey might be pregnant and that it might not be my baby. Kyle revealed to me in the car that it has been confirmed that the baby is not mine. He also revealed that if I don't stand by her side, claiming it to be mine, then Zoey's staff would leak my story as well.

Questions are shouted at me as we exit the car. Flashes of camera bulbs dot my eyes. Security stands in the way to try to block the assaults, but it feels like the elevator takes forever to arrive.

When the elevator finally arrives, I am whisked away up to the quiet ninth-floor lobby. The quiet is almost deafening and disorienting after the mob downstairs. Zoey sits in the glassed-in conference room. Her big sunglasses are pushed up on top of her head to hold back her dark waves of hair. Her halter dress shows off her very nice tan and very nice chest. Our eyes meet and her gaze never waivers from mine. I know she is here to make a deal. I excuse myself before even entering the room.

I need to make a phone call.

29

HARLEY

I sit in my car until the plane had been gone for a long time. A knock on my window startles me. A man in a security uniform informs me I am well past my stay. I nod reluctantly. I don't want to leave, but I have to. My time with Reed is over. I am just not willing to accept it yet.

At the stoplight to get on the highway, I can't make myself go home. There is nothing waiting for me there. The auto shop didn't need me. George has proven to me he is capable of managing it and the bar was doing fine without me. With Reed gone, it's more obvious to me now that I am a third wheel to Nikki and Milo. *There is absolutely nothing for me back in Middleton.*

The light turns green and I move forward. I skip the exit to head home. I had spent so much of my life taking care of what I thought were my inescapable responsibilities in Middleton. Now I realize that I am not as needed as I had imagined. The only thing needing my attention is me.

I drive and I keep driving. I end up on the street where my mom's house sits. I park a few houses away and know that coming here is a mistake. Nothing in this place feels right. The neighborhood is nice, with beautiful manicured lawns, ornate street lamps, and well-kept flower beds. I watch Lance get out of his car. He spots me. Like the bruises all over my body, his face has not finished healing either.

I used to be afraid of him, but for some reason his menacing look doesn't make me back down like it used to. He stalks off towards the house, leaving my sister looking dumbfounded as to what caused his mood change. She never once notices my car.

My family's lives continue as if nothing has ever happened. I never wanted to be a part of their world, but I didn't want to feel like a virus in their world either. I sit in my car a little longer and work on letting go of what I once considered family. They will always be tied to me and they will still affect me. But at this moment, I really don't care.

Putting the car in drive, I flip a quick U-turn with the intention of heading home. But a few turns later, I find myself at the last place I thought I would be. Staring at the apartment complex, with its paint-faded siding, and orange-yellow lights lighting the stairwells, I climb out and make my way over to park bench. I start reminiscing about all the parties and cookouts we had here when Milo and I shared an apartment during college.

The cold from the bench seeps through my jeans. The complex has no real character to it other than the typical cream-colored siding and tan bricks. It's close to campus and a little nicer than the dorms. The only drawback is that the air surrounding the complex carries faint odors of pizza and macaroni and cheese.

I find myself missing those days and I wonder if I went wrong somewhere. I wonder what my path might have been like if I would have stayed here. My dad offered to hire a nurse to take care of him so I could stay in school. He didn't want me to quit, but I couldn't deal with something happening to him and not being there. We all knew he wasn't going to survive and I could not let that happen without trying to help. He was angry with me for a while, but stopped fighting me as he got worse. Not because he was grateful for me sticking around, but because he was tired.

What if I would have gone on to become an architect like I had always wanted to be? Would I have switched majors to become a doctor? Would I have graduated with a generic degree to find myself in the sea of hopeful students waiting for that perfect job offer? Would I still have ended up right where I am now, questioning my life choices?

A group of people move down the stairwell and fill it with laughter and shouts. They are all clad in stylish bar clothing. All of them are in dark jeans. The girls are dressed in flashy tops and the guys in button-ups. They look ready for a night out and a long morning. Amidst the flirtatious looks they are throwing to one another, it's easy to see something will go down tonight.

"Harley, what are you doing here?"

A concerned, familiar voice fills my head. I don't have an answer. The lamppost shines bright behind him, but I know who it is. Thatcher stands in front of me. His ever-present smile peers down at me.

"Are you ok?" I can hear the concern in his deep voice.

"Yeah, I just thought I would stroll through my old stomping grounds. What are you doing here?

"I live here," he confirms.

"Still? I thought you would have moved out and got a nicer place with your law degree and fancy job."

"Why pay more for a place that you only use for sleep?"

I shake my head at how cheap Thatcher can be at times. He may come across glitzy and all show, but he is always looking for deals and ways to cut costs. He and Jake still probably room together to save money.

"What are you guys up to?" I glance over at the group. Jake is waiting there with the two girls.

"We are headed over to the bar to end the weekend. Are you here by yourself?"

"Yeah, I just dropped Reed off at the airport." *A few hours ago*, I add in my head. How did I waste that much time?

"You can come with us," Thatcher adds. I glance back to see a couple pouty faces at the thought of a newcomer.

"It's ok. I should be heading back home," I say. I see their faces lift in what they might consider a friendly smile but which actually screams at me to go away.

Thatcher watches me for a minute and rubs his smooth jaw. "Hey guys, I'll catch up with you in a bit," he hollers over his shoulder without turning away from me. That rewards me with chilling dagger eyes from the girls. I roll my eyes and head for my car.

His long strides almost leave me behind. He reaches the driver side before me and opens it, motioning for me to get in. I give him another eye roll but get in.

"Where are we headed?" I ask, trying not to show how happy I am that I'm not by myself right now.

"You said you were visiting your old stomping grounds and I think that sounds fun. What's next on your list?"

I look over at him to see his grin and I know just the place.

30

HARLEY

We order our drinks at O'Shay's Pub. This is where I met Thatcher. Like most college bars, it has pool tables. Back in college, as usual, Nikki, Milo, and I were playing 8-Ball and totally trashing one another. At a nearby pool table, Thatcher Sutton first attempted to pick me up and has continued his pursuit of me for the last several years.

Thatcher has always been adorable. At times, he even seems attractive. To his disappointment, he has always been, and will always be, a friend. I always thought it would be nice to be more, but it just never could have happened.

He notices I am staring at our pool table. "You know I promised myself that day that I would never stop trying to win you over."

"Why did you then?" The question startles me and apparently him too. "You were standing at my bar a few weeks ago and you said 'I think this is where I leave you.' As if that comment was you parting ways with me. If I recall correctly, I was dating Lance when we first met and that didn't derail you from your promise. So, what changed?"

"You did." His comment is light as if that should be enough of an answer. He picks up another fry but pauses before eating it. He catches my confused look. "I saw a change in you the day we went skiing. I'm not saying that Reed is the one for you or that you are meant for one another. I don't believe in fairy tales. I do believe, however, that people come into our lives for a reason." This is why Thatcher and I are great friends.

The irony is not lost on me as those are the exact words I told Reed almost twenty-four hours ago. He drops the fry on his plate and really looks at me.

"I saw how happy you were that day. I saw the old spirit of Harley that I fell for that day at that pool table." He points over to the pool table where we first interacted. "You lit up like the Fourth of July. I noticed the light inside you was dimming as your relationship with Lance continued. My commitment to winning you over stayed steady and true because I wanted to bring that light back." He smiles at me and I see how sweet Thatcher is and how genuine his heart has been for me.

"That day on the mountaintop… I saw the light again, only to find out someone else had brought it back. I knew I couldn't compete with him. He had only been here a short while, while on the other hand… I had been there for four years."

"I'm sorry," I said meekly.

"Don't be, because I'm not." He leans over and kisses my forehead while pulling me into a one-sided hug. I wince and he notices. "See, I can do this and it's not weird. I can come see you and it won't be awkward. I am glad I have spent the last four years trying to make the sourpuss in you happy. All because I cherish the friendship I have with you." He pauses and gets a little hesitant.

"What?" I ask because I don't like the look he is giving me.

"Something happened." He eyes my neck and cheek. I hadn't re-applied makeup so the light shade of discoloring is starting to show through. "Please tell me the bruise on your cheek didn't come from him," he asks quietly. His eyes search for the truth and I can tell he is making sure to watch for any signs of a lie coming.

I smirk. "Which him?" He doesn't like my sarcasm. "That would be Lance," I say matter-of-factly.

"Did Lance hit you while you guys were dating?"

This is one of the many realities I hid from. "A few times," I finally admit after deciding I am no longer going to let this control my future.

"You don't fit the battered woman stereotype. What happened?" Thatcher asks, shocked.

"When we started dating, he seemed nice. Did you know we kind of knew each other before college?" I rhetorically ask.

"His family is well known in the next town over. Lance's parents owned a bank and Lance always had whatever he wanted thanks to their wealth. He was pretty spoiled and threw tantrums when he didn't get his way. The tantrums got bigger as Lance got bigger. When my dad got sick and I went home to take care of him, and I was slightly shocked that Lance stood by my decision to leave school and come home. Hind-sight I guess it put him at ease to know exactly where I was and freeing him up to cheat whenever he felt like it."

"Our first incident happened when I came back to the city to visit over a weekend. Lance had some study group he was involved in. It was probably a cover for him meeting up with my sister. Nikki and Milo took me out. When I got back to his apartment, he was livid that I wasn't there when he got home. We fought and he shoved me pretty hard. I knocked over a lamp as I fell and got cut on the glass. I thought I was okay, and he apologized profusely, so I let it go. I realize now that that was my first mistake.

"Where it went south was after my dad died. My dad was the only blood family that genuinely cared about me. I knew deep down that I needed to cut Lance loose, but I just didn't have the energy to leave him. I was trying to run a business and grieve for my dad. We only spent some weekends together, so as long as I kept him happy it wasn't bad. It was pretty easy to keep him happy."

"I don't need to know how you kept him happy," Thatcher interrupts. I laugh and punch him in the arm. I know he is serious about what he said, but I also know Thatcher needs a break from the heaviness of this. Humor is how he copes with what I am telling him.

"Since he had proposed before my dad's death, the wedding was still scheduled and our moms were planning the event. I just had to show up, which meant I found him cheating on me with my sister. After that, it all became a sick, twisted game. Lance's angle was only to get one thing. He cheated because I wasn't around to fill that need."

"Harley…" Thatcher warns me to let me know he doesn't want to picture it.

"Shelby's game was to get back at me for her daddy issues," I continue. "She didn't like how close my dad and I were, so taking something away from me made her feel like she was winning. After the wedding was canceled, the game changed completely. I thought since Lance and I were over he would move on. Instead, he used Shelby to show me he wasn't going away. Shelby believed he was choosing her over me. Lance told me those details once as a twisted addition to his attempts to manipulate me. I kept the lines of communication open in hopes of protecting Shelby."

"Why was he so obsessed with you? I mean, you're a great girl, but if he was going to cheat, what did it matter if you were a part of the picture or not?" Thatcher asked.

"Lance is the jealous type. If he can't have it, no one can." I stare blankly at the television screens hanging from the ceiling. I feel sick about how much control I had allowed one guy to have over my life.

"What aren't you telling me?" Thatcher's practice in law has aided him in knowing when details are being omitted.

"I always wondered how our relationship would have gone," I admit. "I've thought about how you would have been an equal partner to me. When people asked why we weren't together, I always told them it was because you wanted to stay in the city."

Thatcher looks at me, stunned. "I would have gone wherever I needed to if it meant being with you."

"I knew that, and still know that, but we could never be together. Lance was threatened by you."

"Reading between the lines, Lance hurt you because of me," Thatcher concluded, "and not just with a punch or a kick?"

Thatcher can't bring himself to say the word rape any more then I can, but I didn't need to confirm his statement. Nor did I need him to know in what way I was hurt that night. I had relived that night way too many times in my nightmares.

"I could have taken this to my grave with me, but I need you to know that your feelings were never just one-sided. After the wedding was canceled and we went on a few of those dates, I was reminded too much…" I left the statement hanging. I was not sure how to finish it. "Bet you hate him more now than you ever thought you could?" I ask sarcastically.

His jaw clenches. "More than you know."

I take sips from my beer just to give him a few minutes to digest this information.

"So what caused this lashing?" Thatcher motions towards my bruises.

"Lance found out that Reed was staying with me. But this time, Reed kicked his ass and I pressed charges."

He looks satisfied with the story's outcome. "I'm not sure I liked that Reed was staying with you either, but I'm thankful that the guy was around. I would have liked to kick Lance's ass too. I am glad, though, that you chose someone decent, otherwise my ego would have been deflated like a grandma's saggy boobs."

I laugh out loud. "That's just unattractive and not true. Your ego would have gone from a double D to C cup, but never deflated." He knows it too and chuckles as he nudges me away. I can tell that Thatcher is not his relaxed, carefree self yet. He is still bothered by the history of Lance in my life. I see him trying to move past it all because that's what Thatcher does. He doesn't hold on to things he can't change.

"Lee, you know I love you."

I'm sure at one point his love was an infatuated love, but the way he is looking at me right now is a much more understanding kind of love. There is a sweetness to it.

I kiss his cheek and look him in the eye. "Thank you." Two simple words carried so much weight in them. Thatcher's cheeks heat with the slightest blush. I have never seen that on him before. I hope he finds someone who can cherish him like he cherishes me.

When dinner is gone and all of our memories of college and the last four years are accounted for, we head back to the car.

"Why did you come by the apartment?" His question is still one I don't have an answer for. In the past, I would have shrugged and not said much. After spending time with Reed, I learned it isn't bad to let people in.

"With Reed gone… I guess I just feel a little lost. It got me thinking that most people get lost while they are at college. It's where they get to change majors and figure out who they are. I never got that chance. I guess my chance is now though. The businesses are perfectly fine. They have people who know how to carry them on; therefore, I'm not needed as much anymore. I want to figure out where I want to go from here."

"So… where are you going?"

"I thought I would travel, since that's what some college kids do after graduation."

"Want company?" he asked. I glance over to give him my full attention. "I never got to backpack across the U.S."

"I thought you backpacked across Europe?"

"Like I said, not across the U.S. Besides, I think you need a wingman at the bars we will be hitting along the way."

I know he is just looking out for my safety. He is the one full of adventure though. He will expand my life experiences much more than me just driving in a car, going from town to town.

"I would love to have a partner in crime."

"But…" Thatcher's lawyering kicks in again.

"If I don't leave tonight, I don't know if I will."

"Then let's go." His eyes gleam with excitement.

When we reach his apartment complex, Thatcher dashes out of the car with his phone to his ear. Not even five minutes later, he dashes out the door with a handful of crumpled clothing. He shoves them inside a small duffle bag as he quickly moves down the stairs.

"Highway," he says while he continues making arrangements with someone else on the other end of the phone. I put the car in drive and we are off.

Highway signs zoom behind us as the city lights disappear. It's never too late to turn around, but the more distance that is between the car and the city, the less the fear takes over me. The car is completely quiet, but I feel like I am in an overcrowded dining hall in my head. Every concern I have is echoing and bouncing around in my head.

"Lee, relax. It's a vacation," Thatcher says, taking one of my hands off the wheel. He massages my white knuckles as I sheepishly grin at him. "Roll down the windows," he instructs, cranking up the music. I do as he requests and he lets out a crow. I laugh when he nudges me to join him. He continues to crow until I join in. I laugh even harder as stress and tension leave my body. I let out a shout of freedom.

31

REED

I plow into my hotel bed late one night after a long day of work. We have hit the major European cities for a series of "World Premier" parties for a movie Zoey and I did before I took my vacation. There are tons of screaming fans at each location and countless interviews. Everyone has the same types of questions, though maybe worded a little differently. There are autographs, film screenings, celebrity one-on-ones, and then we can head back to the hotel. The same rituals with different faces, in different cities - all of which we have been to before. It's all part of the job.

I breathe in the clean smell of the bed, which I realize is probably covered in someone else's dead skin cells. I roll over onto my back and quickly try to erase that thought. I lay there, fully clothed, with every light on in the tiny room and the television on a low hum. I am too tired to do anything but stare at the ceiling.

My cell vibrates in my pocket. Retrieving it, I see my parent's phone number appear on the screen. I couldn't help but smile at karma for making them call me at this moment. They always call when I'm in a sour mood.

"Hello," I say in the best *normal* voice I can muster.

"Happy Thanksgiving kiddo!" Lisa's voice rings through. She told me once that no matter how old I get, I will always be her kiddo. I stopped arguing with her years ago.

"Happy Thanksgiving," I respond back.

"Just thought I would check to see how you are doing?"

She has been checking on me quite a bit since I called them when I got back to L.A. When I saw Zoey sitting in the conference room, I realized how done I was with the game.

Being around Harley helped me see who I want to be. I had excused myself before even going into the conference room with Zoey. All I wanted to do was talk to Jerry and Lisa. I needed to make sure they were going to be okay with the ramifications of whatever I decided in that meeting room that day. I needed to make sure they understood my actions would affect their lives. They reassured me that they have had, and always will have, my back. My story would always be theirs too and nothing could ever change that.

"I'm doing good." It's not a lie, but it feels like it is.

"I may not have raised you from when you were a little boy, but I still know my son. Tell me how you really are Reed."

The sound of her calling me son tears at my heart. She may not have known me before I was fourteen, but she could always see through any wall I put up.

"I'm good. Just tired."

"Well, good news, no gossip leaks have happened here on the home front." I am silent for a beat and she continues, "You miss her?"

When she found out that I spent time in Middleton, I told her about Nikki, Milo, and Harley. She quickly decided that I had interest in Harley. She said her woman's intuition pointed her in that direction.

"Always." I decide it's not worth lying to her about it.

I think about Harley a lot. My mood sinks a little more now that we are talking about her. I think about what she is doing. I glance over at the clock to check the time. I can picture her at the bar closing up. Alone. I can't fight my worry for her safety.

But I also think about what she said about playing Drew. "Hey, I got the roll of Drew in the movie *A Single Rose*," I tell Lisa.

"Wow, Reed. That sounds great." I hear her trying to be happy for me but clearly she's worried about how playing someone so evil will affect me. I try to ease her worries because I don't need any more worry in my head right now.

"It doesn't start filming until next fall," I say, hoping that will give her time to get better at lying to me about her support for the role.

She changes the subject. "How is Zoey?"

"She is still angry at me," I confess. Zoey's been mad at me since our meeting in L.A., because I wouldn't agree to be the baby's father publicly. Unfortunately, she has miscarried. "Publicly, she's handling the miscarriage part fine, but I know it tears her apart when she's alone," I add, feeling Lisa's motherly instincts also resting behind that question.

We talk for a little longer about Thanksgiving dinner and who was there. She shares the family gossip. She warms my heart and I get homesick. I tell her that I have more interviews to promote the current movie when I get stateside. After that, in the mix of everything surrounding Christmas, I am supposed to start shooting another rom-com with Zoey.

"I feel like Middleton changed you. You seem more at peace, but a little lost." Lisa knows how to move conversations from heavy to light back to heavy, with no hesitation.

"When I was there, I realized that all I had been doing over the last several years was running. I thought I was running from who I didn't want to be, but I was actually running from who I really am. I can't take away my past because my past made me. I just can't let it control my future, but that is exactly what I have been doing."

"Sounds like you needed Middleton, kiddo." She pauses but I can tell she's not done talking about Middleton. More likely she's not done talking about Harley. She finally gets to her point. "How did you and Harley part? Are you trying to make the long-distance thing work?"

"No… we know it won't work. Our paths were only meant to touch." Harley had used those words a lot and I find myself using them as well.

"I agree. I feel like that path was only set up for heartache with the distance and different lifestyles. Do you think it's time to close that chapter and move on?"

I know she's trying to be supportive, but I am not mentally ready to let Harley or Middleton go yet.

"It's not just about Harley though," I get a little defensive. "It was the town and the experience. People there were so kind and didn't care about who I am or what I can do for them. It was like a big extended family. They gossiped just as much as the tabloids but their hearts were genuine."

"Sounds like a small town." I could hear the nostalgic smile in her voice, but I knew she didn't trust small-town people. Lisa and Jerry raised us in a small town. Once we all left, they did too. In her mind, there are two types of small-town people. Type one: the ones who want everyone to stay in the small town, to never grow, and to never go anywhere. Type two: the ones who would do anything to get out of a small town.

"You wouldn't understand," I mumble to myself.

"You're right," she surrenders, "I wouldn't understand, nor do I care to understand. All I want is for you to be okay. I'm worried about you taking on this 'Drew' role all because some girl thinks you should." She wasn't even keen on me being involved with any part of the movie to begin with. I wasn't surprised at all when I only received disapproval from her when I announced the part I had been picked for.

"Mom," I say endearingly, knowing this will get her attention, "I know you are scared, but please trust me. Give me a chance to show you that I am stronger today about my past than I ever have been." Since she hasn't seen me since I left the east coast a few months ago, she must still think of me as the broken son who showed up to tell them bad news. I understand her point of view. "I'll come see you when the tour is over, before I start filming the movie. I think that will help you relax."

I hear her take a deep breath and let it out slowly. "Okay," she says. I take the opportunity to turn the conversation light again. She takes the bait and we end the conversation on a positive, upbeat note. When I end the call, I am more exhausted than I was when I first reached my room.

There is tapping on my door in our code.

"I'm not here for that," Zoey hisses at me when I open the door with a huge grin. Her red-rimmed eyes are swollen and my heart sinks a little. I wasn't in the mood for "friends with benefits" either. I can't deny, though, that since she's been mad at me because of our meeting, I was looking forward to turning her down. The obviousness that she has been crying is a game changer.

"Nice to see you too, Princess," I say in my usual sarcastic tone with her, trying to bring back our old banter. "What brings you by then?"

"I've been doing some thinking and I miss having my friend. I've realized that I've made you my scapegoat for a lot of things. So… I am hoping you can forgive me."

We used to be close, but with celebrity rumors, drama, and the push and pull of our lives, we've ended up fighting most of the time. I step aside to let her in. She crawls into my bed and curls into a ball. "So how do we start this friend thing back up again?" she asks.

"By being honest with each other." I plop on the bed next to her. "How are you holding up?

"Fantastic," she says distantly. "I thought we would talk about you first. I'm not ready to deal with all my mess yet." She gives me a small smile.

I chuckle and abide, "Okay, where do we start with me then?" After my vacation and facing a lot of my past, I'm ready to talk about anything Zoey throws at me. I miss having friends around. Thanks to Middleton, I realize how much more fun friends can be.

"Where did you disappear to?"

"I first went to see Jerry and Lisa. I knew those drug accusations were going to hit the news when I left, thanks to *your* team, and I wanted them to be prepared. I also went to my brother's parole hearing."

I look her in the eye, waiting for her judgment. Zoey is three people in one body. She can either love you, judge you, or hate you. I have seen and been affected by all spectrums of Zoey. When Zoey loves you, she can become a true, concerned friend, which will outweigh the other two Zoey's. Tonight, her eyes are full of concern.

"The tabloids have some facts correct, but most are incorrect. Surprise, surprise," I mock.

This statement leads to a flurry of questions. Zoey heard the rumors from her staff about how my birth father murdered someone and that I grew up without a mom. She admits that when she met Jerry and Lisa, she assumed it was all gossip. For the first time in our friendship, she asks to know the details of my upbringing. I share about the murder and how it has affected me. I tell her about Blaine and his drug abuse, along with his police record. While Zoey sits there listening intently, I find myself grateful that I refused to claim Zoey's baby as mine. If it weren't for that decision, her team never would have leaked my past, and Zoey and I would not be discovering such a deeper understanding of each other.

She asks questions about Blaine's trial hearing. I explain that I feel guilty for being happy that he is still in jail. The Blaine that I saw on that stand looked so devoid of humanity that I feared for what he would do if they released him. His psych evaluations proved that he still isn't remorseful for any of his actions. It just makes me sick. I tell her that I'm sad that the baby brother I knew has turned into that kind of person.

As much as I am grateful for the rekindled friendship with Zoey, this discussion drives my pain about Harley deeper. I miss Harley and our fireside chats. I miss her cocked smiles and sarcastic laughs. I miss the spunk she brought to my life. Zoey has had her fair share of struggles, but my heart aches for Harley's deep understanding about deeply broken families.

"From there, I started heading back to L.A., but my car broke down." I hesitated after that. I thought I was ready to talk about everything with Zoey, but Middleton was something I wanted to keep for myself. The conversation with Lisa tonight put a damper on me wanting to talk about Harley and Middleton. I know Lisa means well, but she hadn't gone through the experiences I did while I was there. I feel like there is a disconnect between my reality and what Lisa is mistaking as my romanticizing a small town. I question Zoey's capabilities to understand it as well.

"What's her name?" Zoey asks. She catches me off guard.

"What makes you ask that?"

"Will, your lip twitched into a slight smile when you said your car broke down. Then you just stopped talking. If there wasn't a girl, you would have continued with how you worked your way back," she smarts off at me.

I've heard the name Will for a few weeks now, but it still feels strange to be called that in private spaces. It makes me miss Harley and Reed that much more. But to try and correct Zoey and have her call me Reed after all this time seems pointless.

"There was a girl," I concede. I had also forgotten how well Zoey knows me. "But she has a life set up in Middleton and I have this life. I travel and work all the time. It would never work."

I pause, sensing or maybe hoping that Zoey will understand my experience in Middleton. "It's not just the girl though. The whole trip allowed me time to realize that when I left the Montgomery's house after high school, I was trying to find myself. Looking at everything I've accomplished, I always thought that would have helped me identify who I am."

"But you realized it amounts to nothing. We've been playing parts, not just in movies, but in our real lives," Zoey concludes for me.

I beam because she really does get it.

"I was mad at you for not playing the part anymore. I had all this pressure to be the 'it' couple and you just walked away from me and the baby."

"Zoey, I only walked away from the part, not from you. Besides, there would've been no way Isaac, *the real father*, would have agreed to being a closet dad. I know you guys had a few fights about him being pushed into the background. He really cares about you. So do I."

She breathes out a shaky breath, "I guess it doesn't matter now since there isn't a baby."

I scoot closer to her, pull the blankets over us, and wrap her into a hug. "I'm sorry." The words aren't much and will never heal the pain. Only time will, but words are all I have to offer.

We sit in silence the rest of the night.

32

HARLEY

Weeks have passed. Thatcher and I are stopped somewhere in Ohio for a late afternoon lunch. The quaint diner has antique tools mounted on the walls and the staff is busy decorating for Christmas. The booths have seen better days and the smell of grease hangs heavy in the air.

It wasn't long after Thatcher and I started our trek that Milo called to inform me that my sister is suing me for my father's estate. Milo was a great help to me in finding the paperwork that Thatcher needed to represent me in the lawsuit. During several phone calls between Milo and Thatcher, we were assured that my father had protected me. Thanks to my father's clear directions in his final will, the business and the house would remain with me. Milo was able to locate documents which will be strong enough to hold up in court. I wasn't worried about the shop or my money as much as I was worried about Bromley. If Shelby would have been able to take over my father's house, she would have easily kicked me out. Then I would have lost what I had left of my childhood and the roof over my head.

Our waitress brings our food out. Dousing the perfect greasy burger with condiments, I feel Thatcher's hand pat my arm. I glance up to see his eyes trained over my shoulder. I turn around to see what has his attention and then a rock sinks in my stomach.

A small television behind the counter flashes a gossip news show with a bar scrolling across the bottom of the screen: "William Montgomery is the son of a murderer." They were displaying pictures of him and what I assume are his adoptive parents, his incarcerated father's mug shot, and a few other random pictures.

This was bad. When Reed left, I could tell he wasn't looking forward to going back. He had expressed a few times how desperately he had tried to keep that part of his life a secret. Now it was all over the news.

I walk over to the television to see if I can hear what they are saying, but the story has changed to focus on Zoey and how there had been rumors about a possible pregnancy. The report went on but my mind zoned out. Flashes of Reed's face before he left kept repeating in my mind. He looked so discouraged and defeated. My mind was trying to connect pieces of why this information had been leaked.

Thatcher walks up behind me and startles me. "I paid, we can go." Forgetting about the food, we walk out of the diner.

We are silent for several miles. The newsreel of Reed keeps playing through my mind. In all of the snapshots, Reed's shoulders were always back and strong. Even in the few where his head was hanging in efforts to avoid the cameras, he looked strong and confident.

"So… is it true?" Thatcher's voice breaks my thoughts.

"Yeah," I answer softly. "He never wanted it to leak but it appears it did anyway."

"You swear he never laid a hand on you?" he presses.

I want to crassly tell him that Reed never laid a hand on me I didn't want, but I didn't feel like right now was the time given the way Thatcher was looking at me.

"I promise."

He doesn't say anything for a while. Time passes and we finally find our groove again.

Town by town, city by city, we make our way across the states to the Big Apple. Christmas is around the corner but I can't bring myself to go home yet. Nikki has been pestering me to go back but the thought of home doesn't feel welcoming.

Thatcher has been gone from his job too long and his father is hounding him to come back. Knowing our time is ending, we pool our money and decide to splurge on the famous Plaza Hotel. Figuring we would finish our vacation with a bang, we requested a suite with two rooms to give us space to sprawl out. We spent several days in New York doing all the big touristy attractions we could think of.

"What are you going to do now?" He asks me over lunch on our last day together.

"Long-term plans, I don't know. But current plans are to go see some of the smaller museums we have missed."

"I think I will pass. I am museum'ed out. Will I see you at the room later for dinner before I have to leave for the airport?"

I nod and grab my coat. Thatcher remains seated at the table. I glance back at him and raise my hand to wave but stop as our waitress pauses to talk to him. She leans in flirtatiously and he chuckles while winking at her. Typical Thatcher - always wooing the ladies no matter where he is. The image of the two of them reassures me that he will be fine, as always.

Walking in New York is amazing. There are people from all walks of life around me and it is a great place to people watch. Across the street, a man hurries along the sidewalk checking his watch. He crosses the road and horns blare at him for not using the crosswalk. I make up my own story for why he is in a hurry but continue on my way.

Down a few streets from the restaurant, there is a hipster in a hat, bright red lipstick, and high-wasted shorts and leggings. I pull my coat tighter around myself as I feel the cold winter air whip around me. I wonder how she isn't freezing. She passes by, walking as though she hasn't a care in the world.

I cross the street and have a few more blocks to go before I reach the first museum I want to see. As I approach, the crowd gathered around one of the main news media buildings gets much louder than a typical New York City street. The closer I get, the more curious I become about who they are getting autographs from.

Then it dawns on me. It's the movie... It's *his* movie. I see the top of a blonde head bent down signing someone's poster. When her face pops up, it is tan and covered with a wide, movie-star-worthy smile. Zoey is several feet away from me but it feels like she is mere inches from me.

To her left, he stands. His smile is genuine and kind. It's the smile I saw so many times when cleaning up the bar or glancing up when I needed a break from working the books. My heart hurts knowing that this sight is all I will get of him. We have become the classic Romeo and Juliet, star-crossed lovers from two different worlds.

Zoey's eyes catch mine and it's obvious on her face that she recognizes me, but I don't know how. I duck through the crowd and head to the museum across the street. I let my heart sulk as my feet carry me away from him. After seeing Reed, I know that he is the reason I don't want to go home. He isn't there. I liked coming home to him. I liked his random pop-ins at the shop. I liked closing the bar down with him. I miss him and I'm not sure I'm ready to go back to life where he isn't there.

I blankly stare at the abstract art in front of me. I am lost in my gloom.

"Did you come here for him?" The voice startles me. Zoey, in all her perfection, stands and watches me. I glance at my watch to see that the museum is closing and I don't know how long I have been standing here.

"How did you know it was me?" I ask.

"He's mentioned you and your friends, showed me a picture of all of you, but he doesn't really like to talk about you guys."

"No." I glance back at the art in front of me answering her first question. "I didn't come here for him. It's just a coincidence that we are both here." I turn to face her again. "When he left, we stopped talking."

She stands there studying me. "How is he doing?" I ask. My voice is softer then I would prefer.

"How do you think he's doing?" Her statement comes out surprisingly gentle.

"The pictures the tabloids show try to make him seem ashamed, but he always has his shoulders back and he looks strong to me. But that's a picture." I sadly realize that this will be the only Reed I will now see.

"I think you know him better than you think you do." Zoey sits on the bench that is facing the painting and studies it. "He's changed... he's more settled."

"I think it's time for me to go," I abruptly state. I can feel my heart in my throat. "Please don't tell him I'm here."

"Why?" She asks puzzled.

I want to tell her that it's killing me to be in the same city with him. That I want to move on from him. That any further relationship would only end in frustration. But I settle on, "because seeing each other won't change our situation."

She nods slightly and I quickly turn to make my way out of the museum. I feel my heart breaking. Each step that takes me away from Reed leaves a piece of my heart behind.

Back at the hotel, I kick my shoes off and stretch out on the couch. Thatcher is a procrastinator and, as always, is running around trying to gather all his belongings. He crams them into his small suitcase. I chuckle quietly as I remember how we left with almost nothing and now he is struggling to get it all in the one single bag.

Thatcher pauses in the middle of the room. After scanning to make sure he has gathered everything in the main quarters, he rushes back to his room.

There is a knock on the door and I begrudgingly swing my legs over to the floor. Rule number one: always check the peephole to see who is on the other side. I neglect this rule and swing the door wide open.

His eyes are wild with disbelief, shock, excitement, and anger. His body fills the door frame and his hand thwacks the door to make sure it can't be closed on him. I am frozen. I don't know how he found me, but I am so thankful he has.

I throw myself at Reed. My lips lock onto his. He hesitates for a second. Then his hands find my waist and push me up against the nearest wall inside the room. Our kiss draws deeper and heats with need. We have been separated for weeks but this kiss feels like we've been separated for years. I can't get enough and I want more. I want to be closer to him.

Reed gently pulls back with heaving breaths. "I thought I saw you today. It's really you," he says in a whisper as his fingers move over my swollen lips, over my cheeks, and into in my hair. Reed is pawing me like crazy and I giggle with excitement. I am lost in him. I kiss him again and draw him back to me.

His hands grab the backside of my thighs and he hoists me up. My legs wrap around his hips. A very noisy hitch in my breathing causes a low chuckle from him that I feel reverberating all through my body.

Needing him closer, I start tearing at his clothes. Between kisses he asks the question, "Why didn't you stop?"

In that moment, Thatcher emerges from his room. My head doesn't turn but Reed's does. His body stiffens and he sets me down. Turning slowly to see Thatcher standing there with his bags in hand, I see Thatcher's regretful face as he realizes that we have company.

"It's not what you think," Thatcher says as he sees Reed's confused expression.

Reed's confusion is quickly replaced with a hurt. Then his eyes begin to harden as his mind seems to cross a line I can not redraw and I'm sure he won't listen to my explanation. I can see his mind is made up. My face must show my increasing anger because Reed looks startled for a slight moment when our eyes meet again, but his shifts back to disgust.

"Seriously?!" He deadpans at me.

"No matter what I tell you, you have your mind made up," I bat back at him.

"Try me? Why is he here then?"

"I wanted company." Jealousy brews in his jaw and I'm annoyed that he thinks so little of me. "I thought you knew me better than that."

"I thought I knew you better than that too."

"You're an ass! You can leave the same way you came in." I wave my hand in the direction of the door. Reed is frozen in his spot so I shove past him and make my way over to Thatcher. "Thank you for coming with me and have a safe trip home." I hear the door shut behind us.

"I didn't know. I'm sorry. I would have just stayed in my room if I would have known he was here."

"Thatch, it's not your fault. It's his. Now go before you miss your flight." I kiss him on the cheek, turn on my heel, and head towards my room. I am ready to scream because my anger is too much right now, but instead tears well up behind my eyes.

33

REED

I impatiently hit the elevator call button. I want to get out of this hotel as fast as I can. I text my driver to be ready. Frustration is brewing as I had seen Harley so many times in my dreams that I thought I was dreaming today when I saw her on the street. I kept telling myself all afternoon that there was no way it could be her in New York City, but I couldn't shake off the feeling that she really might be here.

Throughout the day, my publicist kept critiquing my facial expressions in between interviews. She thought I was holding my shoulders weird or my mouth was too pouty. Zoey was silently watching me too, but for a different reason that I could not figure out. Then she finally revealed what I had been struggling with all afternoon.

"You saw her," Zoey states with a sigh, like she found the missing puzzle piece. We are alone in the press junket room waiting for the next interviewer to come in and fire the next round of questions.

"How do you know?"

"I saw her too and talked to her."

"What?" I shriek. "When and why are you telling me now?"

"I saw her this afternoon, but I didn't tell you because she didn't want you to know she was here. But I am a true romantic at heart, so… go find her." She is grinning at me.

Having Harley back in my arms was indescribable. I never wanted to let her go, but when I saw movement out the corner of my eye and realized it was Thatcher, everything just fell apart. I knew they had a history, but after the connection we had I thought it would have taken her longer to move on. Lord knows I haven't moved on. *How could she?*

The elevator doors finally ding open. I get in, press the lobby floor, and repeatedly smash the "close door" button. When the doors start to close, I feel a weight lifting off my chest and my breathing starts to ease. Just like in my movies, a hand slams on the door to stop my hasty escape from someone I would rather be running to.

Thatcher looks pissed off and glares at me. He steps into the elevator and blocks me in so I can't get around him without a fight. I refuse to let him get the better of me, so I stay, but the pissing war is very present.

"Really? That's how you want to leave it?" Thatcher says calmly, but heat rests firmly in his face.

"Fuck you," I snarl.

"You don't know her at all," he retorts as he steps closer to challenge me. This only pisses me off more and I square my shoulders. Thatcher continues talking calmly. "When you left, she looked lost."

"So you thought you would save her? Get in her bed?"

"No, and fuck you back for thinking so little of her. Harley never needed saving. Everyone thought that, but what she needed was strength. She needed someone to believe in her."

"And that was you?" I spit out.

"No Reed, it was you! It has always been you!" His angry glare bores into me deeper.

I'm caught off guard and stay silent as I get even more pissed. Does he really know her? She did need saving. She wasn't living. She was only existing.

The elevator doors open. "You better fix what broke before she shuts you out completely." Thatcher shouts and slings his bag over his shoulder and walks out.

People in the lobby stare at us, waiting to see if a fight is about to happen. My heart is pounding in my chest, but I have no words to yell back at Thatcher and he is already out the doors anyways. I slowly become aware of the fact that the on-lookers are pulling out phones and taking snap-shots. I duck my head and make my way out of the lobby to the town car that is waiting for me to take me back to my own hotel.

Back in my own suite, I slam the door and kick my shoes off. One slams against the wall.

"Wow, I never thought I would see that temper tantrum again," Zoey chides as she checks for damage on the wall my shoe hit. "Didn't go well?"

"No!" I bark and storm into the small kitchenette to grab the first bottle of liquor I can get my hands on. I take two giant swigs. I see Zoey watch me with disapproval. That frustrates me more and I take another long pull from the bottle.

"What happened?" She tries coaxing the story out of me and sits at the bar stool nearby. "And pour it in a glass, you were raised bet-ter...and pour me one too while you're at it?"

My head snaps to her.

"What? I want a drink." Zoey shrugs and then nudges me, "So what happened?"

"I went to her room and she was with Thatcher," I huff out.

"The ex?" Her shock makes her voice squeaky.

"No, that's Lance. Thatcher is a *friend*." I make air quotes around friend before taking another swallow.

"Glass!" Zoey corrects me one more time. I grab two tumblers, set them in front of us, and pour us each a good-sized amount. "Since when do you drink?"

"Not now. So, if they are friends, what's the issue?"

"You make me sound petulant."

"Well, you threw your shoe and you are drinking because you are pissed over a *friend,*" she states.

"Well, you don't know them."

"No, I don't, but what did she say?" I don't want to answer this question because I sense a trap so I take another drink. She pulls the bottle and glass away from me.

"You're not getting drunk over this. You're going to deal with it. Now what did she say?"

"I left before she could explain. But you don't understand." I start to defend myself from her judgmental look. "Thatcher followed me out and we got into a pissing war." My head is starting to buzz a little and all I see is Thatcher glaring back at me.

"I feel like you aren't being honest with me." Zoey and her ability to cut through my crap is kicking my ass right now so I snag her drink and she presses her lips into a thin line.

"Fine, it appeared he was leaving, but that doesn't mean they weren't sleeping together." Then Thatcher's words ring in my head. "I think I messed up, Zoey."

34

HARLEY

I spend the rest of the night in restless frustration because of how Reed left. After all that time we spent together, it cut me deep that he assumed I'd run to Thatcher in that way. I was ready to go home. I was ready to move on and get back to my regular life. I was done running. Reed's exit today helped close a revolving door that hoped we could be together - that there might be a way for "us" to work out.

In the morning, I book an afternoon flight home. I figure I can have my car shipped back. Sadly, continuing the trip had lost all appeal to me. I pack everything up in the suite and check the clock. There are still several hours before I need to leave.

Bundling up, I head down to the park for a stroll to stretch my legs and waste time. Rounding a corner, my heart jumps when I see a movie crew adjusting cameras, shouting directions, and calling for more help to do this or that. I approach the barricade to see what is going on. That's when I see Reed. He looks frustrated and flustered as Zoey hangs on him. My temper spikes.

I glance around me to see that no one is paying any attention to me. I scale the barricade like a farm girl hopping a country fence. I roll my shoulders back as if I belong here. The hurt is raw and exposed. I push pass people as I make a direct line towards Reed. Some take notice of me but most don't put much thought into what's going on. I pass the cameras and I have clear shot at him.

"You!" I shout before I can second-guess myself. He clambers out of Zoey's snake-wrapped arms and strides confidently and angrily towards me. "You had no right to be angry with me." I yell, "There was never anything between us except a few make-out sessions here and there. You never expressed feelings and neither did I. You have no right to be jealous, mad, or have any feelings that stem from a relationship status that never existed. Besides, you where the one who bust into my world and left without a second glance back."

He screams back at me. "Don't play stupid or innocent!" All heads snap in our direction to listen to us.

I gesture over to his shocked co-star. "You're all over the media hugging and kissing. But to be honest, it has been two months since I have seen or talked to you. How am I supposed to take that?"

"How was I supposed to take Thatcher leaving your hotel room?"

"He has been a friend for several years versus the mere few months I have known you. He flew back yesterday to get back to work. I have been trying to get over you and it hasn't been by getting under someone else." I could feel my blood pulsing through my body. My eyes were set on him. "What kills me is that you honestly think I am that kind of girl. After everything you know about me, you just assumed." My voice has grown soft with disappointment.

I turn and walk off the set. I hastily apologize to the guy sitting in what I am guessing is the director's chair. His face is blood red and he looks like he is about to explode.

"Do you want to be with me?" He asks pleadingly. I pause in my tracks. Of course I want to be with him, but not if he thinks that is how I deal with a break-up. Then I chide myself as we were never even dating.

"Not if that's how you view me." I climb the barricade again and head back towards the hotel. It's time to leave.

After checking out of the hotel, I drive myself to the airport. Once the plane lands, Milo is waiting for me in the baggage claim area. We don't speak of Reed or my trip the whole way home. I drop Milo off first since his house is on the way to mine. Since I currently don't have a car to get to work, he lets me borrow his. When I pull into my drive-way, the headlights flash on the exterior of Bromley. The house sits there with paint-chipped siding; loose, worn steps; and a complete lack of the luster it once had. I am done. I climb out of the car, march up the steps, and yank down the porch swing. I drag it off to the shed.

Hours pass and the swing has been sanded down and repainted. I walk back to the front of the house to let the fresh paint dry. Taking in the neglected sights of Bromley, I study the flower beds. They have become overgrown with weeds and vines. I rip into those and pull everything out. It's cold and dark now but I don't care. I take out my frustration by digging and plowing. I am driven to make some changes to this old house.

This is my home and it's time I start making it mine rather than just living in it.

35

HARLEY

In the weeks that I have been back, I won the lawsuit brought by Shelby. This is something that no one thought would end differently. Through the legal battle, I lost my family but I came to realize that I really lost them a long time ago. That pain crashes through me when I am alone. I wake up from nightmares of the crushing weight of loneliness.

My obsessive work habits have returned with vengeance, probably because of the nightmares. I have hired a construction company to remodel Bromley. She is coming along beautifully and is turning more and more into *my* house. I have finally taken over the master bedroom. I never felt comfortable sleeping in there because it was my dad's room. It took a while to get used to the change. It was hard not to reflect that the last person to sleep in this room was Reed. That first night he stayed here, I never put much thought into why I was okay with him sleeping in my dad's room - a place that felt off limits to me.

Time is ticking by slowly. According to the media, Reed has taken on the roll as Drew in the movie *A Single Rose*. I smiled when I heard that news. I let my mind wander to him for only a few minutes when he pops into my head and then I force myself to move on. A few pictures of our fight at the movie set had shown up in the news and caused a frenzy in our town.

I mostly think about him when I am in the bar alone. I am most tempted to research him online when I enter the spreadsheets into the computer. The Montgomerys have made appearances in tabloid pictures. They walk beside their son, probably coaching him to hold his head up high. Reed's eyes are always shaded with sunglasses but his jaw is tight. My heart aches when I see those pictures because he has a mother and father to walk beside him through this rough valley.

Unfortunately, it wasn't lost on everyone that the character Drew was a little too familiar to Reed's past. Reed has been vague about his past to the media and has handled their inquisitions very well. He's using it as a platform to talk about domestic abuse and to bring awareness to how much of it is present in the country. During interviews, Reed looks the same as he does in the pictures. He holds his head up and keeps his jaw tense, but I can see that his eyes hint at the anguish he's dealing with when discussing this personal matter.

I hear a creek come from the back room and stop washing glasses to listen for a minute. The bar is in an old building and most of the time I ignore it. Tonight I feel a little off though, mainly because Reed has flooded my head more than I usually allow.

The jukebox switches songs and the silence is filled again. I start scrubbing the next glass and trying to distract my mind. A hand slides around my mouth and a low chuckle rumbles in his chest. "You were always a little bitch." His voice reverberates in my chest. "Always thought you were invincible. Thought you were always tougher then everyone. I tried to break you so many times."

Lance presses his body up against my back and I can tell he is enjoying every bit of the power hold he has on me. He kisses my neck and my ear lobe. Fear seeps into my breathing. I fumble for the panic button under the counter but my fingers can't find it.

"I'm done with this game Harley." His voice turns harsh and his free hand begins to grope hard on my body. "You have abandoned your family and me. I think it's time we break the rebellion out of you." He breathes heavy against my neck and my stomach turns.

"I've noticed that your body guard is nowhere to be seen here." He snickers. "Except all over the television and newspapers." He turns me to face him. "What's so disappointing about you, Lee, is how easily you can be manipulated. Buying into his ruthless ways. Following his steps into walking away from family. I didn't think you could be that stupid."

My fingers find the button finally and I press. I hear Reed's voice echo in my head, *Stand strong, shoulders back. Take up space.* Lance notices a change as I straighten my back. His eyes grow angry.

"You think you can win this? No one is here but you and me. I made sure of that." *Fight to get away - not to win,* nonexistent Reed coaches. I jab my fingers in his throat, right above his collar bones, and hook them, shoving downward. Lance backs away in pain as I hoist myself up on the bar to climb over the top. I make sure I keep an eye on him. My eyes catch a glimpse of the lump on his back hip but my brain doesn't register what it is. I focus on his red face and his eyes on me. I used to be afraid but now I'm in a scary calm. I look back towards the door while keeping my body squared towards him. I rhythmically move between the tables and chairs, only slightly bumping into them but not enough to slow me down.

Lance scales the bar with ease and rushes at me. His fist snaps out. I duck but not fast enough. It hits above my ear and is followed by another swing from underneath that forces me on my back. He rushes on top of me. Instinctively, my palms collide with his shoulders. My legs are stretched out to where I can't get any momentum to throw him off and get out from underneath him.

He sneers at me and grinds against me. "Still thinking you can get away?"

He is still too far away for me to gain any leverage. I let his weight break my lock on my arms and he moves closer to me. Vomit climbs the back of my throat with the nearness of this monster. I force my head up off the ground as hard as I can and head butt him in the nose.

Blood gushes out all over me but I am able work my knees up. He has gained his ground again and has shoved up between my legs. He leans forward. Again, my hands connect with his shoulders and my elbows lock. Just like I was taught. I quickly turn my hip and prop my opposite foot on his hip. I shove my other foot into the correct place. My hands are at his elbows within seconds. Shock causes him to pull back but I grip his wrist and hold him where I want him. I kick hard. First, my foot connects with his crotch. My grip on his arms stay firm. I try to kick again but miss his chin. Instead, my heel collides with his broken nose again.

I let go and scramble out from under him. The door swings open. I see flashing police lights and hear a loud cracking sound echoing in my ear. Pain radiates down my back and throws me forward. Officer Meeks catches me before I hit the ground. Gun fire explodes around me. But my body screams in pain. My vision fades out.

36

HARLEY

My mind is clouded with cobwebs but I see flashes of Lance above me. I hear beeping in the background and feel like it's a timer running out. I try to get away from Lance and the beeping picks up speed. Panic rises. I hear a gunshot and my eyes snap open.

Tubes and wires are attached to me everywhere and the only thing I'm aware of now is pain. It's coming together slowly in my head. I recall the events that led me up to where I am now. The door flies open and my heart rate jumps even more. The nurse looks apologetically at me. His kind eyes soften my racing heart.

He checks the monitors, presses buttons, and then turns to me. "How are you feeling?" "Just in pain," I tell him through a very parched mouth. He hands me a button and instructs me how to release the painkillers. He states it is on a timer so I can't overdo it. I make a disappointed face and am rewarded with a cute grin. He leaves me be but tells me he will be back to check on me in a little bit with some more medications.

I settle back into the bed only to be startled again as a hand touches mine. Luckily, this time the machine doesn't beep but I can see the spikes on the monitor. I glance over as I suddenly realize I'm not alone.

My voice squeaks out, "What are you doing here?" Reed reaches over to a table and picks up a cup of water with a straw. I try lifting my head to take a sip but every move I make hurts.

"I was heading back to New York to work on some reshoots, but I couldn't do it." His eyes bore into mine. "So, I changed my flight plan and came here instead. Only to find out what happened." Even with the time spent apart, I can tell he's keeping something from me. The intense stare gives him away. It's like he's pleading with me to leave his statement alone. We hardly hid anything from each other before but I let it pass for the moment. I assume he will come clean about the truth later.

I grin at him. "I beat the shit out of him."

"That's what I heard." His chuckles are quiet and put me at ease.

"I just can't outrun bullets," I say solemnly.

"No, you can't." His voice is soft. His hand softly strokes my hair.

"What are you keeping from me?" He is hesitant and watchful, both of which are normal for him but something feels off.

"Lance… he died." The words leaving his mouth don't sound right but there is no doubt in my mind as to their truth. "I'm so thankful you guys put that panic button in the bar." His eyes glass over. Panic flutters in my stomach as I recall the severity of the situation I was in.

When I pushed the panic button, the police station was signaled and Officer Meeks and Officer Kane knew there was trouble at the bar. They got there right as I was bolting for the door. By that time, Lance had pulled his gun from his back hip and fired. Seeing this threat, the officers pulled their guns and fired.

"Reed, I fought to get away," I reassure him.

"Harley," his voice cracks, "I know that." We sit in silence to let everything soak in.

"Have you seen Nikki and Milo?" I ask, trying to break the tight tension between us.

"They left about half an hour ago to go get some fresh air and some food. I told them I would watch over you." He doesn't look at me. His eyes are focused on the television.

"Reed, look at me." He reluctantly turns his head. His eyes are red. "I survived because of you. I need you to understand that. There is nothing that could have protected me from a bullet. No move, no technique, not even your physical body could have stopped it from happening. I need you to understand that I was able to get away. Because I got out from underneath him, I was able to be shot at a distance rather than close range."

That thought sinks heavily in my stomach at the same time that it puts power behind what he taught me. He nods his head and takes a deep breath. I am grateful for what Reed has done for me. He leans over and kisses me deeply.

I feel his fear, his concern, and his relief, pour into our kiss. I clearly hear each unspoken word. I am thankful that he is the one sitting here beside me.

37

Nikki and Milo show up. They are mad at us for not letting them know that Harley was awake. She had only been out for a day due to surgery and was heavily medicated to allow her body to rest, but it felt like weeks. After she woke up and explained that self-defense allowed her to get distance from Lance, Harley confirmed my fear that he wasn't there solely to terrorize her. It was evident that Lance was there to cause more damage than just fear. I didn't really know how lucky she was until that moment.

I glance over in amazement that Harley is still here. Nikki is sitting on the bed cooing over Harley and I can't help but smile. Harley's on a medical high right now and if it weren't for the drugs, she would already have snapped at Nikki.

"How bad was she?" I ask to break the silence that settled on us when Harley fell asleep. Milo looks over at me. For the first time since I have arrived and Harley has been awake, Milo's gaze cools. "I can see the circles under her eyes," I continue.

Milo tries to defend her. "It could just be the medication and everything she has been through." I know he is upset with me for the way things ended in New York, and he can tell I am not buying his first excuse.

Milo starts again, this time giving in to the truth. "Pretty bad. Shelby filed a lawsuit against her and used Ben as her attorney. They went after the shop and Bromley. Harley won of course, but she lost what was left of her family over it. Her mother and Shelby have cut her out completely. Ben isn't mad but he definitely is using a hands-off approach like always. Elan just went missing. Harley dove deeper into work and when that wasn't enough, she started remodeling the house as a distraction. The house looks great, but she was clearly slipping away from us." He takes a tight breath. "We've been worried about her for a while."

The evening creeps up on us and Nikki and Milo head home. I offer to stay with Harley and she doesn't argue. I don't ever want to leave her again, even though Lance is gone. Harley and I have been civil towards each other. Even though we've kissed since I've been back, it's not the even flow we used to have. I had not expected to go back to our old comradery quickly, but I am really missing it.

"It's killing me," she says when everyone else is gone. My head snaps up from my book. I am concerned that she is in pain. "I can't keep going on with the elephant in the room. Why are you here?"

"I couldn't go back to New York. I was getting ready to get on the private jet to go back for reshoots, but all I kept thinking about was how you left me in New York. So like I said, I switched flights to come see you, but then Milo called."

Despite how mad Milo had been at me for jumping to conclusions about Thatcher and Harley, he still felt it necessary to let me know about the attack. I will always be thankful for that. The moment that call ended, all I wanted to do was see Harley. I kicked myself for not going after her when she left New York.

"After I walked away from your hotel room in New York, Thatcher chewed me out in the elevator," I start to explain. "What he said didn't soak in until I got back to my hotel." I pause with a slight smile as I reflect on my reaction to her in the park when she crashed my filming session. "I don't handle being yelled at very well, so when you started in on me the next day, I fought back, even though I knew I was wrong."

Harley doesn't say anything. She just watches me. I've missed her so much. I regret letting her walk away. It's a moment I wish I could go back and correct because I should have known better. But I didn't do anything. I just let her go.

"When the story about my dad leaked," I continue, hoping to shed some light now about what she really means to me, "at the end of the day, I only wanted to talk to you." Harley is eyeing me with a stone-cold poker face so I don't know how well my explanation is going. "You were always only a phone call away but, like we have said, we are in different worlds. I wanted to let you go and I tried. I swear there were so many times I thought I had seen you. My mind was constantly trying to find you. So, when I thought it was you in New York, I chastised myself for thinking of you again but I couldn't shake the thought that it might've been you. I could have sworn I was going crazy."

I give Harley a pointed look. "Zoey finally admitted she had talked to you. She relayed your message that you didn't want to see me. I had all these questions to ask when I tracked you down. When I saw you, all my questions and anger melted away."

"Then Thatcher made his appearance," she interrupts.

I nod. "I have no excuse for my reaction. I should've known better."

"Yes, you should have." Her arrogant statement makes me laugh. I feel her coming back around a little, even with all that has happened. "So… why are you here?" she asks again.

I know what my heart wants me to say but I'm not sure that this is the time I want to tell her that I love her. I don't want the first time I tell her it to be mixed with an apology or even tied to a fight, or even worse, an attack. "I'm still trying to figure that out," I concede. I know it's a cop-out, but I need some space between professing my love and the horrific event that put Harley in this hospital.

She smiles at me and motions for me come over to her bed. She wiggles over and winces. Before I can say anything, there is enough room for both of us and I settle in next to her. "I'm glad my friend is back," Harley says as she lays her head against my shoulder. We start to watch the movie on television.

A few minutes later, Harley pipes up: "Did you really think I was sleeping with Thatcher?" My jaw clenches. I don't want to answer the question.

"I hoped you weren't, if that counts for anything."

"Not really," she says deflated.

"I'm really sorry about that. I really am." I pull her chin up to look in her eyes.

"I know." She settles back against me and I gingerly pull her tight into my side.

After her release a few days later, Harley settles in at home. Milo and I changed all her personal phone lines to protect her from Shelby. Her sister had been calling several times a day since Lance's death to harass her.

Harley acts strong with everyone around but I know the truth. Her nightmares reveal how she really feels. I have taken up residency in her home again, but this time on the couch since she now sleeps in the master bedroom where I used to stay. Due to her nightmares, I don't want to be in any of the upstairs bedrooms.

"Where is this going?" Zoey asks one night over the phone. She sounds coy. She's hoping for a fairy-tale ending. When I glance down at the sleeping beauty on my lap, I'm reassured I might just get that.

"Reed, I like her and I approve of her…"

"What do you mean you approve?" I cut her off.

She huffs a sigh, which tells me she said too much but can't go back now. "When I talked to her in New York, she told me she didn't want to see you because she knew this wasn't going anywhere. So, why prolong the inevitable?"

"I don't want to lose her again." My hand runs through her hair. I want to keep her close to me, but I am right back where I started the night I left. She and I are from different worlds. I voice one of my many concerns: "The media would drag her through the mud."

"Yes," Zoey confirms. "What are you going to do?"

"I don't know," I confess. We end the call with nothing left to say.

38

HARLEY

I'm wiping down the bar top. People are laughing. Pool tables are full of loud cracks. The place is swamped and full of life. The silence that suddenly falls on the crowd is deafening. I glance up to meet Shelby's eyes. They glare at me and fill my bones with ice. Behind her, Lance stands with a gun aimed at me.

When I hear the crack, I scream and rip myself out of the nightmare. Outside, a storm rages with bolts of lightning and claps of thunder. I am thankful to realize it's only a storm and not real gunfire. I scoot to rest my back against my headboard. My body still aches from the attack but I'm managing. It's not long before Reed appears in my doorway and rests against the door jam. Another flash of lighting streaks across the sky and floods the room with a brief moment of light. I can see concern on Reed's face.

"Can I get you anything? One of those sleeping pills?" I shake my head at him, remembering how I am when I'm on those. The sleeping pills keep me trapped in the nightmares not allowing me to wake up from them.

The scenes change night to night but the nightmares are on a loop. Tomorrow, I will probably dream about the empty bar where I can't find anyone. Or it will be the one of Lance actually attacking me but in that nightmare I lose the battle.

I motion for Reed to come in. His long body stretches out beside me. I snuggle down into bed against his chest and let him coax me out of my head and back to reality. Each nightmare leaves me cold and exhausted. Reed is my security blanket. "Want to tell me about this one?" he offers.

"It was the one with Shelby and Lance," I say against his chest.

"I have never met her, and bitches be crazy…" he says, making me laugh, "… but I don't think she is crazy enough to do that. She is angry but not a murderer." He rubs his palms along my spine to ease some of my tension.

"When do you have to leave?" I ask quietly.

I find that I ask this question all the time and he never answers me. He either shushes me or changes the subject, but this time he responds.

"I don't know." He sounds exhausted. My guilt wrecks me because he has been spending his time taking care of me instead of living his own life.

"Reed, you don't have to stay here to protect me. I never needed a knight," I say, feeling like maybe he needs permission to leave. Something has sparked in him though. Reed stands up and walks to the foot of the bed. I can feel his frustration. Sitting up quickly, I hiss as pain radiates up my back. I reach to turn on the side lamp so I can see him.

"It isn't always about you or what you need." He rakes his hands through his hair. "I thought I knew who I was when I left home after graduation. I was a son of a murderer but I didn't want that to define me. Then I met you."

"Listen, don't let my baggage become yours." I interrupt him, my voice matching his frustrated pitch. I refuse to be blamed for someone else's issues.

"Damn it, Harley. Whether you like it or not, what happens to you does affect me and it becomes my baggage." His voice is stern, but he pauses to reign in his harsh tone. "Again, this isn't about you."

In an instant, he looks like he is crumbling and it snaps me into silence.

"Back to what I was saying," he continues, "I met you and you've been showing me that my father doesn't define me. It's what I do with my past that defines me. But as the movie deal gets closer… I don't want to be Drew. I'm basically running right now and I am running to you for reprieve. I *need* you."

I study him for a moment and let his words sink in. I'm unsure if the needing me is an admission to his true feelings about me or if he needs our fireside chats. I think back to our conversations on the couch and from the time we have spent together. "In order for you to portray Drew correctly, to give the character justice, you have to think like a predator," I conclude, choosing to focus on the idea that me just needs my friendship.

"And looking at you right now… knowing what has happened…. knowing what my mom went through…" He physically pales.

"What happens if you walk away?" I am sure it can't be that easy but I need to understand why he won't.

"A contract will be broken. So what, right? But I feel like if I do the part then I'll be set free." He crawls back in bed beside me and sighs. He pulls me against him. "But I know the truth. Nothing ever really sets you free. You just learn to cope with it."

I feel his body cave in to the weight of the situation. "So, you don't need me?" he teases after a moment, trying to lighten the mood. Or maybe he is just finding any reason to continue procrastinating on his decision about the movie role.

"I can't believe I got shot and it's not about me," I playfully jab him.

Reed chuckles and kisses the top of my head. His statement of needing me still lingers in my mind and I pause to ask myself if I need him like I'm hoping he needs me.

"I don't want to be dependent on you." I say out loud to answer my nagging thoughts. "Depending on people in my life only resulted in me getting hurt," I admit.

"Lee, you can be with someone and not become dependent. You can live alongside someone and share life together without relying on them for everything. I mean that is what you, Nikki, and Milo have."

I feel my heart sink a little...*Was I hoping for more from him?* He strokes my hair and we don't say much more tonight. We both seem to be lost in our thoughts. I eventually drift back to sleep.

I don't wake again until late morning. This has become our new routine. Usually, I wake up to catch Reed reading a book. This morning, however, he smiles down at me as if our early morning conversation had never happened. Per our new routine, we get up and fix something to eat. After brunch, I stay at the kitchen table letting Reed clean up while I field phone calls and emails to keep up with my businesses.

"Lee, Nikki and Milo invited us out tonight, are you up for it?" Reed asks me while I am finishing up an email. My heart skips a beat. I have left the house for walks but we stay on the wooded path behind the house to avoid people in town. Sure, visitors have stopped by but I have yet to leave the security of the house or walking path.

When I don't respond, Reed asks the question again. "I...I don't think so." I fidget horribly in my seat. Reed doesn't say anything right away but I sense something is about to tumble out of his mouth.

"Lee," his voice is right behind me, "this is part of moving forward." He coaxes me like I'm a skittish animal. I know he is right but I have no words. He kisses the top of my head before moving to sit down next to me. He reaches for my legs and shifts my body to face his. "Lance is gone. Shelby isn't bold enough to face you. Nothing bad can happen." I start to roll my eyes. "Harley." The edge in his voice grabs my attention. "You own this town. Stand strong against your fears because you are not alone. Nikki, Milo, and everyone in this town is here for you. I am here for you."

I look into his eyes. "I just don't know what to expect. What if I flip out with everyone watching?"

"We already thought of that." He grins at me. "Kayden said he shut the bar down for a couple hours today so we can go if you want to. If not today, he will shut it down when you are ready. We all understand that you need time to adjust. I just know you haven't left this house other than to walk in the woods and that has been with me. It worries me." His eyes are kind.

"I feel like this is an intervention," I joke.

"I figured if the other two were here, you would have been more apt to fight with Milo and brush off Nikki." Then he chuckles. I laugh because he is right. I sigh because I know that time isn't going to heal this part of my life.

"Let's go face the music then."

We are out the door and in the car in what feels like no time. In actuality, it took us a few hours. Now we are in front of the bar. With the car parked and off, my heart is racing. When the first attack happened, Lance was alive and I saw Reed as my protector. But for this last attack, I was on my own. Not only that, but Lance died in this building. His death freaks me out more than the actual attack.

"You went through your childhood home where your Mom was killed, didn't you?" I ask. His eyes never leave mine but I know the answer. "Will you tell me about it?"

I'm feeling really uneasy about going back to the place I last saw Lance and knowing he died here. My dad passed in a hospital and I've had no reason to be around other crime scenes. This is a first for me. I'm hoping Reed can tell me what to expect when I walk through those doors.

Reed stares ahead at the bar for a bit before he speaks. "I know you're trying to prepare yourself for what to expect when you go in, but I walked back to where a murder happened and it was someone that meant something to me. It will be different for you as this attack happened to you here."

"But Lance died here. A death is a death, and I knew him," I say quietly. I am unable to take my eyes off the bar the whole time we have sat here. Suddenly, my vision is blurry.

"The relationship was tainted though, right?" He finally turns to me. "The blood is gone and the bar has been up and running for a few weeks now. But Harley, he won't be in there and he's not coming back."

As I sit, I realize that a few months ago I was in this exact same spot in front of the bar, forcing myself to move on past Lance's first attack. I feel discouraged that I have to repeat this process all over again. With a big sigh, I raise my eyes and bring the bar into focus.

"How's your family?" I ask, stalling.

"Do you really want to know?" Reed asks skeptically.

"I thought talking about something else would calm my nerves but it's clearly not working."

"I thought so. Harley, nothing is going to make this first step easy. It's like a Band-Aid that has to be removed. You just have to do it." He tries coaching me. "But you don't have to do it today. This is the farthest you have come. I really thought we would make it only halfway here then have to go back."

I smile through tears that have welled up in my eyes.

"I'm right here," he encourages me as his hand massages my neck.

My shaky hand reaches for the car door. I won't let fear control me any longer. I am not turning back now.

39

REED

We enter the empty bar. Harley is frozen just inside the door. I hear her shallow breathing and my heart aches for her. I am prepared for all spectrums of emotions: anger, tears, and silence. I remember all those feelings rushing through my own body all at once when I went to my old house.

What I don't expect is my own outpouring of emotions about her situation. I have flashbacks of the four of us playing pool for the first time, cleaning the bar late at night, the music, the conversations, and everything about us that we experienced in this bar. This bar was ours, but now Lance has tainted this place with his sinister actions.

I reach for Harley not for her sake, unfortunately, but for my own support as anger and sadness rake through my bones. She jumps at my touch as if she forgot I was standing next to her. Glancing over, I see silent tears flowing down her cheeks.

Harley stands stock still and stares at the floor where I assume she had been trapped under Lance. I move to wrap her up in my arms. Her head stays trained on the spot. My stomach turns with bile as I imagine what went on here.

Tucking her head against my chest, she adjusts her gaze. I feel her inhale deeply while her tears soak my shirt. My own eyes glass over and I thank God that she is still here. Everything could have gone wrong that night, but she escaped, not unscathed, but she did escape.

I step back to see for myself how she is handling this. Her eyes are large but she nods to me to reassure me that she is doing okay. We are back to our instinctive communication and this brings a glimmer of how things used to be, even in the midst of all the tragedy. She moves towards the bar, taking deep breaths as she moves. I make my way over to the pool table. I want to bring back more of the good memories and chase away the tightness in my chest.

She fixes herself a drink. "Lee, you shouldn't do that with your medications," I caution. She looks at me then throws back a shot, gagging.

"I think I deserve one too," I concede and she fixes another shot to pass over to me. It burns down my throat.

"I have to agree, that does help," I admit. Looking at the bottle in her hand, I set my glass down and remark "poor choice in liquor for a shot, but I agree that the burn is a welcomed one." She giggles. Her laugh is a little off but that's understandable.

She moves over to the juke box and selects some music. "Let's play a game. A game of truth." Her coy smile appears as she stands next to the pool table.

"Are you sure?" I'm worried that hanging around this place for this long so soon is pushing her too much. I figured we would come here and slowly adjust to the new atmosphere a little at a time over the course of a few different trips. I walk over to her and study her face.

"I know I sound crazy, but you're right. This is my bar. I am still adjusting but it's easier with it being the two of us. I can handle your two watchful eyes, but not the whole town yet."

"Rack 'em," I say as I snatch the pool stick from her hands. She starts to turn away from me, but I catch her hip and lightly brush my lips against hers. Harley's arms snake around my hips and pull me deeper into her. I feel the tension melting from my body. Our kiss lasts only a few seconds then we pull away from one another and begin a game we played many moons ago.

With the first ball in the pocket, she looks at me to ask her question. "Last night, when I said I didn't need you...It wasn't true." She moves around the pool table and comes closer to me. "I realize now that it was easy to talk to you when I didn't think you were ever going to really enter my world, but now that you have, I don't ever want you to leave. At the same time, I don't want you to be my everything either."

"I thought you got to ask me a question if you made a shot," I tease, but she shrugs it off.

"We always shared the deeper stuff here in this room or on my couch. Right now, I need you to know where I am coming from," she says.

I rub my scruffy chin and eye her. "I don't believe in love at first sight and I don't believe that there is only one person meant for another. But I do believe there are soulmates and many of them. I believe that a soulmate is someone who changes your life. Someone who creates a before and an after." I step closer to her. I am excited to finally tell her what I've wanted to for a while now. "I don't know where we will be in ten years, or even ten months, but I know that I'm in love with you."

Her eyes glimmer with joy. "So, what now? What do we do with this revelation of yours?"

My brow furrows because I don't have an answer. She continues. "Neither of us wants to leave each other, but are you willing to give up your career?" Again, Harley leaves me with a question I have asked myself so many times but I have yet to find the answer for. Likely that's because we have never talked about it.

"Why can't we compromise?" I offer. "You have proven to yourself that you can leave your businesses in capable hands. Why don't we split the time? We will travel together. Explore the world, but call this place home."

She processes this by turning back to the table and lining up for her next shot. The ball falls in, followed by another line up, and another shot made. I want to pull my hair out from not knowing what she is thinking.

"When are you supposed to leave?" she finally asks.

"Three weeks ago," I answer slyly.

"And you stayed for me?" She can't hide her smile.

"Don't flatter yourself. I'm not only here for you," I reply, with a ghost of a smile playing on my lips. Her mouth pops open in shock which makes me chuckle.

"Wow, I don't know what to do with that exactly," she teases.

"I'm trying to figure out what I want to do."

"Are you getting any closer to a decision? How pissed is the production company?"

"Pretty pissed." I laugh. "I did use you as a cover-up though, just to be completely honest. I told them I had a family matter that I needed to take care of and to give me a couple of weeks. They are pacified for now. But I need to know... do you love me?"

"You'll have to sink a ball before I answer that question," she says playfully.

EPILOGUE
HARLEY

After our game of Truth in the bar that afternoon, Reed had to go back and finish shooting the movie I interrupted back in New York. The production company penalized him for jumping ship but he didn't care. Since he's been gone, we video chat regularly. My inability to sleep has come in handy for once. Due to his erratic movie schedule, we talk at all hours of the day and night.

I'm slowly going back to work. I still have doctor stipulations on what I am allowed to do and George is adamant that I stick to them at the garage. Milo and Nikki help me in the evenings when I close the bar. It is comforting to be in a small town where people look out for one another.

Bromley's transformation is finally complete. It is a cute little house now, with light green paint and white trim. There are extra safety features as well at Reed's request. And the flowerbeds are starting to take root as the spring morphs into summer.

I sit on the porch swing and stare out at the oak tree that I chastised last fall. It has given birth to a new round of leaves. I don't feel so much hatred for the tree now because I realize that sometimes a tree has to let go of decay in order to spring new.

Milo walks up the gravel drive and eyes the house. "Looks great, Lee." I beam at him as he joins me on the swing. "You're looking good too, even though you still have sleep circles under your eyes. You look happy."

"I am." I have felt the weight on my shoulders disappear as time has set me apart from my biological family. It took me awhile to grasp that Milo and Nikki are my real family. "Thanks for never letting go of me when you could have easily given up."

"I wanted to," he says honestly, "but I knew you were capable of change and you would come around." Milo rests his arm around my shoulders and pulls me against his side.

"Are you packed for your trip tomorrow?"

"Yes! Reed says the beaches are perfect this time of year." I have been approved to travel. To celebrate, I am flying to meet up with Reed in Florida for a little R&R for both of us. "I'm nervous. My scars aren't the prettiest."

"They aren't but don't shy away from them. They are proof that you are a fighter." He nudges me and I giggle. "We should go. Nikki's already at the bar."

When we get there, the bar is full. Noise bleeds out of the closed doors. "It's a party!" I say sarcastically as Milo opens my car door.

"What did you expect? We are all excited that you are finally leaving this place!" He wraps one arm around my head and roughs up my hair with his other. I squeal and laugh. "Man, it's been a long time since I have heard that noise from you." Milo looks at me all gooey eyed.

"Stop it!" I yell. His sentimental moment is weirding me out but I can't help but laugh.

Milo opens the door for me. When I step through the threshold, everyone welcomes me with cheers and hugs. Making our way to the bar, we spot Nikki holding two seats for us. Milo and I join her, order food, and raise our steins to one another.

"We have time for one more game of pool before you go." Nikki bounces with excitement.

The thought of Reed makes my heart leap. It feels like it's been years since I have seen him.

Since he left, I learned what Reed meant when he said a soulmate marks a beginning and an after. A soulmate never wants to be a fairytale prince or princess. A soulmate is someone that changes you for the better. Someone that makes you realize what life can be like and that you can have someone to share it with.

I watch Milo and Nikki fuss over how to rack the balls. Even after all the times we have played, they still like to playfully pester each other over the simple task. They love each other and they really love living life together. Watching them makes me sentimental. My two best friends, who have always been by my side, will be staying here while I leave. I know I will be back in a few weeks but this feels different.

I feel different.

I feel free.

And it's all because I found myself on the county line.

ACKNOWLEDGEMENTS

To everyone who believed in my book. You gave me the confidence to keep writing.

To Jess Richter. You once told me you didn't normally read fiction, but you took the leap with me anyway. You spent hours poring over my grammatical errors. I will forever be grateful to you for this experience.

To all my Kickstarter Backers…. YOU GUYS ROCK!!!

To my wonderful husband. You walked this six-year long journey with me. You encouraged me to keep going, even when I wanted to throw the whole project away. You stood behind me when I struggled with decisions and you always believed in me.

To my parents. I couldn't have done this project without you. I reflect on my time in high school and how much of a carefree person I was. I'm sure I scared you since I believed everyone was nice and no harm could come to me. Good news, no harm came to me, but it's because you taught me to be cautious. I learned how to read people from you.

To Becklyn. May you fight like Harley, be bold like Reed, love deeply like Milo, and always find happiness like Nikki.

Made in the USA
Coppell, TX
01 May 2023

Being dispatched for a gunshot wound is one of those types of calls that usually get your juices flowing. Depending on the neighborhood, the call itself can vary from a superficial wound to a hypercritical wound to the head where the only thing you may be attempting to do is to save an organ donor. The shooting we were dispatched to was for a gunshot wound to the chest. As with any wound that invades the chest cavity, they're nothing to fool with, as they can quickly and easily be fatal or certainly life threatening.

At the time I was working with a basic EMT named Mike Kushman. When we received the call for this gunshot wound, we quickly jumped in our ambulance and blasted out of our ambulance garage like we were shot out of a cannon. We were en route to this particular high rise where this kind of thing was not out of the everyday normal way of life. As we arrived, there were several squad cars already on the scene.

As I exited out of the ambulance, one of the several officers there said, "He says he's been shot in the leg."

I don't know why, but I was really primed and ready to treat a really serious and life threatening chest wound. As we were rocketing over to where our patient was to be, I was already thinking about all of the complications that I might encounter. Sucking chest wound, massive blood loss, airway management problems, or profound shock were a few of the things I was contemplating. So when the good officer informed us that we had a gunshot wound to the leg, it was almost anticlimactic.

I know that sounds a little macabre to most people but those in EMS know exactly what I am talking about and at the time, feeling. The man was sitting on the ledge of a walkway by this high rise and was complaining about a wound to his leg that's just under his knee. Well, nonetheless, we helped this guy to our ambulance by getting under each arm of our patient and basically we carried him to our side door of the patient compartment. We then let him down so as he could hop up into the ambulance.

As Mike followed him into the rig from that side, I ran around to the back of the ambulance and entered the patient compartment from the rear doors, mostly so I wouldn't have to step over him and Mike in my attempt to examine our patient. As I looked at his leg, I noticed a small tear in his jeans just below his knee.

"Well, there doesn't seem to be much blood on your pants. In fact, there are only a few drops around this small tear in your pants," I said to him.

He said back to me, "I'm telling you man, I just got shot!"

"Okay, okay, let's get a good look and see. Hike your pant leg up."

After all he may have had a serious leg wound. It's certainly possible that a gunshot wound to the leg could damage the leg beyond the capability of saving it. So I could see where this guy might be a little excited about it. As we attempted to pull the pant leg up, it's readily apparent that it's too tight.

So I said to him, "This isn't working for us. Just drop your pants and let's get a good look at your wound."

He unbuckled his belt and one of the police officers pokes his head into the ambulance from the side door and said, "What do you guys got?"

Without looking up I said, "I'll let you know in a second or two."

As he drops his pants to around his ankles, I was able to clearly see his wound. What this big tough guy of five-feet ten inches tall and carrying around roughly 180 pounds, had was a small abrasion just under his kneecap that was almost (but not quite) the size of a dime. For a split second I have to admit I was a little confused. I think mostly because I was really anticipating at least a moderately serious injury and instead I had essentially, nothing. After another split second, I got mad.

"Shot? SHOT? You haven't been shot!" I yelled. "You got a tiny, little scrape on your knee! Get the hell out of my ambulance! Pull your punk-ass pants back up and get the hell out of my ambulance! Officer, you can take this dumb ass to jail for all I care, just get him the hell out of my ambulance."

As I'm having my little snit over this whole stupid call, Mike stood there, bent over with laughter. In fact, both he and the officer were laughing so hard they are both nearly in tears. Before I knew it, the officer who heard my little tirade was escorting our would-be patient to the nearest squad car and at the same time telling a few of the other officers what I said. Now it seems as though everybody was having a good chuckle over the whole matter.